## A DOCTOR'S CAREER
### vs.
## A PATIENT'S LIFE

They were both at stake in the malpractice suit against Dr. Dubic.

Dan Lassiter was an expert witness, but he didn't expect to be cross-examined by a beautiful female with a computer brain. He also didn't expect her to become his mistress.

But the real shock came when Lassiter found himself trapped in a white-hot triangle of medical emergency, violent crime and human lust that threatened to shatter an entire hospital . . .

### SKELETONS
The page-scorching blockbuster
by MARSHALL GOLDBERG, M.D.
bestselling author of *Critical List*

Bantam Books by Marshall Goldberg, M.D.

CRITICAL LIST
SKELETONS

# Skeletons

## Marshall Goldberg, M.D.

BANTAM BOOKS
TORONTO · NEW YORK · LONDON

SKELETONS
*A Bantam Book | June 1979*

ISBN 0–553–12622–9

*Published simultaneously in the United States and Canada*

Bantam Books are published by Bantam Books, Inc. Its trademark, consisting of the words "Bantam Books" and the por-
trayal of a bantam, is Registered in U.S. Patent and Trademark
Office and in other countries. Marca Registrada. Bantam
Books, Inc., 666 Fifth Avenue, New York, New York 10019.

PRINTED IN THE UNITED STATES OF AMERICA

Dedicated to my children
(in order of appearance):
Brett, Carey, Sandra, Jeffrey and Dara

## ACKNOWLEDGMENT

Having been trained in medicine, not law, I knew very little about malpractice litigation at the inception of this novel. At its conclusion, I knew a great deal, perhaps more than I cared to, thanks to the expert tutelage of trial lawyer-novelist, Robert Beltz, of Flint, Michigan. I am also deeply grateful for the advice and assistance I obtained from my sister, Dr. Toby Goldberg, Associate Professor of Communications of the University of Wisconsin at Stevens Point; my close friend and co-author of two novels, Lieutenant Colonel (ret.) Kenneth Kay, of the University of Southern Florida at Tampa; my superb secretary, Miss Frances Pope; and my editor, Linda Price.

Humbly and deeply, I thank them all.

Marshall Goldberg, M.D.

# 1

Milos Bednarik was in the habit of stopping off at a neighborhood tavern, the Tam-o'-shanter, on his way home from work each afternoon. He went there to quaff a few beers, shoot a few games of snooker, and ogle the bouncing breasts of the braless, T-shirted waitress. Above the bar a block-lettered sign read: TODAY IS THE FIRST DAY OF THE REST OF YOUR LIFE! Unknown to Milos Bednarik, it was also his last.

Milos, a Croat by birth and a machinist by trade, was a robust man in his mid-forties whose youthful ambitions gradually had been pared down until he fit uncomplainingly into the slot his adopted country provided for him. Though a passably talented metal sculptor, he accepted the meager recognition of his artistry along with the meager rewards of his clock-punching, union-protected factory job without complaint.

Years before, shortly after emigrating from Yugoslavia, he had been drafted into the U.S. Army and sent to Korea. He vowed then that if only the Lord let him survive the gook infantry, he would never complain about anything again. The Lord, busy as He must have been at the time, had kept His part of the pact, and so had Milos. Not that he had much to complain about. So what if he was going bald and his gums were riddled with pyorrhea? He had a steady job, a devout and frugal wife, and his own home in a Springfield, Massachusetts, suburb.

His childhood in Nazi-occupied Yugoslavia had given Milos the instincts of a survivor, which had helped extricate him from many dangerous scrapes in adult life. Ever since Korea, though, he could not shake the notion that he was living on borrowed time, and lately he had begun to suffer qualms that this extra time might be running out. He had no idea what was producing this morbid state of mind and he didn't take it too seriously. In his younger years, such a premonition would have kept him constantly on guard, but living so long in America had instilled such a sense of security, even complacency, that this once he chose to ignore it.

Along with most people, Milos Bednarik had long ago learned that too much of any good thing, be it fast cars or favorite foods, could be harmful. What he had no way of knowing was that in his case "too much" would turn out to be a single molecule.

He had wakened that morning with a stuffy nose, a scratchy throat, and a dull ache behind his eyes, which signaled the start of another head cold. He had medicated himself with several aspirins, which made him sweat, and antihistamine pills, which parched his mouth. But by afternoon he had grown feverish, and the air-conditioned coolness of the tavern made him shiver periodically.

"Nervous from the service, honey?" cracked the waitress as she waited beside Milos for the bartender to fill an order.

Woozily he twisted his neck around while still leaning against the bar and tried to focus on the twin mounds of cotton-covered flesh inches away. Talking boobs? Milos wondered for an instant. Then, he straightened, turned to look her up and down, and grinned.

"Coming down with a cold, I guess."

"Yeah?" she said with mild interest. "Head or chest?"

"Head," said Milos.

"Then you ought to see a doctor."

"What for?" Milos protested. "It's just a cold."

"Yeah? Well, you never know about colds. My boyfriend thought he had a cold and the doctor told him it was hepatitis. Bet you didn't know you could catch hepatitis from screwing?"

"No," Milos said, bemused. "I sure didn't!"

"Well, you can. So now he's my ex-boyfriend. But if I were you, I'd go see a doctor. Why take chances?"

Milos Bednarik left the Tam-o'-shanter at five P.M. and drove across town to the office of Dr. Emil Dubic. He had met Dubic, a fellow Yugoslavian emigrant, shortly after Dubic arrived in Springfield. Milos had been one of his first nonmedical friends in the area and one of his first patients after he entered private practice. Initially he had liked Dubic's zest for life in the United States and his dedication to his intern's duties at the hospital. But marriage to the daughter of a wealthy local banker had changed his friend. Dubic's wife, who doubtless would have preferred a Boston-trained specialist for a mate but settled for a Yugoslavian-trained general practitioner, made sure he dressed properly and moved in the right social circles —which did not include evenings out with factory machinists, even if they were fellow Croatians. Although Dubic still worked long hours in his office, Milos was well aware that the time he gave each of his patients grew shorter and shorter while the list of lab tests he ordered on them grew longer. That was the reason Milos had not gone to see him when he developed a prostate infection a year ago. But now, despite the waitress's warning, he was reasonably sure he had only a cold.

Dubic's office was located between two sprawling, low-rent housing developments. Milos pulled his Chevrolet into a parking space beside a sleek, silvery Mark IV Lincoln that he knew belonged to Dubic. He was relieved to see only two patients, an obviously pregnant woman and an elderly man on crutches, seated in the waiting area. Dubic's receptionist took his name, located his medical record, led him to one of six examining stalls, and told him to disrobe.

Milos had barely managed to shed his street clothes and slip on the skimpy johnny handed him when one of Dubic's nurses entered the stall to take his temperature, pulse, and blood pressure. She then asked if he'd had a chest X ray, electrocardiogram, complete blood count, and serum cholesterol taken on him in the last six months. Ignoring her skeptical look, Milos claimed that he had. The last time he had answered honestly, it had added eighty dollars to his bill.

"Well," the nurse said brusquely, "what's wrong with you this time?"

"A cold," Milos said.

"That's all?"

"Maybe a little sinus trouble," he speculated.

"Have you had sinus X rays in the last six months?"

"No," Milos admitted sheepishly. "Think I should?"

"Well, I would. But we'll let the doctor decide. You just wait here for him."

Milos nodded. Where else could he wait in his johnny?

A few minutes later the door opened, and Dubic boomed, "Milos, my dear friend and countryman! What's ailing you?"

Milos shrugged. "A little cold. Maybe sinus."

Dubic did not question him further. His examination was almost as brief as his history-taking. "Open your mouth wide," he ordered, and pulling out a penlight and tongue blade from his pocket, thrust the blade deep down Milos's throat until he began to gag.

"Hmmm," Dubic murmured after a quick look.

"Hmmm, what?" asked Milos, but he was ignored.

Dubic pressed his thumbs hard against Milos's cheek-bones until he winced. "Hurts, huh?"

"A little," Milos admitted. "So?"

"Lungs next," Dubic told him. "Take deep breaths through your mouth."

The initial touch of Dubic's metal stethoscope head against his warm back made Milos hunch his shoulders and shudder, but after that he complied.

"Well?" he asked anxiously after Dubic had removed the stethoscope from his chest and pocketed it. "What do you think?"

Dubic made an equivocal gesture. "Your throat's a little red, your lungs are a little congested. Either you got a bad cold or a touch of pneumonia, and since a cold I can't cure, I might as well treat you for pneumonia. Sit still for a minute and I'll have my nurse give you a shot of penicillin."

"You sure I need one?" Milos looked dubious.

Dubic frowned. "Am I sure? What kind of talk is that? You want me to be scientific and run up a big bill, I'll do it. Take a throat culture, sputum culture, and blood culture. Then wait a few days for the results —by which time you'll either be feeling better on your own or have double pneumonia! Besides, if you ask me, there's infection in your sinuses, and I can't culture those without poking a hole in one with a sharp instrument. So just trust me, Milos. A shot of penicillin isn't that big a deal."

"No," Milos reluctantly agreed, "I suppose not."

"Good!" Dubic beamed and patted him on the shoulder. "I'll send the nurse right in."

Without understanding why, Milos Bednarik suddenly felt uneasy. He almost called after Dubic to ask if he could take penicillin tablets instead. But he was afraid of angering Dubic by questioning his judgment again. So he meekly submitted as the nurse injected the syringeful of penicillin into his left buttock. Then he started to get dressed.

Bending over to step into his pants, Milos suddenly felt dizzy and had to steady himself on the examining

5

table. The room had barely stopped spinning when he was struck by an array of even odder sensations. His scalp and tongue tingled, and a wave of intense heat swept over him, making his face burn and drenching his body with sweat. Then the sweat abruptly turned cold, and he began to shake uncontrollably. Milos had received several shots of penicillin before without difficulty, so he neither knew nor suspected that what he was experiencing was an anaphylactic reaction—the body's all-out, sometimes suicidal, attempt to rid itself of a foreign protein. Powerful humors secreted by his white blood cells and lymph glands constricted his small blood vessels and contracted his smooth muscles. His vision dimmed; his vocal cords clamped down. Hungry for air, he sucked in huge lungfuls. But with his throat muscles tightening like a noose around his neck and a strange swelling rising deep in his mouth, exhaling became more and more difficult. With his neck veins bulging and his face suffused with blood, Milos strained to expel the trapped air from his lungs, but it was like trying to breathe under water. Grasping his throat in both hands, he struggled futilely to loosen the imaginary noose around it. Had a knife been handy, he would have cut at it to let the air out of his overinflated lungs. His chest burned like fire, and a pressure mounted in his head until he felt his brain about to burst. His stomach twisted, making him intensely nauseous, and his intestines writhed and gurgled as if filled with enema fluid. "What the hell's happening to me?" he silently screamed. He had never felt so ill before. Then the awesome thought hit him: he was dying. He was leaving this earth, this existence. His borrowed time was nearly up. Panicky, he cried out for Dubic, but only a gurgling sound emerged.

Mustering all his strength, Milos pushed himself up and away from the examining table and lurched into the door of the booth. Despite the blackish haze before his eyes, he fumbled for and found the doorknob. Pushing outward with all his might, he fell forward into the void and landed hard on his hands and knees.

Faintly he heard a female voice shriek Dubic's name, felt hands grabbing and lifting and depositing him on his back on a hard metal surface. A bright light shone in his face, dispelling the haze. He opened his eyes, blinked several times, and focused on the ceiling. Suddenly an astonishing transformation occurred. The acoustic tile of the ceiling dissolved, and the pale light of dawn filled the sky. No longer was Milos in a doctor's office; he was huggng the floor of a sandbagged gun pit, fearfully watching a squad of North Korean soldiers, bayoneted rifles thrust out in front of them, advance on his position. Closer and closer they came until he could actually see their slanted eyes and flared nostrils and cruel snarls. He tried to cry out, to wake and warn his sleeping buddies, but something—his gas mask?—muffled the sound. Then his gas mask was ripped off, and a rifle butt slammed into his mouth. A bayonet blade stabbed his arm. Exploding with rage, Milos struggled to gain his feet and kill at least one of them with his bare hands, but he could not break free of the arms holding him down. Slumping back, he caught a bare glimpse of the glittering point of a bayonet descending toward his throat before a searing pain from his ruptured lungs spread upward to short-circuit his brain, obliterating any ability to feel at all.

Shakily Dubic held the tip of the scalpel against Milos's throat, but he could not bring himself to plunge it in, to perform the lifesaving tracheotomy. Oh, God! he thought despairingly. Not again! Please don't let it happen to me again!

Mary Bednarik was in her kitchen when the bad news reached her. With the dishwasher churning loudly, she could barely understand a word of what the emergency-room nurse was telling her. She asked her to repeat it and then, when she finally did understand, asked her to repeat it again. "What!" Mary cried. "My Milos? Milos Bednarik? What's he doing in a hospital emergency room? How did he get there? . . . By ambulance? From Dr. Dubic's office? . . . Is he very sick?" she asked worriedly. "Dead!" she wailed. "How can he be dead? What killed him?"

Afterwards, Mary Bednarik was unable to remember the taxi ride to the hospital or the content of the papers the nurse had given her to sign; she was in too dazed a state. One thing she would never forget, however, was the sight of her dead husband's face, his swollen tongue protruding from his mouth like a half-swallowed sausage.

Dr. Dubic talked briefly, soothingly, to her. Milos had come to him for a shot of penicillin for a cold, he explained, and then suffered some kind of seizure. Perhaps a heart attack. Dubic had done his best to revive him but to no avail. Feeling lost and forlorn, Mary saw his mouth moving and his consoling hand on her shoulder and nodded numbly. As Dubic turned to leave, however, she whispered, "His tongue. What happened to his tongue?"

Dubic looked uncomprehending.

"His tongue," she repeated. "He didn't choke on his tongue, did he?"

"No, no," Dubic said hastily. "It was his heart. I'm sure of it."

But Mary Bednarik was not so sure. She had been with her father when he suffered his fatal heart attack, and his tongue hadn't swelled up. Neither had she ever seen or heard of anything like that on all the TV doctor shows she watched. It didn't seem right. Something more must have happened to Milos, which Dubic was hiding from her. When the white-garbed intern on duty approached her and tried to persuade her to sign an autopsy permit, Mary at first refused. She could not bear the thought of having poor Milos cut up and gutted of his insides like a slaughtered cow. Besides, none of this was really happening. It was all a dream, a terrible dream. Today was Tuesday, the night Milos took her bowling and then home to bed. Milos wasn't like most men when it came to sex. Beer and bowling both relaxed and stimulated him, and on Tuesdays and Saturdays he made love to her half the night. He had a good heart, a strong heart, so how could he have died of a heart attack? How could he even be dead? But he *was* dead, she knew; otherwise his tongue would not look so awful. Rising abruptly from the chair she had sat slumped in, Mary went looking for the intern who had the autopsy permit for her to sign.

The autopsy was performed the following morning, and after many phone calls to Dr. Dubic's office Mary finally got a copy of the pathologist's report. A nurse-friend interpreted it for her. According to the autopsy evidence, the cause of Milos's death was not a coronary occlusion, she told Mary, but anaphylactic shock, and the probable cause of that was a penicillin reaction.

Mary Bednarik brooded over the discrepancy between the autopsy findings and what Dr. Dubic had told her for a week before deciding to take action. She had heard her sister-in-law, Shirley, a court stenographer, rave about some Boston lawyer who specialized in malpractice cases and how successful he was. Should she go to see this lawyer or shouldn't she? Mary debated. She was not an injustice-collector; she was a stoical, God-fearing woman who had great respect for doctors, and the thought of bringing suit against one of them unnerved her. But she remembered one more thing Shirley had told her about this marvelous lawyer; that he was very selective in the cases he accepted, taking only those involving bad doctors as well as bad results.

Emil Dubic, she was convinced, was a bad doctor.

# 2

Dr. Daniel Lassiter gazed out his kitchen window at the morning sun shining through the birch grove in his backyard. Beside him the percolator gurgled a few last times before falling silent. Dan turned to it gratefully. Of all the many cups of coffee he drank during the day, the first sip of his first cup every morning always tasted best. Dan could have been a happy monk, were he more religious, or a happy forest ranger, had there been forests to range in Massachusetts. Instead, he was a self-sufficient bachelor, nearly healed from a costly divorce and feeling no particular need to share his suburban Wayland home with another wife or even another woman on a night-by-night basis. He was also an internist, an associate editor of the *New England Journal of Medicine,* and, since his appointment to the post three months before, general director of Boston's famed Commonwealth General Hospital.

Fame, along with its price tag, was very much on Dan's mind that morning. Because of it he faced a tough ordeal. At ten A.M. he was scheduled to testify at the malpractice trial of Dr. Emil Dubic.

Malpractice, mused Dan; like cancer, an emotionally charged word for doctors. A ravager of reputations. A malpractice conviction stole both pride and purse. Such was the mentality of many doctors these days that any patient, no matter how badly mistreated, who sued his doctor was considered not only an ingrate but a dupe of some avaricious lawyer. Dan did not quite subscribe to this biased view; nor did he dare contest it too loudly during the current malpractice crisis. It was not only a spreading crisis but a shifting one—the major cause of the shift being the law firm of Sprague, Adams, Rosensweig and Cane.

"Sprague the Plague" its senior partner had been dubbed by Jimmy Dallesio in his syndicated column, and the epithet had caught on. Jimmy, a Pulitzer Prize-winning journalist, was Dan's closest friend. He had wanted to accompany Dan to Springfield and watch him square off against Charles R. Sprague in the courtroom, but Dan had dissuaded him. The two columns he had already written about Sprague had given the man enough publicity.

Dan had testified at malpractice trials three times before, fortunately never as the defendant, and had evidently acquitted himself well. So the prospect of spending most of the day in court did not faze him particularly. But defending Dr. Emil Dubic did.

Dubic had been one of Dan's interns at Holmes Memorial Hospital in Springfield when he was its director of medical education. Under his tutelage, Dubic had apparently absorbed enough American-style medicine to pass the state's licensing exam, but not much of Dan's compassion.

How was he to know that as Dubic dutifully followed him around the hospital like a puppy dog, it was not Dan's medical knowledge he hungered after but the material rewards it could bring? And bring them it did! By that measure Dan's former intern had far surpassed his mentor. While Dan drew an annual salary of $75,000 as director of Commonwealth General Hospital, Dubic had become a "Medicaid millionaire."

So why have I agreed to defend that pissant? Dan wondered. Because he really believed Dubic was innocent of the charge of malpractice, this time anyway? Or to prove to the local medical establishment that, much as he personally despised doctors like Dubic, he was with them in their crusade against the venal lawyers, ungrateful patients, and capricious juries that composed the malpractice monster: the devil's own dragon locked in mortal combat with the shining knights of the caduceus?

How Miltonian! thought Dan, wryly congratulating himself on his choice of imagery. He would have to remember to repeat it to his acerbic lawyer-friend and neighbor, Gordon Donnelly, as they drove the eighty miles to Springfield together. Gordon had handled Dan's divorce for him, and Dan, in turn, handled Gordon's high blood pressure. At times the current malpractice crisis strained their friendship; at other times it added zest to their drinking discussions.

Fortunately Gordon was not involved in the Dubic trial. He had to be in Springfield on an unrelated matter that morning; otherwise the two ethically could not discuss the case or even risk being seen driving there in the same car together.

"Dubic, you dolt!" Dan spoke aloud on entering his bathroom. "You'd better be blameless this time, or surely you'll be reduced to rags and scabs by Sprague the Plague!"

Dan talked to his inner self often these days to prove they were still compatible. Yet he harbored doubts about his way of life. Was he better off married or single? Better off a bedside physician or a hospital administrator? As protégé and successor of the late Dr. Curt Anders Gundersen, founder and first director of Commonwealth General, Dan wondered if he had inherited Gundersen's melancholy along with his mantle.

He had finished shaving and half a carton of yogurt when the phone rang.

"Dan?" said the familiar voice with the unmistakable Boston accent. "They did it again last night."

"Did what, Gordie?" Dan asked innocently.

"Burned a Blue Cross on my lawn."

Dan knew he was being facetious but decided to play along. "What lawn?" he said scornfully. "You haven't even raked last fall's leaves off it. If they caught fire, it was probably spontaneous combustion."

"In the shape of a cross?" Gordon protested.

"Oh, you lapsed Catholics see crosses in everything."

"You 'bout ready?"

"Five more minutes."

"Okay. The word is, Sprague had two scrambled radiologists and one neurosurgeon on toast for breakfast this morning. But he refused a second helping. He's saving you for lunch."

"I'm high-cholesterol and practically indigestible."

"Not after he grinds you up on the witness stand, you won't be! See you in a bit."

Minutes later, Dan slid into the front seat of Gordon Donnelly's crimson Jaguar XJ.

Gordon was a bluff, big-boned man with reddish brown hair, a receding hairline, and a drooping mustache. To Dan, who had known him for the last ten years, he had always looked the forty he now was. He captained an amateur hockey team in winter and played tournament tennis in summer. Otherwise he slouched around his ten-acre property, drank too much on weekends, and railed at the folly of an existential existence. What saved his sanity and their friendship was his unfailing sense of humor.

"All right, Doctor," Gordon said with a sly smile, "let's get the nasty catchwords out of the way so that we can enjoy the ride."

"Contingent fee!" Dan growled.

"Conspiracy of silence!" Gordon snapped back.

"Nuisance suits!"

"License to kill!"

Dan hesitated. "Ambulance chasers. Is that enough for now?"

Gordon nodded and started the engine.

14

"Hey, Gordie," Dan said a moment later, "is it true your firm is bringing suit against Sam Dunlop for malpractice?"

"Yeah. So?"

"So! Jesus, he's past president of the State Medical Society. A pioneer goiter surgeon. An institution."

"So's the Smithsonian—which is where he belongs. Face it, Dan, he's an over-the-hill surgeon with failing vision who doesn't know when to quit. He botched the last thyroid he did pretty badly. The last several, really, only his surgical colleagues managed to bail him out. Nice of them to humor the grand old man by bird-dogging him in the operating room, but not so nice for his unsuspecting patients."

"How come you got the case instead of Sprague?"

Gordon braked for a red light and turned to him with scorn. "Sprague isn't the only lawyer who knows how to try a malpractice case, you know? He didn't write the statutes."

"No," Dan agreed. "But he's sure as hell *re*writing them. My guess is you got it because he turned it down."

Gordon sighed. "Yeah. That's my guess, too. Sort of puzzling. The settlement's likely to be a big one."

"Any ideas?" Dan queried.

"On why he turned it down? Not really. Just a theory of sorts."

"What? Tell me."

"That he only goes after bad doctors. Dunlop may be half-blind and doddering, but that's all. He was a pretty outstanding surgeon in his day."

"You mean that?" Dan gave him a quizzical look. "That Sprague goes after bad doctors exclusively? Hell, that makes him more of a medical nemesis than a lawyer. Good Christ, I knew we did a lousy job of policing ourselves, but I didn't think we'd brought an avenging angel down on our heads. Where does Sprague get his referrals—direct from God?"

"Either Him or a network of accomplices in medical records."

"That's an interesting thought," Dan mused.

"It was, until the Los Angeles Medical Society gave lie detector tests to a slew of them in five hospitals. They all passed."

"If this guy Sprague is such a phenomenon, why hasn't there been more publicity about him? I never heard of him until he started suing doctors around here."

Gordon reflected. "I don't really know. I suppose because he doesn't want it, and the medical profession sure doesn't want him to get it. As your buddy, Jimmy Dallesio, said in his last column about him: to be sued for malpractice by Charles Sprague has become as much a presumption of guilt as being defended by Perry Mason is a presumption of innocence. The doctors in town must've *loved* that!"

Dan laughed mirthlessly. "But what drives a guy like Sprague? Money?"

"I doubt it. He's a bachelor in his late sixties or early seventies who's already won two or three million dollars plus judgments. What's he going to do with more loot?"

"Then what's he after?" Dan said sharply. "Does he want to bring back the Code of Hammurabi, where a surgeon who screws up loses his hand? We'd have one hell of a doctor shortage!"

Gordon accelerated around a lumbering truck and then slowed down. "What's Sprague after?" he repeated. "The obvious answer, I suppose, is justice. Simple justice for his clients. But that doesn't quite explain the peculiar way he operates. Why he so seldom agrees to settle his cases out of court. The other members of his law firm do, but not Sprague. Which is one reason he scares the shit out of insurance company lawyers. Nor does it explain why he moves to a different part of the country every few years. The truth is, Dan, he's pretty much of a puzzle to me, too. Maybe he's got a grudge of some kind against the medical profession. Or maybe he's just trying to put the fear of God into you doctors."

"Oh, come on," Dan protested. "There're screwups in every profession. More in yours than mine."

"Sure," Gordon admitted. "But we rarely bury our mistakes, since we hardly ever execute them anymore. So stop bitching about Sprague. He's really doing your job for you—protecting the public against bad doctors."

Dan gave him a contemptuous look. "*That's* an over-simplification! Like saying all the Salem witch trials were trying to do was protect the townspeople against incompetent witches. You really think that pricing malpractice insurance out of the reach of most doctors is going to get rid of the bad ones?"

"No, I don't. But we both know the malpractice scare's the only thing that's gotten doctors' attention in years. When the hell are you guys going to get rid of all the quacks and butchers that practice with impunity in our city? Take that son of a bitch Mackman, who was doing incomplete abortions on his patients so that they'd have to come back for a second scraping and he could double-bill Medicaid. Just dumb luck that he didn't kill more than one woman that way!"

Dan squirmed in his seat. "Hey, Gordie," he asked, "what's got you so hot under the collar? I thought we swapped insults over our respective professions at the outset, so we could enjoy the ride?"

"Want to stop for coffee?" asked Gordon, as a Howard Johnson restaurant loomed ahead.

Dan looked at him sharply. "Evading my question, counselor?"

"Just wondering if you want coffee," Gordon said defensively.

Dan glanced at his watch. "No, thanks. I promised Dubic's lawyer I'd get there a little early to review yesterday's testimony."

"We'll be there soon. Want to talk about something else?"

"Like why no player in major league history ever batted a thousand? Or why Bobby Orr doesn't score a goal every time he gets the puck?"

Gordon sighed. "Okay, I get your point. Doctors are

human, too. But I must admit, Charles Sprague intrigues me. An old man who up until eight years ago nobody ever heard of; a man out of nowhere . . ."

"What do you mean by that?" said Dan, puzzled.

"I mean, there aren't many lawyers around who specialize in malpractice. In fact, only a handful in the entire country do. So they're a pretty close group, who know and consult each other often. Yet not a one of them ever heard of Charles R. Sprague until he tried his first big case in Los Angeles eight years ago."

"So where in hell *did* he come from?"

Gordon shrugged. "Some say from Europe, where he was working for the World Court. Others say from Canada, where he'd been spending his time fishing. Nobody seems to know for sure, which admittedly is a bit strange. But what's even spookier is how he seems to know more medicine and more about the plaintiff's case than the defendant doctor."

Dan's eyebrows lifted. "Man, that *is* spooky—if true. Maybe he went to medical school?"

"At age fifty-five!" Gordon dismissed the suggestion with a wave of his hand. "Up until then we know where, and what type of law, he practiced. It's a matter of record. Then he allegedly retired and took off for Europe, or Canada, depending on what story you believe."

As Gordon took the Springfield exit off the Massachusetts Pike and pulled up before the toll booth, Dan dwelt on the mythification of Charles Sprague. Gordon's meager description of the man had aroused not only his curiosity but his competitive nature. Rather than feeling the least bit cowed at the thought of facing Sprague in court, Dan was actually looking forward to it. So far it had the makings of an even contest: the courthouse was Sprague's ball park, but medicine was Dan's game. The deciding factor, Dan knew, would be Dubic. Was he really guilty of malpractice or not?

"Any more tales you'd care to pass on about Sprague and his mysterious ways?" Dan asked Gordon as they drove away from the toll booth.

Gordon chuckled tolerantly. "One I'd bet you and your fellow doctors don't know. The trial lawyers' association invited Sprague to conduct a seminar on malpractice last winter. It's not only a mark of prestige to be asked, a good source of referrals, but it pays well. Mel Belli and Lee Bailey love to do them. Yet Sprague turned us down flat. Even after we upped the honorarium to a cool five grand. You know why?"

Dan shook his head.

"Well, I didn't actually see his letter, but I heard on good authority what it said. 'Gentlemen,' he wrote. 'Malpractice trials are tragic events. There are no secrets to winning them, and I disdain teaching lesser lawyers mere tricks.'"

"Wow!" Dan exclaimed. "That's quite a kiss-off! Sounds like it should be engraved in stone." He cocked his head. "You know, Gordie, I might learn to like this Charles R. Sprague after all."

# 3

Gordon dropped Dan off in front of the Hampden County Superior Court building in downtown Springfield and with the cheerful look of a doctor about to jab a hypodermic needle into a patient's backside said, "Don't worry, son, it'll only hurt for a minute."

Men with jackhammers were ripping up the pavement. The din was deafening, the drifting dust strangling. With a grimace Dan started up the two flights of stairs leading to the courthouse entrance with its slender Corinthian columns. It was a miserably hot morning, and sweating men with attaché cases hurried past him. Dan was sweating, too, by the time he entered the building. The lobby was being replastered and repainted and was thick with floating dust.

As he looked around for a place to sit, Ned Josephson, Emil Dubic's defense lawyer, came bustling out of an elevator. Josephson was a short, stocky man in his early forties with salt-and-pepper hair, a handsome round face, and wily eyes. As chief counsel of the Massachusetts Medical Society's mutual malpractice fund, he was generally respected by the membership for his legal know-how and generally distrusted because he knew too much about them.

"Mornin', Dr. Lassiter," he said in a soft voice that bore traces of a Carolinian accent. "Good to see you!"

Dan sized him up further as they shook hands. The lawyer's face was florid, either from sunburn or high blood pressure, and his forehead was dappled with sweat. "How's it going?"

Josephson grimaced. "How? Lemme tell you. I wear my best white suit to show purity, so they start sand-blasting outside and that courtroom's dusty as a coal bin. Also, they're repairing the ventilation ducts, so the air conditioning isn't working worth a damn. So be prepared to sweat, on and off the witness stand."

"I mean the trial," Dan said. "How's that going?"

"Oh! That." Josephson looked pained. Suddenly a din of jackhammers reverberated through the corridor, and fine dust danced. Josephson's pained expression turned agonized. "C'mon," he said, taking Dan's arm. "Let's go down to the cafeteria. We can talk about the trial there."

As Dan munched toast and sipped iced coffee, Josephson reviewed the highlights of Sprague's cross-examination of Dubic the previous day. "Old Emil didn't do too bad," he concluded. "Not bad at all, under the circumstances. I thought he was going to have a coronary when Sprague stared him straight in the eye for almost a full minute before asking his first question. But after that he sort of settled down."

"Sounds good," said Dan.

"Maybe, maybe not," Josephson reflected. "For some reason Sprague went kind of easy on him. Hardly raised his voice in righteous indignation at all. Which, let me tell you, is not Sprague's usual style."

"Any idea why?"

"Well, for one thing he didn't have much of a voice. Real hoarse. Barely above a whisper at times. And he looked mighty peaked. I kept hopin' he'd be too sick to get out of bed today, but no such luck! I just saw him conferring with his partner, Angela Adams. So one possibility's that he just wasn't up to going after Dubic in his usual fire-breathing style." He paused, looking thoughtful and glum. "Then there's the other possibility."

"Which is?" Dan prompted.

"That he's going to save Dubic for recross-exam and zero in on you. So be prepared to bear the brunt of his verbal onslaught."

"But I'm not the doctor on trial. Why browbeat me?"

"Well, you see, Dr. Lassiter, Sprague didn't get too many straight answers from Dubic yesterday, and he probably didn't expect many. But he *does* expect them from you. Aw, hell, why pussyfoot around? It's my guess he's going to *really* lay into you. Dubic's not the only one on trial here; the whole friggin' medical profession is! Particularly the Establishment. And you, Dr. Lassiter, are a prominent member of that Establishment. So be ready to defend not only your fellow doctor, Emil Dubic, but the profession of medicine itself—how it trains doctors, polices them, pays and punishes them. The whole damn shooting match!"

"Is Sprague *really* that good?" Dan asked.

"Good!" Josephson's eyes rolled upward. "Look, Doctor," he said, pointing to his chest, *"I'm* good. At least my record says I am. What we call back home a pretty fair country lawyer. My daddy was a doctor, and I've been defending doctors in malpractice actions for twenty years. Until recently I'd lost only four times. Four out of maybe a hundred. I'm pretty proud of that record; it's why the State Medical Society retains me. But I've been up against Charles Sprague three times now, and I ain't won once. Not one damned time! And I hate to lose a case the way you hate to lose a patient. I won't go so far as to call Sprague uncanny—I wouldn't psych myself out that way . . . Besides, maybe I'll get lucky and beat him this time."

"You should," Dan said. "Dubic's no Albert Schweitzer, but how much of a malpractice case can Sprague make of a patient who dies of a penicillin reaction after tolerating penicillin dozens of times before? It's simply a fluke, a once-in-a-million happening that couldn't possibly be predicted."

"Oh, I know," Josephson agreed. "I've been telling myself the same thing for weeks. Trouble is, I got this feeling in my bones that Sprague knows something more about it than we do."

"How the hell can he?" Dan argued. "Medical facts are medical facts. Even a courtroom whiz like Sprague can't change them."

"He doesn't have to. All he has to do is convince a jury that his version of those facts is closer to the truth than ours. Don't forget, the only truth that matters in court is what the judge or jury can be made to believe."

"Okay," Dan said impatiently. "But I've done my homework. I've read the depositions you sent me and all the literature I could get hold of on anaphylactic reactions. I don't give a damn what Sprague asks me. I just don't see how he can possibly prove malpractice this time."

"I'm sure he couldn't, if *you* were the doctor on trial. But Emil Dubic is. Look, Dr. Lassiter, I'm well aware that a doctor's office is one of the last truly inviolate sanctuaries of our civilization, but I'm also aware of how Sprague operates. I've learned the hard way. It's my guess he knows more about Dr. Emil Dubic and what goes on in his office than you'd believe possible."

"You think he's compiled some sort of dossier?" Dan said incredulously.

Josephson nodded. "Like J. Edgar Hoover's FBI and Hitler's Gestapo only dreamed of."

# 4

In the courthouse elevator one of Ned Josephson's fellow lawyers asked how the Dubic trial was going and passed on a rumor from a doctor he played golf with that the State Medical Society was threatening to replace Josephson with some malpractice specialist from California if Sprague beat him again.

Josephson swore under his breath and grumbled, "Let 'em! Then maybe I could get out on the golf course myself once or twice before Christmas. Come on, Dan," he said as the elevator reached the fifth floor.

Etched in the glass of the double doors they entered were the words *Room Seven* and *Justice James Morton*. The courtroom itself was surprisingly large, and its rows of cherrywood benches were nearly filled with spectators. There were two furled flags behind the judge's platform and a colorful mural depicting the wellsprings of American jurisprudence: Mosaic law, ecclesiastical law, and Roman law. A long, wide table down in front served to display exhibits of evidence and separate excitable lawyers from the judge's august person. Two women sat at the plaintiff's table in the center of the room, and Emil Dubic sat alone at the defendant's table.

The moment Dubic spotted Dan he practically leaped from his chair and rushed up the aisle to greet him. "Dr. Lassiter!" he exclaimed. "I am *so* happy to see you."

Dan smiled and shook hands, feigning a friendliness he did not feel. Dubic's stylish Italian silk suit and jeweled accessories gave him an outward appearance of elegance and prosperity. But his eyes were dark-circled, and his pale face looked pinched and haggard.

"Oh, Dr. Lassiter," he sighed, "I am so grateful you believe I'm innocent of this terrible charge. A man of your reputation! I know you can help me more than anybody."

"I'll do my best," Dan assured him. "How's it been going so far?"

Dubic scowled and shook his head. "Oh, that man, Sprague! You should've seen the way he looked at me yesterday! Like I was a common criminal. That man is a monster, I tell you, who hates doctors worse than Hitler hated Jews. What happened to Milos Bednarik was a tragic accident, and I feel as bad about it as anybody. But to have my ability, my reputation, my right to practice medicine—everything I've worked for all my life—threatened like this is terrible. Such things should never be allowed to happen to doctors like us, Dr. Lassiter."

Dan nodded sympathetically and started to move on, but Dubic impulsively grabbed his arm. "I wanted so much for you to meet my wife, Elizabeth. But she didn't come today. Yesterday was too upsetting to her."

"I'm sorry to hear that," said Dan. "I'm sure we'll meet another time."

"Yes, you must come to dinner soon. And be sure to bring your wife—" Suddenly Dubic faltered, looking acutely embarrassed, almost stricken, and pounded his forehead with the flat of his hand. "Oh, I'm *so* sorry, Dr. Lassiter. I forgot."

"Forgot what, Emil?" Dan said with an edge to his voice.

"That you and your wife are divorced. I can't tell you how saddened I was to hear it. It must've been a terrible blow. My wife's a banker's daughter, too, you know? But not a banker like J. P. Briggs!"

Smarmy bastard, thought Dan, trying to hide his irritation. He hadn't married Lois because she was the daughter of J. P. Briggs—as much a Boston institution as his bank—but in spite of it. He had gambled on the chance that with patience and perseverance he could help free her from her tyrannical father's domination, and he had lost. It wouldn't surprise him if Dubic's marriage were now in trouble too, but he couldn't feel too sympathetic.

Dan was about to end their conversation when the bailiff's voice, cutting through the din of the crowd, did it for him. "Hear ye! Hear ye!" he barked. "The Superior Court of Hampden County is now in session, the Honorable Justice James Morton presiding. All rise!"

A side door to the judge's platform opened, and the seven-by-five-foot doorway was filled almost completely by the black-robed figure of Justice Morton. With an audible grunt he squeezed through the opening and waddled to his chair. Dan stared at him in surprise and bemusement. With his bald head, bulging eyes, and protruding abdomen, Morton bore a remarkable resemblance to the late Sydney Greenstreet. He also had the raspy-deep Greenstreet voice when he rumbled, "All right. Everybody be seated."

Dan sat down in the front row and turned his gaze to the two women at the plaintiff's table. Both looked around forty, but that was their sole similarity. The plain-faced, thickset, fidgety one he guessed was Bednarik's widow. The other woman had swept-back ash blond hair and a mature face whose beauty had been deftly sculptured by the years. Intrigued, Dan tapped Josephson on the shoulder and asked who she was.

"Angela Adams," Josephson whispered, "Sprague's partner. She's not only a looker but a crackerjack lawyer—one of the best women trial lawyers I've ever seen. Too bad."

"About what?"

"She's as aloof and unapproachable as Sprague himself. More than one lawyer I know has made a play for her, but no luck. The rumor is that even though he's old enough to be her father, she belongs to Sprague. I hear she turned down a judgeship rather than leave him and his firm."

As Dan gave her a second look, she removed her horn-rimmed reading glasses. Her hazel eyes reflected intelligence, alertness, and something less easily defined. Cynicism? Disillusionment? Under her sleek attractiveness there was the hint of a certain vulnerability, a forlornness, that made him want to know and comfort her. Would that feeling outlast the trial? mused Dan as he was called to the witness stand.

The bailiff swore him in and stepped away. Dan wet his lips, feeling a faint tremor of stage fright as he looked out at the faces of the spectators and then at Angela Adams, who was resting her cheek against her hand and peering at him intently, almost intimidatingly.

Ned Josephson soon put him at ease, however, with his polite, often plodding line of questioning. He spent the first several minutes establishing Dan's credentials as a physician and expert in the field of internal medicine, emphasizing the special opportunity Dan had had to observe and evaluate Dubic while he served a year's internship under him at Holmes Memorial Hospital. For the next thirty minutes Josephson took Dan step by step through the medical care Dubic had rendered Milos Bednarik, periodically asking Dan to state whether, in his opinion, such care met the standard of medical practice in the community. The defense attorney's questions were carefully phrased, seldom requiring more than a yes or no on Dan's part, and he answered in the affirmative each time.

Surprisingly Angela Adams did not object once during the course of his testimony. Even more surprisingly she did not scribble a single note on the legal pad in front of her. Though her expression reflected skepticism, even disdain at times, she was obviously biding her time. Finally Josephson concluded, and it was her turn to question the witness.

She rose, a single sheet of notes in her hand, skirted the lectern Josephson had been using, and moved to within a few feet of Dan. "Dr. Lassiter," she began, "after just now reading through your curriculum vitae, I must confess it's a pleasant surprise to learn about you and your accomplishments."

Dan answered in kind. "Thank you, Miss Adams. I'm sure I'd enjoy learning more about you, too."

The judge's eyes darted between them, and he guffawed. The jury tittered.

"Perhaps so, Dr. Lassiter," Angela Adams said, her eyes mocking. "What impressed me particularly was your winning the NAACP Humanitarian Award for the two years you spent in Jefferson County, Mississippi, helping provide medical care for that impoverished area. That's certainly quite an honor, and I commend you for it. Now, as a humanitarian—a humane person —am I correct in assuming you believe good medical care is more a right than a privilege for all Americans?"

"You are," Dan said firmly.

"Not all your colleagues agree, you know. In fact, one of them, writing in the March 24th *New England Journal of Medicine,* argued against it. Do you recall the article?"

"Very well." Dan smiled wryly.

"Then, quite naturally, you'll remember the editorial you wrote in that same journal rebutting him. Specifically, do you recall writing the following passage, and I quote: 'Good health care should not only be the right of all Americans, whether they live in Massachusetts or Mississippi, but they should have easy access to good doctors who can provide it. Substandard medical care is barely better than no medical care at all. Steps must be taken to assure the public that a licensed doctor has been as carefully checked for competence as a licensed commercial pilot.' Do you agree that this ideal has not yet been achieved, Dr. Lassiter?"

"Ideals are strived for but seldom achieved by *any* professional group, Miss Adams."

"Then you admit there are some bad doctors—colloquially called quacks and butchers—in practice?"

Dan shrugged. "Unhappily, yes."

"And you're opposed to bad doctors, I take it."

"I don't know anybody, in or out of the medical profession, who's in *favor* of them." He braced himself as he saw Angela's eyes narrow peevishly.

"In that same editorial, did you not make the statement, and again I quote: 'In my opinion, the only thing worse than a bad doctor is good doctors who let him get away with it'?" She paused for effect. "That's strong language, Dr. Lassiter. It indicts a large segment of the medical profession. Are you aware that a law has recently been enacted in New York State making it mandatory for doctors to report acts of professional misconduct by their colleagues to the proper authorities or risk loss of their own license to practice?"

"I've heard of it," Dan said.

"And being the humane doctor you are, I assume you're in agreement with it. But doesn't that create a potentially enormous dilemma for you and your colleagues? I've heard that doctors swap as much gossip about each other in their coffee lounges as women do under their hair dryers. Isn't that so, Dr. Lassiter?"

Dan grinned. "I've never been under a hair dryer, Miss Adams. And since becoming general director of my hospital, I've stayed clear of the coffee lounges. But being under oath, I'd have to say that probably is true."

"And since you *are* under oath, do you also admit that a significant number of licensed physicians are either incompetent or unfit to practice medicine because of some physical or mental incapacity?"

"I admit that a *small* percentage of doctors are incompetent. The same for lawyers. What is your point, Miss Adams?"

"*I'll* ask the questions, if you don't mind," snapped Angela Adams, and Dan found the angry glitter of her eyes oddly alluring.

Justice Morton sighed, "Just what *is* the point, Miss Adams?"

"The point, Your Honor, is that most doctors who practice in hospitals are well aware of the incompetents among them. Which means that if such a law existed in Massachusetts, half or more of all physicians in the state would be guilty of noncompliance. May I proceed, Your Honor?"

"You may," Morton hastily replied.

"Dr. Lassiter, would you consider any doctor who consistently practices substandard medicine a bad doctor?"

"I would," Dan said.

Angela fixed her eyes on Dan's, paused a beat, and said, "Would you consider Emil Dubic a bad doctor?"

Dan did not even blink. He had anticipated the question, had asked it of himself dozens of times, and knew he need not answer it in court. As expected, Josephson sprang to his feet to object.

"Objection sustained. *Really,* Miss Adams," Morton chided. "You know better than that. Let's not have any repeats."

"I'm sorry, Your Honor," she said, suppressing a smile. Dan wondered if Morton reminded her of Sydney Greenstreet, too.

Angela Adams turned, took two steps toward the lectern, then suddenly spun around. Her quick movement made Dan draw back slightly. "All right, Dr. Lassiter," she said brusquely, "I realize your time is valuable, so let's get directly to the key issue of this trial: Did Milos Bednarik's death result from mistreatment on Dr. Emil Dubic's part or did it not? You *are* familiar with the deposition and testimony of Dr. Britt Tangway for the plaintiff, are you not?"

"I am."

"And since the opinion Dr. Tangway rendered was based on accepted scientific and medical fact, I assume you two are in substantial agreement?"

"You can assume that we agree on what is, indeed, established medical fact, namely, those aspects of infection that meet Koch's four postulates and those aspects of antibiotic treatment recommended by the FDA's subcommittee on infectious diseases. As for the application of these facts to this particular case, I'm afraid there's very little Dr. Tangway and I agree on."

She glared. "I'm surprised to hear that, Dr. Lassiter. In fact, quite amazed. I remind you again that you are under oath."

Dan squirmed irritably.

"You do concede that Dr. Tangway is a recognized authority in the field of infectious diseases?"

"Well," said Dan sardonically, "ordinarily I would agree. But since you've just reminded me I'm under oath to tell the *whole* truth, I'll have to demur. In medical parlance, to be a recognized authority means that other doctors at a national, or at least state, level associate your name with a particular disease, diagnostic test, or treatment. Such recognition usually comes through original research done and papers published. I personally searched through the *Index Medicus* for the last ten years and could not find a single paper by Dr. Tangway. Nor do I believe Dr. Tangway has his subspecialty board certification in infectious diseases. Therefore, while I'll concede Dr. Tangway is a competent internist with an interest in infectious diseases, he does not qualify as a recognized authority in that field, even in his home state of California."

"I see," Angela Adams said curtly. "Which raises an interesting and, I believe, pertinent point. Dr. Tangway does, indeed, practice three thousand miles away in California, and here we are in Springfield, less than a hundred miles from the 'medical Mecca' of Boston. Yet we could not get a single infectious-disease specialist from this area, however sympathetic he might be to the merits of our case, to agree to testify on behalf of the plaintiff. That's really quite typical, Doctor. The jury can draw its own conclusions as to whether the medical profession is more interested in seeing justice served or in discouraging malpractice actions in general, regardless of their merit. Take you, Dr. Lassiter. Would you, if asked, be willing to testify against a fellow physician in a malpractice suit?"

Josephson half-rose from his seat. "Objection, Your Honor. Question is immaterial, argumentative, and impugns the integrity of the witness."

Morton mused and then nodded. "I agree, counselor, and I'll sustain the objection, though I, too, am curious. Perhaps you might want to rephrase the question, Miss Adams."

She smiled accommodatingly. "Very well, Your Honor. Dr. Lassiter, have you ever testified against a doctor in a malpractice suit?"

"Yes, Miss Adams, I have. He lost his patient through negligence, and the case, too."

Soft laughter sounded through the courtroom.

"My congratulations, Dr. Lassiter," she said. "And now that I have established what a conscientious and fair-minded physician you are, let's get to the heart of the issue. You conduct your own private practice, do you not?"

Dan nodded. "A limited one, yes."

"How limited?"

"It varies. Up until three months ago, when I shifted to full-time administration, I saw between two and three hundred patients a month in my office."

"And, I'd imagine, some of these patients complained of sore throats at times?"

"Yes."

"Was it your practice to treat all, some, or none of these adult patients with antibiotics?"

"I treated them individually, as all patients should be treated."

"And did you obtain throat cultures on all of them?"

"No, not all. But a large percentage."

"And among those that did not get throat cultures—how did you decide whether they needed antibiotics?"

"I—I relied mainly on my clinical judgment."

"Your clinical judgment? In other words, an educated guess."

"More or less," Dan admitted.

"And guesses can, of course, be wrong. Wouldn't it bother you if you failed to treat a strep throat with penicillin and the patient subsequently developed rheumatic fever? Or conversely, if you treated a virus sore throat with penicillin and the patient suffered a severe allergic reaction to it?"

Soberly Dan said, "Yes. It would bother me a great deal. But obtaining throat cultures on every person with pharyngitis is neither foolproof nor practical. It takes at least twenty-four hours to get the throat-culture result, and if the patient's already had a strep infection for two or three days, he can still come down with rheumatic fever despite antibiotic treatment. On the other hand, if you start penicillin while waiting for the culture report, he can have an allergic reaction. So you still have to rely on your clinical judgment."

"Yes, Dr. Dubic made that point innumerable times yesterday. What surprises me, however, is that you disagree so strongly with Dr. Tangway's checklist of clinical features that help make that judgment."

Dan shrugged. "I take mild issue with him on some points."

"Then let me refresh your memory of his checklist to see exactly where you disagree. With the court's permission, I would like to read aloud certain portions of Dr. Tangway's testimony."

The sigh Morton emitted was almost a groan. "Very well, Miss Adams, you may proceed. But *please* make it a small portion. I'm sure I express the sentiments of the jury when I say we've learned far more about the causes and treatment of sore throats than we need to know."

"I *will* be brief, Your Honor. According to Dr. Tangway, the following clinical features point to the presence of a bacterial, rather than a viral, sore throat: 'One, fever greater than one hundred and one degrees in a patient who has not recently ingested aspirin. Two, painful swallowing. Three, pus patches on the pharynx or tonsils. Four, swollen lymph glands in the front of the neck. Five, absence of cold symptoms such as a runny nose or red eyes.' Now, Dr. Lassiter, would you agree that these are the criteria most practicing physicians use to decide whether or not to treat with antibiotics?"

"I suppose so."

"And would you further agree that, according to Dr. Dubic's meager notes on Milos Bednarik, the deceased did not display a single one of these features?"

"I would," Dan answered without hesitation.

Angela Adams nodded approvingly. "Then you would certainly agree that the fatal shot of penicillin he got was not indicated."

Dan stared back at her in silence for a moment before saying, "As far as the treatment of pharyngitis is concerned, I would agree. But Dr. Dubic believed he was treating more than pharyngitis. His physical examination revealed maxillary sinus tenderness, suggesting possible bacterial sinusitis, and crackling breath sounds at the lung bases, suggesting possible bronchitis or early pneumonia."

"Is penicillin the treatment of choice for sinusitis?"

"It is *a* treatment, an acceptable one."

Suddenly looking weary, Angela Adams turned and walked back to the lectern to consult her notes. Dan glanced at Josephson and saw him gesture approvingly with thumb and forefinger.

"Dr. Lassiter," she began anew, "I remind you that an otherwise healthy, productive man with a loving wife is dead because he received an unwarranted shot of penicillin."

"Objection!" Josephson cried out. "I object strenuously, Your Honor, and ask that Miss Adams's last statement be stricken from the record and the jury given the usual cautionary instruction."

"Objection sustained," Morton said. "Jury will dis-regard the last statement. Go on, Miss Adams."

"I repeat, the issue on which this action is based is, whether or not—" She stopped short as a murmur of excitement rose among the spectators and a lank, stooped, white-haired man, wearing a suit and vest despite the heat, came down the middle aisle and sank into the chair beside Mary Bednarik.

"Your Honor," she said immediately, "I realize we're nearing the lunch hour, but with your permission I would like a five-minute recess to confer with my part-ner."

"The lunch hour is, indeed near," Morton replied, "as my stomach has already informed me. But if op-posing counsel has no objection, I will grant you exactly five minutes. Dr. Lassiter, you may step down if you wish."

"Well," asked Dan as he approached Josephson, "what do you think?"

"I think you're doing beautifully. So beautifully, in fact, that I'm worried as hell."

Dan stared. "What for?"

"Two reasons," Josephson said. "First, you've either held your own or beaten Angela on every point she's raised—and she's not beaten so easily. Which makes me suspect she's spent most of the last hour setting you up."

"For what?" Dan demanded.

"Not what. *Who.* The guy who just came in."

"But he can't cross-examine me now! I know that much law."

"You're right, he can't. Not without my permission, which I have no intention of giving. But he's still Charles R. Sprague, the sharpest legal mind I've ever come up against. So watch the written instructions start flying between him and Angela. And be careful, Dan. Be damned careful. Unless I miss my guess, that witness chair is going to turn into a hot seat very soon now."

"Jesus, Ned," Dan said, "you *are* spooked, aren't you?"

"A little," Josephson admitted. "But not without reason. I've been on the verge of beating that guy three times now and each time he's clobbered me with some last-minute disclosure."

"Look," Dan said, "we both know Dubic's a lousy doctor. I wish the hell I'd never accepted him as an intern. But regardless of that, this time he's not at fault."

"Yeah," Josephson said, brightening. "So if you don't get rattled, and I don't get rattled, and that blind lady holding the scales of justice plays it fair and square, we're going to win and Sprague's going to lose—right?"

"Right!"

"Something's funny, though," Josephson mused.

"What?"

"Sprague. Look at him."

Dan turned to stare at the man between Angela Adams and Mary Bednarik. His white hair, mustache, and short beard gave him a benign look in repose, but when he directed his gaze at the defense table, his lower lip curled and his face displayed a hard, cruel set. "What about him?"

"He looks funny," Josephson replied. "Different. Maybe he really is sick."

When Morton reconvened the trial, Angela Adams took a page of notes from Sprague, avoided the lectern, and again positioned herself a few feet from Dan, who was back on the witness stand.

"Dr. Lassiter," she began with renewed vigor, "would you agree that intramuscular penicillin is the leading cause of death from anaphylactic shock in this country?"

"I would agree that it is the leading *reported* cause of death," Dan replied. "Other drugs, such as aspirin, particularly in asthmatics, may be as common, or even more so. However, there're no good statistics on it because such deaths usually occur at home."

"Yet it is true, is it not, that patients with a history of allergic disease are much more likely to suffer penicillin reactions?"

"In general, yes."

"And you *are* aware that Milos Bednarik was treated by Dr. Dubic for allergic rhinitis two years ago?"

"Yes. But I'm also aware that he subsequently received four shots of penicillin without difficulty in the interval."

"Dr. Lassiter, you stated earlier that until recently you conducted your own private practice. Did you, or your nurse, give many office injections?"

Dan shrugged. "Not many, but a few. Mainly testosterone shots to patients with testicular failure."

"What about antibiotics? How often did your patients receive injections of procaine penicillin?"

Dan tensed slightly. "I don't recall ever giving that particular penicillin preparation to any of my patients."

"Oh?" said Angela Adams, feigning astonishment. "Why not?"

"Well, as I suspect you already know, there's not much advantage to intramuscular penicillin over the oral form, since all it does is achieve therapeutic blood levels a few hours earlier."

"Isn't penicillin still the treatment of choice for syphilis?" she asked him.

"It is."

"Then wouldn't you agree that the only justifiable indication for the office injection of procaine penicillin is venereal disease, specifically, gonorrhea or syphilis?"

Dan hesitated. He could see from the anticipatory look on Angela Adams's face that the trap she had laid for him was about to be sprung. Nonetheless, he and Josephson had discussed this issue and decided it wouldn't weigh that heavily with the jury. So what if Dubic did make a few extra bucks off Medicaid by giving his patients penicillin injections instead of pills? It was common practice.

"It's a debatable point," Dan finally said. "Some physicians prefer to give a shot of procaine penicillin in combination with a longer-acting preparation if they feel the patient cannot be relied on to take the full seven-to-ten-day course of oral medication."

"That's *not* what I asked you," she said sharply. "We're not talking about penicillin mixtures. I repeat: apart from the treatment of venereal disease, do you know of any indication for the office injection of procaine penicillin?"

"No," Dan admitted. "Offhand, I don't.

"Thank you, Dr. Lassiter," Angela Adams said with mild sarcasm. "Now, you consider yourself a well-read physician, do you not?"

Dan gestured. "Reasonably."

"And as general director of a large hospital, you *do* receive the monthly bulletin of the Massachusetts Department of Public Health?"

"I do."

"Do you read it?"

"Not word for word."

"But you would be aware of any major epidemic of VD that has recently broken out in the state, would you not?"

"I probably would."

"Are you aware of any such epidemic in this area?"

"No, I'm not."

"Then, since you'd agree that the only indication for the office injection of procaine penicillin is veneral disease, and you are not aware of any VD epidemic raging in Springfield, how do you account for the fact —and we can, indeed, establish it as fact—that Dr. Dubic's nurses give an average of twenty-four injections of penicillin a day to his patients?"

"Objection, Your Honor!" Josephson shouted. "What Dr. Dubic did in other cases is irrelevant and immaterial. The only issue before the court at this time is whether the administration of procaine penicillin was appropriate under the existing circumstances."

Reluctantly Morton nodded. "Objection sustained. Strike that last paragraph from the record."

Suddenly Dan heard Sprague whisper Angela Adams's name and beckon her over to pick up another note. She read it, nodded, and slowly walked back to the witness stand.

Studying her, Dan got the impression that the slight smile on her face did not reflect confidence so much as relief.

"Dr. Lassiter," she said at last, "in the year before your appointment as director of Commonwealth General you were in charge of its emergency room. Have you ever treated acute anaphylactic shock?"

"Yes," said Dan. "Twice."

"Successfully?"

"Yes."

"Would you briefly and simply describe to the jury what happens to a person stricken by this condition."

"Well, certain protective substances produced by the body's white blood corpuscles are immediately attracted to, and attach themselves to, an invading foreign protein, such as penicillin, to form what is called an antigen-antibody complex. This, in turn, releases very powerful chemicals, which contract smooth muscle, particularly the muscle fibers lining the bronchial tubes, and dilate the small blood vessels in the gut, drawing blood away from the heart."

"Excuse me, Dr. Lassiter, but it does cause swelling of certain structures like the tongue, does it not?"

"Yes. The generalized vasodilatation that occurs causes a leak of plasma out of the capillaries into what's called the soft tissue spaces—leading to swelling of the face, tongue, hands, and feet. The throat muscles and vocal cords can swell severely, further blocking air entry into the lungs and reducing oxygen delivery to the brain and heart. When this lack of oxygen becomes critical, the patient experiences severe chest pain, convulsions, and collapse."

"Can these unfortunate patients be saved by the proper treatment?"

"Sometimes, if such treatment is given in time. The survival rate is much higher, of course, if a person suffers an anaphylactic reaction in a hospital, where trained personnel and the necessary resuscitative equipment are immediately available."

"Well, let's say—as happened to Milos Bednarik—he suffers it in a doctor's office. Does he have any chance of survival then?"

"He can, if the doctor is prepared to deal with such an emergency."

"And would you agree that any doctor who gives his patients dozens of shots of penicillin a day should be so prepared?"

"I would."

"Now, Dr. Lassiter, according to Dr. Dubic's own testimony, and the corroborative testimony of two of his office nurses, Milos Bednarik collapsed within a few minutes after Miss Hochman injected two cc's of penicillin into his left buttock, and was found on the floor outside his booth. I assume you have carefully read the description of the emergency treatment Dr. Dubic administered."

"I have," Dan said.

"And, in your expert opinion, do you consider the initial treatment rendered the deceased—namely, oxygen by face mask, Adrenalin by vein, and cortisone by vein—proper?"

"I do."

"Would you consider the subsequent treatment he received—mouth-to-mouth resuscitation, Adrenalin by direct intracardiac injection, and external heart massage—proper as well?"

"Yes, I would."

"*Yet* the patient died. Therefore, I must ask you a very direct and crucial question. Do you consider the treatment Milos Bednarik received not only proper but *adequate?*"

Dan's face creased in confusion. "I'm afraid I don't quite know what you mean by adequate."

"Very well," she said patiently. "Let's backtrack a bit. You *did* read the results of the autopsy performed on the deceased, did you not?"

"I did."

"*This* report," she said, handing Dan a duplicate copy. "Now, if you would kindly refer to page two,

41

paragraph five, entitled 'External Appearance,' you will find the pathologist's description of the deceased's tongue as being swollen twice normal size. Isn't that so, Dr. Lassiter?"

"Yes."

"And on page three, paragraph three, under 'Gross Findings' you'll find the statement 'massive edema, punctate hemorrhages, and severe narrowing of the vocal cords.' Now, I ask you, Dr. Lassiter, based on these autopsy findings and your own experience in resuscitating two similar patients, could anything more have been done to save Milos Bednarik's life; namely, a tracheotomy?"

Slowly Dan nodded. "That's a possibility."

"Did you, in fact, perform tracheotomies on the patients you successfully treated for anaphylactic shock?"

"On one of them," Dan said. "I was lucky enough to slip an endotracheal tube down the throat of the other, obviating the need of a trach."

"I see. Because of the severe swelling of the larynx, or voice box, and spasm of the throat muscles, you realized the futility of mere oxygen by mask or mouth-to-mouth resuscitation and resorted to more effective measures to oxygenate your patient."

"Objection, Your Honor," Josephson said sharply. "That's not what the witness testified!"

"We all heard his testimony, and this is cross-examination," Morton pointed out. "Objection overruled. Proceed."

Angela Adams drew a deep, calming breath. "In the interests of justice, Dr. Lassiter, I must now ask if you'd have performed an emergency tracheotomy to save the life of Milos Bednarik if you, not Dr. Dubic, had been treating him?"

"*Objection,* Your Honor!" Josephson cried, jumping to his feet.

"On what grounds?" asked Morton.

"On the grounds that any answer the witness gave to that question would be sheer speculation on his part. Each medical emergency must be treated individually, and Dr. Lassiter, not having been present at the time of Mr. Bednarik's collapse, cannot possibly be sure what he would or would not do."

"Hmm," Morton pondered. "Objection sustained. Jury will disregard the question."

"One final question, Dr. Lassiter," said Angela Adams with calm assurance. "We've already established that Dr. Dubic completed a rotating internship under your supervision. Could you briefly describe to the jury what this type of internship consists of?"

"It consists of four months of medicine and two months each of pediatrics, obstetrics, surgery, and emergency room."

"And during the two months each intern spends on surgery, is he taught to do a tracheotomy?"

"Yes, it is a requirement of the surgery rotation."

"So you can state with reasonable certainty that Dr. Emil Dubic, while interning at Holmes Memorial Hospital, acquired the necessary skill to do a tracheotomy?"

"Yes," Dan said.

She nodded pleasantly at him, turned, and walked back to the lectern. "I have no further questions of the witness, Your Honor."

"And you, Mr. Josephson," Morton asked, "do you have any questions for Dr. Lassiter before we break for lunch?"

"I do, indeed, have questions, Your Honor, but none so pressing that they cannot keep until this afternoon's session."

"Good!" Morton beamed. "Court stands adjourned until two P.M."

# 5

"Well," Dan said to Josephson after they settled into a booth at a nearby restaurant, "what do you think now?"

Josephson gestured futilely. "I don't know. Should Dubic have done a trach?"

Whether he should have or not was their main topic of discussion through lunch and the first question the defense counsel asked Dan once he was back on the witness stand.

"That's hard to say," Dan answered cautiously. "It's far more difficult to do one in an office than in an operating room." What he didn't say was that an emergency tracheotomy took guts as well as skill. No doctor liked to leave a dead man with a hole in his throat in his office for family members to see and wonder whether disease or a clumsily wielded scalpel actually killed him. "Nor would there be much purpose to it," he went on, "if the patient's heart had stopped. Restoring an effective heartbeat would certainly take priority."

"And since you agree Dr. Dubic tried every ac-

45

ceptable means to restore such a heartbeat, can you fault the emergency treatment he gave the deceased in any way?"

"No, not with the equipment available to him. If he'd had a cardiac defibrillator in his office, he might've tried electroshock to restart the heart. But lacking this equipment, what he did was acceptable."

"Then it's fair to say that Dr. Dubic did the most any doctor could possibly do under the circumstances?"

Dan hesitated briefly. "It's fair to say that anaphylactic shock is a very rare occurrence in a doctor's office, so not many, perhaps hardly any, general practitioners possess defibrillators. Since Dr. Dubic failed to restart his patient's heart by other means, a tracheotomy would not have saved him."

Josephson nodded vigorously. "Thank you, Dr. Lassiter. No further questions, Your Honor."

Justice Morton stirred from his postprandial lethargy and sat up in his chair. "Does counsel for the plaintiff have any more questions for the doctor?"

Angela Adams said, "No, Your Honor, not at this time. But we reserve the right to recall Dr. Lassiter later, if necessary."

"Witness may step down," the judge said.

Dan took a seat at the opposite end of the courtroom in order to observe Charles Sprague at closer range.

As Angela Adams studied the latest page of notes Sprague had handed her, Morton said, "Well, Miss Adams, do you have rebuttal witnesses?"

"I would like to recall Dr. Emil Dubic to the stand," she announced.

Dan saw surprise in Josephson's face and alarm in Dubic's. Slowly, shakily, Dubic mounted the witness stand. He nodded as the judge reminded him he was still under oath, and waited tensely for Angela Adams's first question.

"Dr. Dubic," she said sternly, "you have heard Dr. Lassiter, your former supervisor at Holmes Memorial Hospital, state that you were trained to perform a

46

tracheotomy during your internship. Did you, in fact, perform them?"

"Yes," Dubic replied firmly.

"Approximately how many?"

"Four, maybe five."

"I see. And since finishing your internship, have you done any more tracheotomies—either in the hospital or your office?"

"No," Dubic said.

"Why not?"

"Why not?" he repeated, puzzled. "Because there was no need. The necessity never arose."

"Never?" Angela Adams challenged. "Are you quite sure? I remind you, you are under oath."

Dubic squinted at her suspiciously. "No, not once."

"You do treat cardiac patients, do you not?"

"Yes, some. To the extent I feel able to. Otherwise, I refer them to a cardiologist."

"Yet you do not have a cardiac defibrillator in your office."

"It is an expensive piece of equipment," Dubic said feebly. "I never needed one."

"And, despite the large number of penicillin injections you give your patients each day, you've never before had one suffer an anaphylactic reaction—correct?"

"Objection, Your Honor," Josephson said.

"Oh?" Morton queried. "Why?"

"On the grounds that Dr. Dubic has already testified to that fact yesterday, and it is in the record."

"Do you wish to withdraw the question, Miss Adams?" Morton asked.

"For the time being, I do," she replied. "In Nurse Hochman's deposition, she stated that when she found Mr. Bednarik on the floor outside his booth and helped Dr. Dubic carry him to an examining table, he was gasping for breath. To quote her exact words: 'His breathing was very noisy and labored.' She then went on to state that Dr. Dubic ordered her to administer oxygen to the patient by face mask, and this was done as soon as the portable oxygen tank could be wheeled into the room. Is that your recollection of the events, too, Dr. Dubic?"

Dubic looked wary. "I suppose so."

"And once the oxygen tank arrived, you did administer the oxygen immediately, did you not?"

"Yes, I did."

"How much time would you estimate elapsed between your ordering Nurse Hochman to get the oxygen and your giving it to the patient?"

Dubic shrugged. "Two, maybe three, minutes."

"And *then* you administered it?"

"Yes!" Dubic exclaimed, looking more and more perplexed.

"Before or after giving mouth-to-mouth resuscitation?"

"Before, of course. It does no good to give mask oxygen to a patient who's not breathing!"

"No," she said, "I'd imagine not. And during this three-minute interval, what were you doing?"

"What?" His lips tightly pursed, Dubic paused thoughtfully. "I think—I'm not sure—but I think I was injecting Adrenalin into his vein."

"You were injecting Adrenalin to start his heart beating?"

"Yes—to start his heart beating."

"Is it usual for a patient to continue to gasp for breath after his heart has stopped?"

Dubic blinked his eyes. "It's possible."

"It's possible for him to gasp more than a few final times?"

"Yes. Definitely."

"I think not," Angela Adams said coolly. "It's possible for the heart to continue to beat for a few minutes after a person's stopped breathing, but it's not possible for him to keep breathing for two, three minutes after a heart stoppage. Isn't that so, Dr. Dubic?"

Dubic looked confounded. "It's—it's—I don't know."

"It *is*, in fact, impossible, isn't it?" she said flatly.

Dubic did not reply.

"So, the truth is, Dr. Dubic, that in all probability Milos Bednarik's heart kept beating for at least three minutes after his collapse. Which leads me to conclude that you had sufficient time to perform a lifesaving tracheotomy if you'd acted at once. Isn't *that* so, Dr. Dubic?"

"It's . . . It's . . ." Suddenly Dubic faltered and looked plaintively at the judge. "I—I don't remember," he stammered.

"Now, I ask you directly, Dr. Dubic, did you even consider a tracheotomy?"

"I . . . I suppose I did . . ."

"Did you, in fact, do more than that? Did you grab a scalpel from your emergency tray and actually intend to do one before changing your mind?"

Dubic dropped his gaze to the floor. "I . . . I might have. I don't recall. Everything happened . . . so fast" His voice trailed off.

Angela Adams paused, giving Dubic a chance to regain his composure. "I now ask you again, Dr. Dubic, if you've ever before had one of your patients suffer anaphylactic shock in your office? I assume your attorney has already advised you of the penalty for perjury; you could be put in jail for it. So think carefully before you answer."

Hesitantly Josephson said, "Objection, Your Honor." Then, more forcibly, "Counsel is intimidating the witness."

"Well, Miss Adams," Morton said, "it seems to me you've touched on this ground before and backed off. Exactly what do you hope to accomplish by this line of questioning?"

"I am determined to establish the truth of the matter, Your Honor, and by so doing, spare the defendant the added charge of perjury."

"Hmm," Morton murmured. "Considerate of you. Proceed."

"Thank you, Your Honor," she said and glanced at Charles Sprague, who slowly nodded. He then reached into his vest pocket and withdrew a small pillbox. Watching intently, Dan saw him fumble momentarily, one pill dropping to the floor before managing to grasp another and slip it into his mouth. Dan leaned sideways and strained to see if Sprague swallowed the pill or let it dissolve under his tongue. But before he could be sure, Angela Adams brought the trial to a sudden climax by asking, "Dr. Dubic, do you remember a former patient of yours by the name of Morris Bender?"

Dubic's eyes widened and his jaw quivered.

"I repeat, do you remember treating a patient by the name of Morris Bender five and a half years ago?"

"Bender . . . yes," Dubic muttered disconsolately. "He died."

"*Where* did he die, Dr. Dubic?"

"He . . . he died in my office."

"Of what, Dr. Dubic?"

"Of what?" Dubic repeated, looking dazed.

"Yes, of what?" she demanded harshly.

Dubic remained mute as a detached look came into his eyes.

"Witness will answer the question," Morton ordered.

Numbly Dubic nodded. "He just collapsed—and died," he said tonelessly.

"Yes, Dr. Dubic," Angela Adams said, "he did just collapse and die, ten minutes after your nurse, a Mrs. Mason, gave him an injection of procaine penicillin. We obtained this additional information only yesterday. Mrs. Mason is presently in a convalescent home recovering from lung surgery and so could not be here today to attest to this personally. Now, Dr. Dubic, did you, in fact, attempt a tracheotomy on Mr. Morris Bender?"

"Did I attempt . . . yes. Yes!"

"Did you complete it?"

"I tried to—I tried, but I couldn't. He was dying. I lost my nerve."

"Did you lose your nerve with Mr. Bednarik, too?"

"I . . . I . . . no . . . I don't know," Dubic said before his voice cracked. Wild-eyed and desperate, he appealed to his lawyer for help, only to see Josephson wince and turn his head away. At that, Dubic emitted a long, low moan. "Oh, God! Oh, dear God, forgive me! Milos was my friend! My countryman! I never meant to . . . How was I to know? I tried to save him. I tried, but I couldn't," he sobbed and covered his face with his hands.

The next instant Mary Bednarik began to weep, too, and Sprague gently put his arm around her.

Wearily, Josephson rose to his feet and said, "Your Honor, if opposing counsel does not object, I would like to request a short recess to confer with my client."

"Miss Adams?" Morton inquired.

"I have no objection, Your Honor."

"Very well. Court will take a ten-minute recess," Morton said.

Once Emil Dubic broke down on the witness stand, the lawyer responsible for bringing him to trial virtually dismissed him from his mind. A verdict for the plaintiff being a foregone conclusion now, and an appeal unlikely, the law would punish Dubic for the negligence that had cost Milos Bednarik his life and Mary Bednarik her husband. But that knowledge barely eased the hurt and hollowness he felt inside.

Angela Adams saw the look on his face and recoiled from him, unable to endure the excruciating torment he suffered after each of these trials and the sickness within him she was helpless to heal.

They had not talked openly of his sickness for a long time now. But his sickness, if that's what it was, had to be talked about, he knew. So when he got back to his Boston apartment, he telephoned Nate Clineman, a Los Angeles psychiatrist and the only outsider who knew the origin of his vendetta against certain unworthy members of the medical profession. As always, they talked cryptically on the phone because of the unlikely, though increasing, chance that their conversation was being monitored.

"Nate," he began upon hearing the familiar and unfailingly calm voice, "it's over. The verdict won't be in until tomorrow. But Dubic cracked under Angela's questioning, so I'm pretty certain we won."

"Good," said Nate. "But I still think it was madness for you to risk it. You could've been discovered so easily."

"I know. But I felt I had to. Lassiter was the key witness, and Angela couldn't have handled him alone. Besides, hasn't it been sheer madness from the start? Today was only a bit more extreme."

"When will it all end?" asked Nate with compassion and concern.

"For me? I no longer even think about it. For as long as Billy lives, or I live, I suppose."

"How's Angela?"

"Tired. Her case load's been unusually heavy lately. Otherwise okay. She was as brilliant as ever today."

"And you? Are you sleeping any better?"

"So-so. I've cut back slightly on the lithium and decreased the thyroid to three grains. Seems to work."

"What about your palpitations?"

"I had a few runs in the courtroom today, but an extra Inderal quickly relieved them."

"Are you sure it isn't anything more serious?"

"Reasonably sure. My exercise tolerance certainly hasn't decreased any."

"Has your death wish?" asked Nate.

"That's a nasty dig. You've cured me of that—remember? You helped plot my transformation."

"I know," Nate sighed. "It was better than homicide. I never would've believed you'd carry my reality testing so far! Some day I'll write a paper about you. Or maybe a book. But I still can't quite condone what you're doing, and I wish you'd stop."

"Do you? Surely you've read Edmund Burke: 'The only thing needed for the triumph of evil is for good men to do nothing.' "

"Your logic doesn't impress me. I like Burke, but I dislike zealots. I only wish I could disapprove of what you're doing more strongly. Unfortunately, doctors are such an untidy bunch these days; they need a good housecleaning."

"They need more than that! They need a fumigator. Which, like it or not, is what I've become. Too bad you're so ambivalent about it, but it'll soon be over. I'm bound to be discovered, especially if I'm forced to do again what I did today. Then you can write your book."

"Who's your next target?" Nate asked.

"A GP-surgeon by the name of Gormann. He wiped out an entire family with his bungling. His hospital was so appalled by the incident that both its medical and surgical review committees sent him letters of reprimand. No suspension, no loss of surgical privileges, just letters. Hardly a punishment to fit the crime."

"How did you get onto him? From the inside or outside?"

"Inside. An outraged medical resident. We're getting more and more cases like that."

"That must feed your messianic complex."

"You're lecturing, Nate. And though I normally enjoy your erudition, right now I'm too exhausted to absorb it."

"My apology. But you fascinate and frustrate me. I can't help feeling partially responsible for your obsession, your need for scapegoats." Nate chuckled softly. "It's already cost me thousands of dollars in higher malpractice insurance premiums. But it's futile, you know? And quite damaging. Not just to you but to Angela."

"Yes, I know. She's been quite moody lately, even despondent. It worries me."

"And yet you go on. Come out to see me soon, so we can talk."

"Why? You won't persuade me."

"I'm aware of that. But perhaps I'll finally persuade myself that what you're doing is wrong."

"I'll call you again soon, Nate."

"Yes," said Nate with resignation. "I know you will. Good night."

# 6

Hands gripping the steering wheel, eyes peering straight ahead, Gordon Donnelly listened to Dan's account of the dramatic climax to that afternoon's court session. Then he said, "Dan, level with me. After hearing all the evidence in the Bednarik case, what's your feeling now? Did Emil Dubic commit malpractice or didn't he?"

"Well, obviously I didn't think so this morning or I wouldn't have agreed to testify for him. Even now I'm not one-hundred-percent sure. But failing to buy a defibrillator for his office after one of his patients had died of a penicillin reaction is inexcusable, so I'd have to say he is."

Gordon braked for a red light. "But by that reasoning," he said, moving forward again, "any doctor who gives penicillin shots ought to have a defibrillator in his office. Or in his car, if he happens to make house calls. Are you prepared to go that far?"

Dan gave him a cross look. "What are you getting at?"

"I'm getting at the standard-of-care-in-the-community concept. How many Springfield GPs own defibrillators? Dubic might've defused that line of questioning if he'd come right out and admitted he'd lost a previous patient under similar circumstances. But he didn't, because Emil Dubic is not an honest man."

"So?"

"So, from what you've told me, it sounds like Sprague's strategy was to prove just that to the jury, and he did. Which is why you were on the witness stand so long. All that verbal fencing between you and Angela Adams wasn't to establish that the penicillin shot Milos Bednarik got was medically wrong. It was to establish your professional integrity and Emil Dubic's lack of it. Why? Because in the minds of a jury a dishonest doctor is much more likely to err fatally than an honest one. And even if Dubic didn't exactly commit malpractice on this patient, he doubtless did on others, so they don't mind so much finding him guilty. Jury psychology, Dan. Sprague is a master at it—as you'll find out when they render their verdict."

"Hey, hold on," Dan protested. "Don't give Sprague all the credit. Angela Adams was on the firing line today, and she's a pretty impressive trial lawyer, too."

Gordon smiled. "Damned impressive, and not just for her legal mind either."

"Meaning?"

"Meaning there's not a male lawyer in the state who, after seeing her in action, hasn't fantasized about her in another kind of action."

"Including you?"

"Sure!" Gordon admitted. "Why not me? I even had a try at her once. At a trial lawyers' meeting in Miami. Four of us went out drinking one night—me, Angela, and two guys who couldn't hold their liquor. So after a while that left just Angela and me . . ." Gordon sped around a pair of diesel trucks and then eased the Jaguar back into the right lane.

"So what happened?" asked Dan.

Gordon laughed ruefully. "Just as the hotel bar was about to close and I was about to make my move, she said, as sweetly as my kid sister, 'I know you think you want to go to bed with me, but you really don't.' "

"You protested that, I hope?" Dan said.

"I did! But not to the point of absurdity. After all, she was right. It was mainly my male ego pushing to dominate her physically after failing to do so intellectually. Since we obviously hadn't had time to fall in love, sex merely represented a power game between us, so why pursue it at the risk of one, maybe both of us, getting hurt?"

Dan glanced at him curiously. "So how did it end up?"

"Oh, we parted in the elevator, me feeling very virtuous, and staggered back to our rooms. About fifteen minutes later she called to thank me for a delightful evening. And just in case I had any doubts, to tell me she found me physically very attractive. It really firmed up our friendship. She's a classy dame."

"Interesting about her and Sprague. Josephson filled me in a little about that."

"*Very* little, I'll bet. Look, if lawyers who are envious of Sprague's success get their kicks imagining that he and Angela frenziedly fall into bed after each courtroom triumph, let them. But it's just malicious gossip! That answer your question?"

"I never asked one," said Dan innocently.

But there were questions about Charles Sprague and Angela Adams on his mind. Particularly puzzling was the look they shared the moment Dubic collapsed on the witness stand. Instead of triumph, or even satisfaction, it seemed to reflect a strange melancholy, as if they were commiserating over some loss. Then Angela's eyes had searched the crowd until they fixed on someone in the rear of the courtroom, and the same look was repeated. Dan had half-risen to see the recipient of her look, but spectators blocked his view. Ever since, he had suspected that far more than the outcome of a malpractice trial was at stake for her and Sprague.

Gordon dropped him off at home, declined the offer of a drink, and drove on to his own place a few miles down the road. Dan trudged up the front walk in the fading light, feeling physically and mentally drained.

Thirty minutes later, after showering, slaking his thirst with lemonade, and eating a warmed-over pizza, Dan got into his Datsun and headed for the hospital. He drove slowly, pondering the events of the day. Stern, silent Charles R. Sprague and his comely law partner had certainly made an impact on him. He even felt a twinge of sympathy for Emil Dubic after the devastating attack the Sprague-Adams team had unleashed on him. But then he thought of Mary Bednarik, sitting forlorn and uncomprehending at the defense table, and promptly dismissed Dubic as unworthy of his sympathy. Losing the lawsuit would cost him some adverse publicity and a steep increase in malpractice insurance premiums, but that was all. What Mary Bednarik had lost was not comparable. However good a marriage the Bednariks had enjoyed, Dan remembered from the trial that it had lasted twenty years. In contrast, his own marriage to Lois had barely lasted three—all of them as turbulent as a sloop caught in a Cape Cod squall. Even so, he missed her presence at times, particularly in the evening hours when the isolated, tree-sheltered home they had built together became a veritable morgue of unsettling emotions.

There was no denying that sex had been good between them—so good that for months after the divorce Lois would periodically turn up at his door and entice him into letting her spend the night. He didn't mind that she was usually boozed up, since that had often been a precondition to their lovemaking. Nor did he mind hearing her compulsive confessions that all the men she was dating or bedding were callow boys compared to him. It was simply that she was costing him too much sleep, both by her presence and by the painful reminder of how miserably he had failed in his first sustained effort to live with another human being. Eventually Dan had put a stop to her impromptu visits. So he had tried hard to convince Lois that her visits were damaging both of them, and when that failed, he'd resorted to more drastic, shameful tactics.

Knowing how infuriated, even apoplectic, Lois's father, J. P. Briggs, would be to learn that his daughter was still carrying on with her ex-husband, Dan had taunted her into calling him late one night. Lois had been drunk and sexually explicit with her puritanical father, and he had reacted predictably. God only knew what steps J.P. took, but that was the end of Lois's nocturnal visits.

A seven o'clock news report on his car radio captured his attention. The broadcaster announced that a bill before the Massachusetts legislature to abolish or severely reduce the contingent fees lawyers collected in successful malpractice actions had been sent back to committee for further study. Dan accepted the legislative stall with equanimity. Contingency fees were exclusively a lawyers' device; instead of setting a standard charge or billing the plaintiff by the hour, the lawyer would take a healthy chunk—usually one-third to one-half—of any cash judgment contingent on winning the case. And since many legislators were lawyers by training, the contingent fee system doubtless appealed to their gambling instincts. This development only affirmed what Dan already believed, that despite all the high-sounding oratory by doctors and lawyers over the malpractice issue, the economic component ruled supreme.

Ah, well, he thought philosophically, as the face of Commonwealth General Hospital loomed ahead, he had probably seen the last of Charles R. Sprague. And he would certainly think twice before agreeing to testify at any more malpractice trials.

Dan's office was on the top floor of the twenty-story structure. It was nearly fifty feet long by twenty wide, with a bank of windows lining one wall and a frosted skylight in the ceiling. During Gundersen's regime as general director the office had been called "the throne room" by underlings, and Dan still thought of it as such, which only added to his sense of annoyance at its outlandish size.

Hedley, his private secretary, long departed for the day, had left a stack of memos on his desk, the top one marked urgent and reading: "Contact Dr. Hermanson soon as possible. Trouble with one of Dr. Trombley's patients."

Dan groaned.

"People get trembly when they deal with Trombley" was the saying among the house staff. And there was good reason for it. Dr. Peter Trombley, a tall, distinguished-looking man in his mid-fifties, was the bane of Dan's existence at Commonwealth General. An internist, arthritis specialist, and adroit medical politician, Trombley shamelessly overutilized the hospital, the laboratory, and the medical residents, who did most of the work on the twenty or more patients he kept hospitalized at all times.

Dan and Peter Trombley went a long way back in the twenty-year history of the *new* Commonwealth General Hospital. Trombley had been one of Dan's first attending men during Dan's medical residency, and perhaps because Dan was athletic enough to give him a good workout on a handball or tennis court, Trombley had sought him out socially, inviting him home for dinner or aboard his boat for weekend cruises. Gradually their socializing ceased as Dan's training advanced and his medical knowledge surpassed Trombley's. But the animosity between them now had not emerged until Dan had been vaulted from chief of the emergency room services to general director of the hospital.

In deference to Trombley's past services, Dan had kept him on the teaching staff, despite the house staff's dislike and distrust of him. The female residents, who bore the brunt of Trombley's insecurity with women, called him a "neck-biter"—the sort of attending man who would withhold comment on a case until he could deliver a cutting one. Dan's clinical superiority protected him from the neck-biting but not the back-stabbing—and Trombley was a political back-stabber of fearsome cunning. Worse yet, he was spokesman for the old guard of the medical staff, those members who resisted change as they resisted Christian Science, chiropractic, and socialized medicine, and who seemed to believe that private patients were not so much a doctor's responsibility as his exclusive charges, to do with as he saw fit.

Upon becoming general director of the hospital, Dan had tried to placate Trombley by seeking his advice on policy matters and appointing him to various committees. And for a while it had worked. But then the chief of medicine, a Gundersen appointee, had retired, forcing Dan to make a difficult choice: whether to respect Trombley's seniority in the department and give him the job or give it to Spencer Walt, a much younger and more able internist. Dan had ended up by making two decisions, hoping one might temper the other. Knowing how reluctant Trombley would be to relinquish his lucrative private practice, he had persuaded the hospital board to create a full-time, salaried position for the medicine department chief. Secondly, he had chosen Spencer Walt for the job. Dan well knew the political risk he was running by such a maneuver, but figuring money meant more to Trombley than professional prestige, he reckoned it could work. He was wrong. Trombley resented losing the chief-of-medicine job bitterly, and ever since Dan had repeatedly felt his sting. Time after time, he and his supporters had thwarted Dan's recommendation that the department hire more full-time subspecialists, a move that would markedly improve the teaching program while further limiting the number of hospital admissions each private physician was allowed.

In angry moments Dan longed to deal with Peter Trombley once and for all—if not in the professional arena, then in some back alley. But opportunities for the first remained maddeningly elusive; even though Trombley's competency had deteriorated to the point where he was making mistake after mistake on his patients, none was so flagrant that Dan could really nail him on it. And Dan had obviously outgrown the back-alley approach.

As Spencer Walt had lamented to him a few weeks before: "The two biggest problems I have are Peter Trombley and my hemorrhoids." The remark had gotten around, and the next day two rectal surgeons on the staff had called Walt offering to solve half his problems.

At the moment, however, Spence Walt was on a beach in the Bahamas with the female intern on his service. The fact that Dan had been best man at their wedding did not stop him from being momentarily irked at Walt for being gone at such an inopportune time.

Reluctantly Dan picked up his phone and had the hospital operator summon Dr. James Hermanson, the chief medical resident, to his office. Maybe, just maybe, he speculated while waiting for Hermanson to appear, Trombley had merely committed a faux pas this time— like making an anti-Semitic crack to one of his Jewish residents or really biting the neck of a female one— instead of another medical atrocity. But the way Hermanson, a bull-necked former hockey player, stormed into his office told Dan there was little hope of that.

Waving Hermanson to the chair by his desk, Dan said curtly, "Sit down and calm down—if you can. Coffee?"

Hermanson sat, his jaw thrust out belligerently, and said, "No thanks, Dr. Lassiter. No coffee, no soft soap, and no philosophizing. What I want is backup from someone in authority."

"All right," Dan sighed, "what's the problem?"

"The problem," Hermanson growled, "is that Dr. Trombley would rather let one of his patients die than admit the house staff's right and he's wrong."

"I see," Dan said. "Have you discussed the case with your attending man?"

Hermanson shook his head. "Dr. Lerner's out of town. So's Spence Walt."

Dan grimaced. "So that lays the problem squarely in my lap. All right, let's hear about it."

"Two days ago Trombley admitted a guy by the name of Harry Jukes to the medical service on ten north. Jukes is a sixty-year-old ex-alcoholic who's been off the booze for years; in fact, is a pillar of the local AA community. Anyway, for the past week or so he's been complaining of progressive shortness of breath, hacking cough, leg-swelling, and chest tightness."

"A chronic lunger?" Dan asked.

"No. No history of it. Doesn't drink, smoke, or chew."

"Then what's he got?"

"He's got severe congestive heart failure. Even a junior medical student could make that diagnosis. But because his liver enzyme levels are so high—his serum transaminase is almost 2,000 units—Trombley's calling it hepatitis. What's worse, he insists we treat him for it *and nothing else.*"

"Well," said Dan after deliberating a moment, "a serum transaminase over 2,000 units usually *does* mean hepatitis—with one important exception: acute passive congestion of the liver from right-sided heart failure. Is that what you think he's got?"

"Damned right!" Hermanson snapped. "His neck veins are distended up to his earlobes. And his lungs are wet enough to float a barge! So he's sure as hell in heart failure, most likely from a massive pulmonary embolus. But Trombley keeps insisting it's hepatitis, because his serum ammonia and prothrombin time are also up, and won't let us anticoagulate him."

"Did you get a lung scan?" asked Dan, referring to the radioactive isotope test to detect the presence of blood clots in the lungs.

"Trombley wouldn't even let us get that until I really raised a stink. So he's ordered one for tomorrow morning."

"Good," Dan said. "So what's the problem?"

"The problem is, the patient's so cyanotic and short of breath he's not going to last till morning."

Dan stared at him hard. "Is Trombley aware of this?"

Hermanson thrust out his jaw again. "I told him. I practically shouted it over the phone. But he still hasn't come in to see the patient tonight. And he won't let me start a heparin drip because he says the prothrombin time's too high. So I'm a little unstrung, Dr. Lassiter," he said with a tight smile. "And if you don't do something about that stupid son of a bitch Trombley, I might just commit a little murder."

Dan gestured for Hermanson to calm down. "What about a pulmonary angiogram?" he asked, postponing the issue of Trombley's competency for the moment.

"He nixed that, too. Claims the patient's too sick to be moved to the X-ray department."

"Then what the hell is he doing?" demanded Dan exasperatedly.

"Ordering me to blast him with diuretics until he finishes playing tennis at his club."

Dan's face betrayed his anger. Unnecessary medical guesswork of any kind infuriated him, none more than telephone orders by doctors too lazy to come in and check their patients. And, according to both nursing and house staff, Trombley was one of the worst offenders.

Rising abruptly, Dan faced his chief resident with a look that made Hermanson take a hasty step backwards. "*Did* you blast him with diuretics?" he almost snarled.

"No, sir, I didn't!" Hermanson replied. "Too dangerous."

"What did you do?"

"I tried to get hold of you."

"Well, you succeeded! So let's go see the patient."

Dan followed Hermanson to the tenth floor, and the bedside of Mr. Harry Jukes, collecting the intern and resident on the case enroute. The intern's name, Dan learned from the nameplate on his white coat, was Robelli. He was squat, hirsute, bespectacled, and properly intense. His resident, whose name was Hirsh, stood almost a foot taller in her high heels and appeared more relaxed in the general director's presence. She was a willowy blond with alert but tired eyes and a winsome smile. Commonwealth General Hospital was certainly attracting more and better-looking female doctors these days, Dan mused, strongly in favor of the trend.

"All right, Doctor," Dan said, taking the chart from under her arm, "let's go see your patient and find out what's really wrong."

Harry Jukes's mind was so muddled by lack of oxygen he hardly realized that he was in a hospital bed and that several doctors had just entered his room. Since he had been lucid only hours earlier, this stuporous state represented a rapid and ominous deterioration.

Harry Jukes wanted desperately to live. Eight years before, when his wife, Mildred, had died of cancer, he had set out to drink himself to death and nearly succeeded. But his devoted daughter, a few friends, and above all his AA group had sustained him through this desolation until his will to live returned and became firmly rooted in a project that gave new meaning to his existence. Now, with his lungs burning like fire with each breath and frothy pink mucus gurgling in his throat, Harry knew intuitively he was near death and, with all the resolution his oxygen-starved brain could muster, was determined to forestall it. Just a brief reprieve, perhaps only a month, was all he needed to complete the work that had so enriched his life these last few years and could enrich the lives of others.

Harry Jukes loved books. For thirty-five years he had checked them out to readers at the Boston Public Library. More than that, he had advised people—particularly young people—as to what volumes were most worth borrowing. Over the years he declined every promotion offer, preferring to stay at the checkout desk, where he could continue his daily discussions with young people on the merits of various books and authors.

Harry had his own favorites, C. S. Lewis's seven-volume *Narnia* series topping the list, but he knew hundreds of others by obscure foreign and American writers of comparable charm and imagination. When a youngster asked him for a good book to read, Harry could quickly size him up, race through his mental filing system, and pick one that almost always made the young reader return and enthusiastically ask for more.

If not unique, Harry's prodigious knowledge of children's classics was at least rare, and some five years earlier it had occurred to him that it ought to be preserved. Unlike the many lists of great literary works for adults—the Five-Foot Bookshelf, the Harvard Classics, Great Ideas—there was nothing similar that children, or people picking books for children, could consult that would recommend books by reading age, along with brief synopses of their plots and a suggestion for the sequence in which they might best be read.

A Boston publisher liked the idea, and for the last five years Harry had labored most nights and weekends to compile such a work. Now his great compendium was nearly finished; it needed only a final editing and indexing. One more month of hard work and Harry Jukes's legacy to future children would be ready.

Harry had been generally healthy until two weeks before, when a long automobile ride left him with a cramping pain and swelling in his left leg. A few nights later he was suddenly wakened by a smothering sensation and a stabbing pain in his upper back. Although the chest pain had eased by morning, Harry was sufficiently alarmed by it to go see his family physician, Dr. Peter Trombley.

Dr. Trombley gave him a cursory physical examination, ordered an electrocardiogram and several blood tests, and instructed him to return the next day. That evening, however, Trombley's nurse telephoned to tell him that he had hepatitis and must enter the hospital immediately.

As an arrested alcoholic Harry knew something about liver disease, and he could not understand how an inflammation of that organ could cause such severe shortness of breath and chest pain. When he asked Trombley about it, he was tersely told his blood tests proved conclusively that he had hepatitis and his lung trouble was probably a complication of it.

Harry dimly remembered that one of the young doctors who had examined him earlier had mentioned liver coma and he supposed that was what was making him so fuzzy-headed. But he also remembered another young doctor arguing that it wasn't liver coma at all but some lung disease whose name meant nothing to him. After they left, Harry had managed a brief prayer beseeching God to spare him long enough to finish his compendium, and then had lapsed into his present stupor.

The moment they entered Harry Jukes's room Dan realized the man was *in extremis*. Despite the oxygen streaming into his nostrils through plastic prongs, his color was distinctly dusky and his breathing was rapid and gasping. After Hermanson introduced him, Dan tried to question Jukes but could not get him to stop his continual grunting and groaning. A younger doctor might have considered such noises self-indulgent and irritating, but Dan knew better. Experience had taught him they were the last, desperate signals of a dying man.

Dan fit his stethoscope to his ears and quickly examined the man from eyeballs to toes, eliciting the signs of right-sided heart failure and the presumptive evidence of massive pulmonary emboli. Straightening, he turned to Hermanson and said, "Go ahead and start him on heparin."

Hermanson nodded vigorously. "What about Trombley?"

"I'll handle Trombley," Dan said curtly and strode out of the room toward the nursing station.

Hermanson followed a few steps behind and halted in the doorway as Dan seized the telephone on the desk. Dan saw his uncertain look and waved him in, feeling Hermanson had earned the right to overhear what he had to say to Trombley.

"Pete?" Dan began after reaching him. Trombley's breathless reply indicated he had interrupted him in the midst of a match, and with perverse pleasure Dan could picture him sweating and scowling. "This is Dan Lassiter," he continued. "Sorry to bother you, but Jim Hermanson asked me to take a look at your patient Mr. Jukes in room 1009, and I agree he's a puzzler."

"What's so puzzling?" Trombley replied coolly. "With a transaminase and ammonia level that high, he's clearly got liver failure secondary to hepatitis."

"Oh, he might well have. But Hermanson mentioned you were also considering acute right heart failure, and I tend to agree that's the more likely diagnosis."

"Well," Trombley said after a pause, "you've a right to your opinion. But as far as I'm concerned, it's hepatitis."

"Have you seen him tonight?"

"Not yet. But I intend to." Trombley sounded defensive. "Soon as I get through here."

"How long?"

"Oh, another hour or so."

"Then you wouldn't mind us playing it safe and starting him on heparin in the meanwhile, would you?"

Trombley hesitated. "What for?"

"To keep him alive until you get here!" Dan said scornfully.

"I . . . why . . . Now, look, Dan," Trombley spluttered, "he's my patient, and I don't recall asking you to consult on him."

"I'm aware of that. But this is still a teaching hospital, and as general director I have access to *every* teaching patient. Furthermore, I've just examined the man and I'm telling you he's critical. I'm also trying to spare you an appearance before the medical conduct-and-review committee in case you lose him. Use your head, Pete. You know damned well you can't treat liver failure in someone this far gone, so heparin's his only chance."

"What if he bleeds on it?"

"Then he bleeds! It's easier to treat bleeding than clotting, and right now it's the blood clots in his lungs that're going to kill him."

Dan heard Trombley curse under his breath. "All

right," he finally said, "if you feel *that* strongly about it, Dan, go ahead. I'll just transfer the patient to staff and let you be responsible for him. But I'm sick and tired of the medical residents running to Spence Walt or you every time I don't give them a free hand with one of my patients."

"I can understand that, Pete," said Dan soothingly.

"I'm not so sure you can, since you haven't any private patients of your own. Is the guy's daughter around?"

"Yes. Want to talk to her?"

"No, you do it. You're doing everything else! Just tell her I'm tied up with an emergency at another hospital and temporarily turning the case over to you. But I'm warning you now, Dan, I'm getting damned tired of being second-guessed all the time by medical residents still wet behind the ears!"

"Well, Pete, if it's any comfort to you, my ears feel nice and dry. So let's discuss this matter in my office in the morning. Eight o'clock all right with you?"

"Yeah, I suppose," muttered Trombley after a pause. "But I don't know what the practice of medicine is coming to when a doctor can't call the shots on his own private patients. I never had this trouble when Gundersen was running things."

"Didn't you? Well, we can discuss that in the morning, too," Dan said and hung up. Shaking his head with disgust, he turned to Hermanson and asked, "Think you can save him?"

"We can sure try."

"Then try! My neck's out a mile on this one." Wearily Dan rose, stretched, and added, "I'll be in my office awhile longer, if you need me."

# 7

When Dan finally left the hospital that night, Harry Jukes was still alive but failing fast; his grunts were barely audible, his blood pressure was bordering on shock, his lips and nailbeds were ominously blue. In the event that Jukes should die, Dan ordered Jim Hermanson to go to any lengths to get permission for an autopsy: plead, threaten, lie, tell his daughter he had bubonic plague—anything!—but get it. Hermanson, knowing what a ruckus Trombley would raise over their takeover of the case, and also knowing that when doctors differ on the diagnosis of a critically ill patient the pathologist usually decides, promised Dan that he would.

Ghoulish as it seemed for them to be more concerned about the postmortem than about the patient, it was one of the realities of medical practice, Dan reflected as he walked out of the hospital into the muggy night air. If Jukes lived, their presumptive diagnosis of heart failure secondary to pulmonary emboli would remain unproven and Trombley would be off the hook. Medical conduct-and-review committees seldom disciplined a doctor whose patient somehow survived, no matter how

71

badly he had bungled the case. If, however, the patient succumbed, they felt compelled to take some punitive action, but not too much. After all, they were only a review board; much as they might cringe and grumble among themselves, they were not empowered to deal with negligent homicide. Nor would they submit their findings to a district attorney. Maybe if a colleague were peddling narcotic prescriptions or fraudulently overbilling Medicare they might; but given certain proof that, through inexcusable negligence or incompetence, a doctor on their staff had actually killed a patient, would they report him to the criminal authorities then?

Dan doubted it. It was not that doctors considered themselves above the law; what usually made them hesitate was their state of confusion, even inner turmoil, over how to satisfy the law while upholding the principle of professional confidentiality.

It was a dilemma more and more doctors faced these days. And the malpractice crisis was pressing them hard to find an acceptable solution. When *did* an erring doctor cross the fine line between malpractice and manslaughter? It was a problem Dan had pondered enough to know it defied any clear demarcation. Emil Dubic had been guilty of malpractice, of actionable ineptitude. But what about Peter Trombley? Had he heeded the house staff's advice and started Jukes on heparin therapy a day or even hours earlier, the patient might have recovered. Now the odds were overwhelmingly against it.

Fortunately, at some absolute cellular level, Harry Jukes decided to defy the odds and live. Shortly after four A.M. he stopped grunting and asked the nurse for a sip of water. It was a simple request, and the nurse, having no instructions to the contrary, complied. But when Jukes demanded more, she thought she had better check with Dr. Hermanson, who she knew was still on the floor.

"He actually *asked* for water?" Hermanson said, surprised. "He didn't just gesture?"

"He asked," the nurse affirmed. "At least, the first time. The second time he growled for it. Should I give him more?"

Thoughtfully Hermanson said, "Yeah, go ahead. I'll be right in to see him."

Picking up the telephone, Hermanson dialed the laboratory for the results of the last set of blood tests he had drawn on Jukes. But the technician, swamped with work from the emergency room, told him it would be another ten minutes.

Hermanson did not complain, as he might have had his patient not asked the nurse for water. It took a sufficient supply of oxygen from Jukes's lungs to his brain to activate the cerebral cortex—which meant that the blood clots in his pulmonary arteries were beginning to dissolve. Hermanson's bedside examination confirmed this assumption, and he phoned Dan to tell him the news.

"Good job!" Dan replied after hearing the chief resident's report. "Have you told Trombley yet?"

"No. I thought I'd let you do it. At your eight o'clock meeting. If he still disagrees with the diagnosis of pulmonary emboli, tell him we might've hit on a new cure for end-stage hepatitis!"

A little before eight A.M., Trombley's secretary called Dan's to inform her that a medical emergency prevented Dr. Trombley from keeping his appointment with Dr. Lassiter. Dan was not surprised. Trombley was no confronter, certainly not on a one-to-one basis. He needed an audience to play to, or at least one loyal supporter to bolster his courage. Nonetheless, a showdown between them was brewing, Dan knew, and was bound to come soon.

Dan did not go directly home from the hospital that evening. Instead he drove to the Longway Medicenter, a nursing home on the outskirts of Wellesley, to visit a patient, an elderly, German-born industrialist and *bon vivant* whose company Dan always enjoyed.

73

The place was located on a four-lane highway between a fast-food restaurant and a wholesale furniture outlet. Its brown brick and tinted glass exterior and its almost total lack of landscaping made it look more like an office building or a warehouse than a nursing home. Its lobby was dimly lit, furnished with plastic-covered chairs and vending machines, and drably depressing. With all their bad publicity and burdensome state regulations, nursing homes in Massachusetts had fallen on hard times, and Dan could understand why patients resisted even a short stay in one. But Longway's medical facilities and nursing staff were supposedly the best in the area. Or so Dan had heard.

He began to doubt it after entering and finding no one behind the reception window. He strode down the corridor to the nursing station, but it was deserted too. Dan returned to the lobby and was pacing irritably, waiting for the receptionist to show, when he saw Tom Townes, a young doctor he had taught as a medical student, bustle through the front door.

"Hi, Dr. Lassiter!" Townes said heartily. "What're you doing here?"

"Visiting a patient, if I can find where they've hidden him. Where the hell's the nursing staff?"

"Probably on the second or third floor. Tuesday's the night Nick Sloan and a group of his house staff from Palmer Memorial make rounds."

"Dr. Nicholas Sloan?"

"Yeah, you know him?"

Dan did not, but he had heard the name mentioned in medical circles more and more lately. A relative newcomer to Boston, Dr. Nicholas Sloan was director of clinical services at Palmer Memorial Hospital, one of the largest private hospitals in the area, and was rapidly building a reputation for himself as an expert in geriatric medicine. With a team of neurologists and psychiatrists, Sloan had meticulously examined one hundred patients with the dooming diagnosis of "senile dementia" and had found correctable diseases, ranging from brain tumors to chemical depression, in almost forty percent of them! After dealing with the ravages of old age for so many years, Dan had once doubted that senility was an acceptable alternative to death. But that was before reading Sloan's remarkable report. He looked forward to meeting him.

"You're not interning at Palmer, are you?" he asked Townes.

"No, at Mass. General. But my grandmother was a patient here, after supposedly suffering a series of strokes, until Sloan made the fancy diagnosis of combined hypothyroidism and pernicious anemia on her. So now she's back running her cannery on the Cape."

"That was quite a diagnosis," Dan said.

"Sloan's quite a doctor! A real clinician like you. He's even got me hooked on geriatric medicine, and I plan to go into psychiatry."

"Hmm," said Dan, intrigued. "But where are all the nurses?"

"Making rounds with him. He really involves them in his evaluations. And the patients think he's God's special angel."

"What do you think?"

"Me? I'm a convert." Townes glanced at his watch. "Sloan's probably made his way down to the second floor by now. C'mon. I'll introduce you."

Dan hesitated briefly and then nodded. He followed Townes up the staircase to the second floor and along the corridor until they came to a four-bed ward crowded with people. Sloan's entourage comprised about twelve nurses, nurse's aides, medical students, and house staff.

"That's Dr. Sloan at the bedside," Townes whispered, and Dan saw a tall, lanky man about his own age with steel gray hair, a triangular face, and a stern, almost austere demeanor that was suddenly transformed by a boyishly disarming smile when he responded to a nurse's question. He then turned to the patient in the bed, a florid-faced man in his fifties, and extended his hand. The patient sat up and tried to grasp it, but could not overcome the involuntary writhing and thrashing motions of his right arm. The medical term for such purposeless movements is *choreo-athetosis,* and Dan knew it had many causes, none good.

"So your doctor told you," he heard Sloan say, "that the shaking and thrashing of your arm could be Saint Vitus's dance, but more likely was a bad case of nerves. Is that right, Mr. Barbour?"

The patient nodded. "That's what he thought at first."

"And what did he recommend?"

"Tranquilizers. Strong ones."

"Did they help?"

"Helped turn me into a zombie! Couldn't think, drive, nothing! The truth is, Dr. Sloan," the patient said, his eyes suddenly moistening, "I got pretty discouraged. Even thought about . . . about . . . you know."

"You thought about killing yourself?" Sloan said directly.

"Yeah," muttered Barbour, hanging his head.

"How?"

"Easy. I'm a World War Two vet. Battle of the Bulge. Got me quite a collection of German handguns."

"I see," Sloan said softly. "We'll want to talk more about that later. Right now I'd like to ask you a few more medical questions. Noticed any weakness of an arm or leg?"

"Yeah. My right leg gets gimpy at times and drags. And my right hand's so weak I can't hardly turn on a water faucet. Fact is, I have a hell of a time doing anything in the bathroom."

"What do you mean?" Sloan asked.

"I can't even relax by soaking in a hot tub. Itch like the devil afterwards. With my arm shaking like it does, I almost drive myself crazy scratching."

Watching Sloan's face, Dan could almost read his thoughts.

"Did your family doctor get any blood tests on you, Mr. Barbour?"

"Sure. He ran a whole bunch in his office. Said I had a high uric acid—whatever that means—and it could lead to gout. Other than that, though, my blood was good. He even told me I had more than my share."

"All right, Mr. Barbour," said Sloan abruptly, "slip off your pajama tops and let's examine you."

Dan watched intently as Sloan spent ten minutes or so doing a general physical examination and then, after reaching into his bag for a tuning fork, a rubber-tipped reflex hammer, and an assortment of pins, another ten minutes doing a neurologic exam. Dan was impressed both by his thoroughness and by the way his running commentary held the audience's interest. He could sense the suspense building among them as Sloan finished up. The patient had won their sympathy, and they were hoping something could be done to help him.

Putting his instruments back in his black bag, Sloan turned to the white-jacketed intern beside him and said, "Hal, take a feel of his abdomen and tell me what you find."

Gently the intern dug the pads of his fingers under the patient's right rib cage and had him take a deep breath. Then he repeated the maneuver on the left side. "I think I can feel the spleen," he finally said.

Sloan looked pained. "You *think?*"

The intern smiled sheepishly and removed a plastic ruler from his pocket. "Take another deep breath and hold it please, Mr. Barbour," he told the patient before placing the ruler on his abdomen. "The spleen is palpable three centimeters below the left costal margin," he reported.

"That's better," Sloan said. "So what's he got?"

"That's what *I* want to know," the patient interjected.

Sloan gave him a tolerant look. "I'm not sure yet—won't be until we run a few more tests on you—but I strongly suspect you've got too much blood in your body. A disease that goes by the fancy name of polycythemia rubra vera."

"Is it bad? It sure sounds bad!"

"It *is* serious, Mr. Barbour. Can cause a lot of complications—some of which you've already suffered."

"Like what?"

"Like a small stroke. Which I think is what's causing those uncontrollable thrashing motions of your right arm. It's also what's making you itch after a hot bath."

Barbour paused as if gathering courage to ask his next question. "Can anything be done for me, Doc?"

The entourage seemed to hold its collective breath as Sloan deliberated. "Matter of fact, it can," he finally said. "The treatment might seem old-fashioned, but we're going to bleed you. Drain off a pint of your blood at a time, until what's left isn't so thick. Then we'll put you on drugs to prevent your red blood cell count from building back up again. With any kind of luck, your windmill-imitating days will be over soon."

As the patient closed his eyes in prayerful silence, Sloan said, "Well, see you next week, Mr. Barbour," and walked away.

"Oh, Dr. Sloan!" Townes called out as he reached the corridor. "Here's somebody I'd like you to meet. Dr. Daniel Lassiter."

Dan smiled. "Pleasure to meet you, Dr. Sloan."

"The pleasure's mine, Dr. Lassiter," Sloan replied, shaking hands. "I've been meaning to drop by Commonwealth General for a chat with you."

"Any time," Dan said. "I'm sure we have much of mutual interest to talk about."

"Maybe more than you realize. Curt Gundersen was one of my teachers too, you know."

Dan was surprised. "No, I didn't know! But I should've suspected from the way you do your physical exam." He reached into his inside coat pocket and withdrew a ruler. "I still measure the size of livers and spleens, too. Afraid Gundersen's ghost might return to ridicule me if I didn't. But please go on with your rounds. I'd like to tag along awhile longer, if you don't mind."

"Not at all," said Sloan, looking pleased. "In fact, I could use your help on the man in the end room. I have one more patient to visit, but we could see him directly if you're short on time."

"Not really. I have a patient of my own here, but I can check him later. Go ahead and finish your rounds."

The next patient Sloan saw astounded Dan—an elderly man who had been labeled schizophrenic after having been found sitting alone in his rented room barking uncontrollably like a dog. Subsequently he had spent several weeks in a psychiatric hospital undergoing a variety of treatments, including electroshock, before being transferred to Longway as a hopeless case. In a brilliant diagnostic feat, Dr. Sloan had deduced that the barking sounds were not due to psychotic delusions but to the respiratory spasms sometimes seen in Parkinson's disease, and he had succeeded in abolishing them with proper treatment.

Dan was deeply impressed and said so. "I'd have missed that diagnosis for sure!"

Sloan shrugged modestly. "Not if you'd seen a patient like him before. I once spent a month with George Cotzias at Brookhaven and he showed me one. By pushing L-dopa therapy to the limit, George managed to reduce the severity of the vocal cord tic but couldn't completely abolish it. Fortunately we had better luck here."

"You really ought to write the case up," Dan suggested. "I'll make sure the *New England Journal of Medicine* gives it serious consideration," he added, hoping he didn't sound patronizing.

"Thanks," Sloan said, after dismissing his entourage for the night. "I probably should. Now let me show you the patient I need help on."

Dan said, "Fine. What's he got?"

Sloan hesitated. "His basic problem is dementia. But if you don't mind, I'd prefer not to tell you what I *think* he's got, so as not to influence your evaluation in any way. Believe me, Dr. Lassiter, I'm not trying to test you or put you on the spot; it's just that the case is complicated—in more ways than one—and I could use your independent judgment."

"I understand," said Dan. "Lead me to him."

"He's in the next room. But he's too demented to give you any meaningful history, so let me fill you in on what I know before we go in. His name is Jonathan Hale. Sound familiar?"

"Hale?" repeated Dan, stroking his chin. "Yes, vaguely. Who is he?"

"An architect. Boston-based and much in demand until he retired, at age fifty-nine, a year ago. According to his wife he did so voluntarily so that they could travel, but his partner tells quite a different story. First thing Hale developed was trouble keeping his balance. Fell off one scaffold, suffering a concussion and broken ankle, and almost fell off a couple of roofs before his partner made him swear to stay on level ground. But even there his gait grew increasingly unsteady, until it was frankly staggering. Then his intellectual function, particularly his work on the drafting board, went to hell, forcing his retirement."

"Did he seek medical help during this time?" Dan asked.

"He did. His personal physician gave him a standard neurologic workup, found nothing abnormal, and diagnosed his condition as mental exhaustion. But retirement, including a world cruise, didn't help Hale at all. And when he tried to jump overboard one night off the Azores, they flew him back to Boston. This time his doctor diagnosed presenile dementia, Alzheimer type, and stuck him in here."

"I see," Dan said. "And you think it's something other than Alzheimer's, I take it. Well, let's hope you're right."

Dan remembered Jonathan Hale from a TV talk show as a dynamic, dignified, highly articulate man. That memory heightened his sense of horror as Sloan led him to the bedside of a wild-eyed, disheveled old man lying on urine-soaked sheets and fondling his penis with trembling hands.

Trying to keep the revulsion he felt over Hale's transformation from showing on his face, Dan borrowed Sloan's instruments and proceeded to examine him.

"Well," Sloan said as they sipped coffee in the lobby afterwards, "what do you think?"

"It's not presenile dementia, that's for sure. I'm no neurologist, but I *do* know Alzheimer patients don't show gait disturbances or motor signs, and Hale does. He's also got a gross tremor, urinary incontinence, and *you* interested in him. So, putting it all together, I'd say there's a good chance he has normal pressure hydrocephalus," said Dan, referring to a rare condition, sometimes following head injury but most often of unknown cause, in which a block in the circulation of cerebrospinal fluid produces damaging pressure on the brain. "You agree?"

Sloan grinned. "Damned right! But deciding what's wrong with him is only half the problem. Trying to do something about it is the other half."

"Why? It's treatable in most cases. Even in ones as far advanced as his. A shunt will relieve the pressure on his brain. So why don't you just go ahead and have one put in?"

"Oh, I'd love to!" exclaimed Sloan, gesturing with enthusiasm. "And so would any neurosurgeon in town. But the hangup is his dementia. The court has declared him *non compos mentis* and appointed his wife, Mavis, as legal guardian. I've talked to her twice now, but she flatly refuses to let us operate on him."

"Why the hell not?" Dan demanded. "Doesn't she want him to get better?"

Sloan smiled wryly. "There are a few things you ought to know about Mrs. Mavis Hale. For one, she's Hale's second wife and about twenty years younger. For another she's a devout Christian Scientist and an even more devout spendthrift. I practically have to wear sunglasses to protect my eyes from the glitter of her jewelry. And her chief legal adviser just happens to be her brother. To put it bluntly, she's an avaricious bitch who doesn't want us to operate on, or do anything to, her husband that might help him recover enough to reclaim what's left of his once sizable fortune."

Dan shook his head disgustedly. "Poor Hale. Made me a little sick to examine him in the pitiful state he's in. But what you've just told me makes me even sicker. Well, you asked me to confirm your diagnosis and I have. Now what?"

Sloan sighed. "I've reviewed the surgical literature on his condition rather extensively. Even in the best of hands, the odds of a shunt reversing his dementia are no better than fifty-fifty. Then there are the legal maneuvers we'd have to go through to get him on the operating table. Still, I'm all for chancing it, no matter how much legal red tape has to be cut through. How about you?"

"I'm with you!" Dan declared. "I've also got a lawyer-friend who'll be with you, too. His name's Gordon Donnelly, and there's nothing he likes better than a good scrap for a worthwhile cause. I'm sure he'll be willing to petition the court for permission to operate once he knows the story. In fact, I'll fill him in on it first thing tomorrow morning. We have a handball match at seven A.M."

"Oh?" Sloan murmured with interest. "You're a handball player, too. Any good?"

"So-so."

"What class?"

Dan eyed him warily. Obviously Sloan was a veteran handballer or he wouldn't have asked so knowledgeable a question. "Class A," he admitted. "But barely. I have a hell of a time with any A player under thirty years old."

"I'm close to forty," Sloan said. "We'll have to play sometime."

"Great!" said Dan, rising to his feet and extending his hand. "Let's do it soon. I'll have Gordon Donnelly contact you at your office tomorrow." With a parting wave of his hand he headed back toward the nursing station, hoping somebody there could finally tell him where his own patient was hidden.

# 8

Gary Gogal, who had graduated with honors from the University of Toronto medical school and was now a senior medical resident at Bradford Medical Center in Boston, took his first tentative sip of morning coffee and lazily reached for the newspaper. He was sitting out on the terrace of the studio apartment he shared with his fiancée, Alix.

Though Gary now lived away from the hospital, he still spent most of his time there, seldom getting more than four or five hours' sleep a night. Even on his third cup of coffee this morning, he felt barely awake enough to read the newspaper. But suddenly his eyes opened wide and a surge of apprehension swept the torpor from his brain as he noticed a story in the lower-right-hand corner of the front page: MALPRACTICE ACE CHARLES SPRAGUE STRIKES AGAIN, EIGHTH MASS. PHYSICIAN SUED FOR MILLIONS.

Even before reading the details Gary knew that the defendant had to be Dr. Carl Gormann, a general practitioner on the staff of Bradford Medical Center, and the plaintiff, Darryl Harrison, a seventeen-year-old black orphan. His apprehension came from knowing that he, more than anyone, was responsible for the malpractice suit. Not that Gary was the least bit sorry for what he had done; his dreams had been haunted by the episode for weeks, and his conscience had compelled him to take some action after the Bradford medical hierarchy had proven too spineless to do it. Nonetheless, only a handful of people knew about the key role Gary had played, and he was worried lest Gormann or some other hospital staff member find out about it.

Alix was bringing a plate of eggs and bacon out to him when she saw the look on his face and asked, "What is it? What's bothering you?"

"This." Gary showed her the newspaper story.

Alix put his breakfast before him and read it. "Good God!" she exclaimed shortly. "Is this true about Gormann? That he practically wiped out a whole family with his bungling?"

· "It's true," Gary affirmed. "I took care of Mrs. Harrison myself until she died."

"Then I'm 'atroced'—to use one of your Canadian expressions."

"So was I," Gary replied. "Now I'm a little scared."

"Why? You're not being sued, are you?"

Gary shook his head. "That's not it."

"Well, what then?" Alix prompted. "This Gormann is obviously a butcher. Why should his being sued frighten you?"

Gary smiled wryly. "Because, Alix honey, I'm the one who got Sprague's law firm to sue him."

"*You* did?" she gasped. Gary watched the surprise on her face change to bewilderment. "You told Charles Sprague about him?"

"Not Sprague; one of his partners, Neil Rosensweig."

"Wow!" she exclaimed. "That took guts—the way the doctors in this town are warring with the malpractice lawyers. I'm impressed."

"Don't be. It wasn't a test of guts. I'm not sure what it was, unless maybe an acute attack of conscience.

Believe me, I didn't go to Sprague's law firm out of spite. It was the last thing I wanted to do. But after what Gormann did to the Harrison family, I couldn't stomach his getting off scot-free. So I went to the hospital authorities first and got nowhere . . ." Looking tight-lipped and reflective, Gary paused. "It's a long, depressing story. Sure you want to hear it?"

"Of course, I want to hear it. But eat your breakfast first and then tell me."

As Gary ate, he related the Harrison case to Alix. It had started late last summer, when he was assigned to the Bradford intensive care unit. Dr. Carl Gormann had asked him to check one of his postoperative patients, Mrs. Delia Harrison, a nurse at the hospital who for some obscure reason had developed severe nausea and vomiting following a total hysterectomy five days earlier. Gary soon discovered that the reason was not obscure at all; it was as obvious as it was horrifying. Because she had run a low-grade fever postoperatively, Gormann had started her empirically on an intravenous antibiotic. The antibiotic he chose was tetracycline, a relatively safe drug when given orally but one which could have treacherous side effects if given intravenously, even in the recommended dosage of one gram or less daily. Choosing IV tetracycline for an unproven infection was to Gary's mind highly debatable. But the daily dosage Delia Harrison had received for five days—not one gram but four—was not debatable at all. It was deadly. After examining her to exclude other possible causes of postoperative vomiting, Gary correctly, if reluctantly, diagnosed tetracycline toxicity. He had never seen a similar case, but he had read enough to know that the diagnosis was tantamount to a death sentence, since few, if any, of its victims ever survived.

Tetracycline, Gary explained to Alix, had penetrated and poisoned all of the patient's body cells, causing a severe acid condition of the blood; liver and kidney failure; and massive hemorrhage secondary to a serum calcium deficiency so extreme that it prevented her blood from clotting.

"For the five more days she hung on," he continued, "we did everything possible to save her. Gave her an unprecedented one hundred and forty ampules of sodium bicarbonate and put her on hemodialysis to try to counteract her incredible acidosis. But the kidney machine only ate up her few remaining platelets, and she bled out." He shrugged futilely. "The case was hopeless from the start, but she was one of our nurses, so we went all out."

Alix shook her head in dismay. "What did Gormann say when you told him the tetracycline he'd ordered had poisoned her?"

"Acted like he'd never heard of tetracycline toxicity —which he probably hadn't. Then when the gravity of what he'd done sank in, he tried to cover up. Claimed the floor nurse must've erred in transcribing his telephone order; that he'd only meant for her to get one gram of IV tetracycline daily, not four. Then he more or less turned the case over to me. Told me to order all the consultations I wanted and do the best I could to save her. He hardly bothered to visit his patient at all those last few days. Simply washed his hands of her."

"Nice man," remarked Alix. "Then what happened?"

"On the day of her funeral, her husband, a fifty-year-old hypertensive, dropped dead of a heart attack. Just at the moment they were lowering her casket into the ground." Gary paused to sip more coffee. "But even his death didn't end the tragedy. A week later Charlie Hamilton was working the emergency room when their only child, Darryl, a seventeen-year-old high school student, was brought in after overdosing on heroin. Charlie barely managed to save him."

"He was an addict?"

"Hell, no!" He was a bright, clean-living kid and a star athlete at Dorchester High. One of the best basketball players in Boston. According to his friends, Darryl had never even smoked pot. The heroin OD was almost certainly a suicide attempt, and he didn't recover for five months."

Alix shivered in horror. "Why not?"

"Well, when he woke up in the intensive care unit, the same place his mother had been, he became acutely psychotic. Kept threatening to kill himself. So he spent the next five months at Boston Psychopathic, which made him miss basketball season his senior year and any chance of a college scholarship."

"My God, Gary, that's the most ghastly medical horror story I've ever heard! But I still don't understand why you had to go to Charles Sprague's law firm. After what Gormann did to that poor nurse and her family, I'm surprised the hospital staff didn't lynch him!"

"That's a little extreme," said Gary tolerantly. "But they should've done a lot more to him than they did. The case *was* reported to the medical conduct-and-review committee. The surgical one, too, since the hysterectomy Gormann did on Mrs. Harrison turned out to be completely unnecessary. All the surgical specimen showed was a uterine fibroid the size of a small grape. According to Bill Muller, our pathologist, that's pretty much par for the course for Gormann. Maybe a little below par, since most of the uteri he whips out show less than that. He also does a lot of dubious T and A's, laminectomies, and hernia repairs."

"Is this Bradford Hospital you're talking about or Buchenwald?"

Gary shrugged. "Gormann's an old-timer on the staff, one of the last of the GP-surgeons. He admits a lot of patients, operates on as many as he can get away with, and brings the hospital *beaucoup* business."

Alix groaned. "So what did the hospital authorities actually do?"

"Not much," said Gary, his voice edged with anger. "Because one of Gormann's partners was on the medical review committee, and because several of the surgeons on the surgical committee depended on Gormann for referrals—actually vied for them—they copped out. Instead of condemning Gormann for causing the death of one of their own nurses, they bought his bullshit story that her overdosage of IV tetracycline was the floor nurse's mistake, and had unfortunately gone undetected when Gormann countersigned the telephone order the next morning. So instead of losing his admitting or surgical privileges at the hospital, Gormann got off with a mere letter of reprimand."

"That's disgusting!"

"It's more than that. It's criminal! After word of the whitewash got around, I stewed about it for a few days and then went to the chief of medicine to complain. The chief agreed wholeheartedly that Gormann had gotten away with murder—or, at least, manslaughter—but he already had more political problems than he could handle and had no intention of reopening that can of worms. So all he did was lecture me on how hard it was to get a bad doctor booted off a hospital staff these days because of the right-to-work laws and legal shit like that. He finally weaseled out altogether by claiming that since Gormann was a member of the department of family practice, not medicine, there was nothing he could do. So I swallowed hard and tried to forget it. But a short time later I was called to see another of Gormann's patients, who damned near died from a high potassium level because Gormann didn't know you're not supposed to give tetracycline, even orally, to patients with kidney failure. Jeez!" growled Gary under his breath. "After already killing one patient with that drug, the dumb bastard hadn't bothered to learn a thing about it! So the next morning I went to see the lawyers. Sprague was out of town, so I told the story to this Neil Rosensweig."

"How did he react?"

"Much the same way you did. Horror at Gormann's long list of victims. And disgust at the gutless review committees who let him get away with it. Rosensweig impressed me. He's a studious-looking guy in his early thirties. His brother is a doctor, so he doesn't have the grudge against the medical profession Sprague does."

"He said that?"

"Not in so many words. But I got the distinct impression from what he did say that Sprague doesn't try all those malpractice cases just for the money; that something more personal is involved. I tried to get Rosensweig to elaborate, but he wouldn't. He did admit, though, that in the five years he'd been working in the malpractice field, the horror story I'd told him was the absolute worst, and he'd make damned sure something was done about it."

Alix sighed. "Bring back capital punishment, I hope. So he got Sprague to sue Gormann?"

"Not quite. Lawyers don't sue anybody unless they're the injured party. And in this case the injured party is the Harrison boy. Which presented a bit of a problem to Rosensweig, since it's unethical for a lawyer to initiate first contact with a potential claimant. In some states, it's even a felony. So someone else had to do it."

"You?"

"We discussed that. But Rosensweig advised against it. He felt I'd already done enough by coming to him, and it would be too risky to involve myself further. He asked me to do just one more thing—find out the name of Darryl Harrison's psychiatrist for him."

"Why the psychiatrist?"

"Well, for one thing he wanted to know how the Harrison boy was getting along and whether he could stand the strain of a long malpractice trial without relapsing. Especially after he learned the truth about his mother's death. That really worried Rosensweig. He also wanted to find out if the psychiatrist would be willing to testify on their behalf. The psychiatrist turned out to be John Reaves, an assistant professor at Harvard who occasionally lectures at Bradford. Evidently he felt Darryl Harrison could handle it and gave Rosensweig the go-ahead. I don't know this for sure, but I sort of suspect that it was Reaves, who's brilliant, black, and subtly militant, who encouraged Darryl to contact Sprague's law firm. Anyway, this was all months ago, and I hadn't heard a thing until this newspaper story."

Alix gave him an intense, admiring look. "You Canadians aren't always as cool as you like to pretend. You have strong passions about other things in life besides hockey."

"You already knew that," Gary taunted.

Alix ignored the innuendo. "Are you going to attend the trial?"

"As much as I can. I want to see Gormann squirm."

"Good," said Alix, gathering up the breakfast dishes. "I'll go with you."

# 9

At eleven P.M. on a sultry summer night, Edgar Emmonds, a bantam-sized, fifty-year-old municipal clerk, entered Duggan's Bar in Boston's West End with a prodigious thirst and a meager cash supply. At one A.M., the legal closing time, the burly bartender told him to pay up and leave. When Emmonds refused, he was given an unceremonious heave-ho. Sent sprawling into a row of trash cans on the sidewalk, he scrambled to his feet, trembling with rage, seized one of the trash can lids, and hurled it through the bar's plate glass window.

The shattering noise sobered Emmonds slightly, and he took off running down the street with the bartender in pursuit. Just as his breath gave out and his steps began to falter, he saw a patrol car stopped for a red light. Staggering and stumbling, Emmonds ran up to the patrol car shouting, "I surrender!" and dived into the back seat.

He meekly submitted to handcuffs, cursed the bartender through the rear window of the patrol car, and then settled back for the familiar ride to the precinct station. En route he was suddenly jolted out of his drunken stupor by a sharp pain in his chest. He tried to speak, but the pain cut his breath off and he could only emit an anguished moan. Eyes bulging with fear, he clutched at his chest with his cuffed hands, gasped, gagged, and collapsed back on the seat.

Although unconvinced that Emmonds was anything more than drunk, the policemen gave him the benefit of the doubt and took him to the emergency room of Commonwealth General Hospital, where Dr. Sam Biggs, the intern on duty, attended him. Sam, who had started his internship barely a month before and was pulling the "graveyard shift" in the ER for the first time had already examined four drunks that night and needed another one about as much as he needed a fresh outbreak of blackheads on his chronic acne. Nonetheless, after he and a team of surgical residents had tended the victims of a four-car collision, Biggs finally got around to Emmonds.

By this time Emmonds's chest pain had eased considerably, and he hardly complained about it. Instead of the sense of impending doom that had gripped him earlier, he felt a sense of shameful neglect as his whimpering, rasping, bellowing pleas for a doctor went unanswered. Nurses and orderlies paraded in and out of the room, offering the two policemen coffee but offering him not so much as a sip of water. The more he struggled to wriggle out of the leather restraints binding him to the examining table, the more they bit into his wrists and ankles. Yet despite his insistent promises of good behavior, the straps remained fastened. He was a sick man, goddamnit, Emmonds ranted; just because he'd had a little too much to drink was no reason to persecute him!

When Biggs finally showed up, Emmonds took one look at him and exploded in indignation. He did not want this pimple-faced kid touching him, he clamored. He wanted a real doctor!

Acutely self-conscious about his acne, Biggs's initial impulse was to tell this obnoxious twerp that he was as much a real doctor as Emmonds was a real drunk. But, remembering his supervisor's admonition that serious disease, from subdural hematomas to fractured spines, could be easily missed in acute alcoholics, he proceeded to evaluate him.

Emmonds quieted down as Biggs removed his restraints in order to examine him in the sitting position. With the two policemen gripping him firmly by the arms, he took deep breaths while the intern listened to his lungs, soft breaths while he listened to his heart, and bided his time. When Biggs told him to lie back and stay still so he could run an electrocardiogram, Emmonds complied, while secretly believing that if he were in imminent danger of dying from anything, it wouldn't be a heart condition as much as his horrendous thirst.

Dan Lassiter reached the hospital at six A.M., an hour earlier than usual. He had a lengthy report for the Joint Commission on Accreditation of Hospitals to write and preferred to do it while his mind was fresh and his office was quiet. Entering through the emergency room, he heard someone shout, "I don't want no electro-cardio-gram! I want a *drink!*"

The next instant a small, wiry man burst out of a patient-examining room pursued by two policemen and an intern. Shirtless and shoeless, his breath coming in sniffs and snorts, the man raced down the corridor, his eyes darting wildly for some avenue of escape.

Dan flattened himself against the wall to stay out of his line of sight.

Turning abruptly, the man squared off in a fighter's crouch to face his pursuers.

"Now listen, buddy," one policeman warned, "you're getting yourself in a lot of trouble."

Emmonds said plaintively, "All I want is a drink."

"A drink of *what?*" asked the intern. "We only serve water here."

"Wrong!" Emmonds exclaimed confidently. "How 'bout paraldehyde? You stock that, don't you?"

Biggs hesitated. For reasons he could never fathom, paraldehyde, a powerful liquid sedative with a disagreeable taste, was a drunk's favorite hospital libation. "No," he finally said. "No paraldehyde till I finish examining you."

"Then you got to catch me first," Emmonds said with a smirk.

As the nearest policeman lunged for him, Emmonds took off down the corridor and ran smack into Dan.

"All right, mister, take it easy," said Dan, catching him in a bear hug and pinning him against the wall. The two policemen hastily took over and put Emmonds in handcuffs.

"Okay, Edgar," one of the officers said, "you've had your fun with the doctors. Now you're going to jail."

Emmonds immediately turned docile. "All I wanted was a little drink to wet my whistle."

"Then ask the judge for one," the officer told him.

"What's going on?" Dan asked Biggs.

"He was arrested on a drunk and disorderly, sir. On the way to the police station he complained of chest pain, and the officers brought him here."

"Doesn't look like he's feeling any pain now," Dan remarked dryly. "Did you take a cardiogram?"

Biggs shook his head. "He wouldn't hold still for one."

Dan frowned. Years of working emergency rooms had taught him, too, to be wary about missing disease in drunks. "What did your exam turn up?"

"Nothing significant. But it's not the best exam I've ever done."

Fidgeting, one of the policemen said to Biggs, "Well, thanks anyway, Doc. You did your best. C'mon, Edgar. Let's go downtown."

Dan watched the two policemen drag Emmonds off. Then, turning to the intern, he smiled and said, "Rough night, huh?"

Biggs nodded. "He was the fifth alcoholic the cops dumped on me."

# 10

By ten A.M. Dan had finished his report and was ready
for his first appointment. "Has Jimmy Dallesio got here
yet?" he asked Hedley over the intercom.

"Yes, he has," she replied.

"Send him in."

Dan had no idea why Jimmy wanted to see him, but
he never dropped by without a good reason and he
never wasted anyone's time.

The two had first met fifteen years earlier, when
Dan was an intern at Boston City Hospital and Jimmy
was a second-string political reporter for the *Globe*.
Although having little in common except a tenacious
idealism and intense curiosity about the human condition, from its political processes to its physical ones,
they had formed a firm and lasting friendship.

The quality Dan admired most in Jimmy was the
way he worked: listening to the big people, the pundits
and politicians and financiers—listening so well that he
was dubbed "Jimmy the Priest" by his press colleagues
—but learning more from the little people who knew
best what the populace was thinking. Each week he

made his rounds of local bars, barbershops, and business establishments, talking to owners and patrons and reporting what they told him with accuracy, gentle wit, and respect.

Dan brought Jimmy coffee and moved with him to the cluster of chairs in the middle of the office. "How're Nora and the kids?" he asked casually.

"Fine. She worries about you—and with good reason. You look like you've lost weight."

Dan shrugged. "A few pounds. Too many TV dinners. But what brings you here?"

"Oh, a couple of things. I haven't seen you since the Dubic trial and I want to hear all about it."

"Don't remind me," Dan groaned. "Dubic lost the suit and deserved to. He's poorer—at least his insurance company is, which I help support—but I doubt wiser."

"I heard you almost pulled it out for him."

"From whom?"

"A reporter-friend of mine in Springfield. Said some of the exchanges between you and Angela Adams had the spectators on the edge of their seats. One thing puzzled him, though. You're a well-trained internist and supposed to know your stuff. But who was feeding Angela Adams all her facts?"

"She can read!" Dan snapped. "She has access to the same medical books I do."

"That's not what I mean. Some of her disclosures about Dubic's medical practice weren't in any books."

Dan nodded glumly. "Yeah, I know. But don't ask me where she and Sprague dug up that information, 'cause I haven't a clue. Ask her, why don't you?"

To his surprise, Jimmy answered, "I already did. I met Angela a few months ago while doing my first column on Charles Sprague, and we hit it off. Since then, whenever we run into each other at the courthouse, we have coffee."

"Imagine that," Dan remarked wryly, "my closest friend consorting with the enemy. Well, don't keep me in suspense. What'd she tell you?"

"Nothing too revealing except that Charles Sprague knows a lot of medicine."

"Does he?" Dan mocked. "That's a comforting thought. Any idea how?"

"Not offhand. I'd have to consult my file on him."

"I'd like to see that file. Sprague is really beginning to intrigue me. But to get back to you and your lovely lady-friend, Angela Adams. Did she spill anything else to you?"

Jimmy looked askance at him. "You're not asking me to divulge a confidence, I hope? I wouldn't ask you to violate your Hippocratic oath."

"You would if there was a good story in it. Seriously, though, Jimmy, what can you tell me?"

"Well, she never came right out and said so, but I got the impression from what she did say that some inside medical source is feeding, or at least screening, their cases."

"A doctor?" said Dan with distaste.

Jimmy shrugged. "Most likely. How else could they have that almost perfect record of verdicts for their clients? Someone inside the medical profession's got to be advising them who the worst offenders are. A nurse couldn't. And despite the rumors about medical record clerks selling copies of incident reports to lawyers, there's no proof it ever happened. So it has to be a doctor, don't you think? A local doctor who knows his fellow doctors pretty well."

Dan scowled. "I was afraid of that. But why? What does the doc-fink get out of it? A bounty?"

"Maybe it's more a matter of conscience with him?"

"Conscience!" Dan snorted. "What kind of conscience lets a doctor make his unsuspecting colleagues prey to malpractice suits! If he feels they're practicing bad medicine, why doesn't he turn them over to the proper disciplinary committees, instead of the wolves in the malpractice arena?"

Jimmy drew a deep breath and exhaled sighingly.

"Well, Dan, I hate to throw your own words back at you, but you've bitched to me more than once about how ineffectual those committees are."

"Sure," Dan admitted. "Sure I have. And you know who makes them that way? The lawyers! The damned lawyers get us poor bastards in the medical profession coming and going. It's hard as hell to try to remove a bad doctor's hospital privileges these days without risking a slander suit and God knows what else. Believe me, I know! There's one guy on this staff I'd love to get rid of, but I shudder to think what I'd be letting myself in for—endless meetings with his lawyer demanding proof that he violated hospital rules or failed to meet the accepted standard of care in treating his patients. And we simply haven't formulated standard-of-care directives for every disease. Either we don't know enough or can't get a panel of experts to agree on the best form of therapy. Each has his own favorite recipes. But despite all my frustration, I've never considered taking unfair advantage of my position, the access it gives me to every patient here, and squealing to some malpractice lawyer."

Jimmy gave him a sharp, skeptical look. "You'd be taking unfair advantage of your position by turning in a bad doctor who's taking unfair advantage of his patients? You sure you've thought that one through?"

"Whose side are you on anyway?"

"Yours, I think—once you decide what it really is. There's a lot of ambivalence in what you're saying."

"Look," Dan said defensively, "I admit doctors, in general, do a piss-poor job of policing themselves, and I despise bad doctors as much as anybody. But that's not to say I'm ready to side with the lawyers, even a vigilante type like Charles Sprague. Too many of my really competent colleagues are losing too much time and sleep over nuisance suits. Take Jim Gibson, who's a hell of a fine general surgeon. Awhile back he operated on a guy with a ruptured retrocecal appendix."

"What's a retrocecal appendix?"

"An appendix that's tucked underneath the junction

between the small and large intestines, instead of sitting on top of it, making a hot one very hard to diagnose. Well, Jim did diagnose it, and while inside the abdomen found out the guy had a mild case of regional enteritis —inflammation of the small bowel—too. So he included that finding in his report to the patient's insurance company, which promptly upped his health insurance premiums. Now, instead of a grateful patient whose life he'd saved, Jim has a malpractice suit pending for allegedly delaying the operation until after the guy's appendix ruptured."

Jimmy gestured sympathetically. " 'Life is unfair'— as the late President Kennedy said."

"Damned right!"

The telephone buzzed and Dan picked it up. His caller was Ned Josephson. "Good morning, Ned," he said.

"I've had better ones," Josephson remarked ruefully. "You know Craig Andrews, don't you?"

"Sure. We've served on a couple of committees together." Andrews was the new executive secretary of the Suffolk County Medical Society, and Dan was impressed with him. He had a master's degree from the Harvard Business School and a pragmatic approach to the society's problems based on a clear separation between its members' wants and needs.

"Well, Craig and I are downstairs in your cafeteria right now," Josephson continued, "and wonder if you could spare us a few minutes."

"What for?"

"Charles Sprague's latest barrage against the medical profession."

"Sprague, huh?" said Dan, curious. "Who's he after now?"

"Have you read the morning paper?"

"No, not yet. Why?"

"Well, part of the story's on the front page. But only part. Look, Dan, I'm at an open phone. If you don't mind, I'd rather discuss this with you in private."

Dan hesitated. "All right. But Jimmy Dallesio's with me. Okay if he sits in?"

It was Josephson's turn to hesitate. "I suppose so. Long as he realizes what we have to tell you is highly confidential."

"Don't worry, Ned," Dan advised. "We're all professionals. But just to make sure, I'll grab Jimmy's notebook away from him. He can't remember his own telephone number without it."

"What was that all about?" Jimmy asked after Dan hung up.

"Ned Josephson and Craig Andrews are on their way up to see me. Evidently Sprague hit another nerve, and they're howling about it."

"I'm not surprised," Jimmy said. "It was the main topic of conversation in the city room this morning. Another of the reasons I'm here." Jimmy reached for the newspaper on Dan's credenza and pointed out the story about the Gormann trial.

Dan skimmed it and said, "Yeah, I've heard talk about the case. And about Gormann. But why's Ned so upset about it?"

"Well, I hate to steal Josephson's thunder," Jimmy said, "but this time Sprague's using a shotgun approach and going for mass casualties. If he's successful, there's a good chance your mutual malpractice insurance fund will go broke!"

"What do you mean?"

"The word I got is that Sprague's firm is not just bringing suit against Carl Gormann alone. Gormann's merely at the top of his list. He's also suing Bradford's board of managers, chief of staff, executive committee, the membership of its medical and surgical conduct-and-review committees, and maybe even a janitor or two. In short, *anybody* who knew *anything* about the Delia Harrison case."

Dan's eyes widened. "How's that possible?"

"If you're asking me to explain its legalities, I can't. You'd better ask Josephson that."

Minutes later, Dan did.

Tensely Josephson rubbed his eyes with the flat of his hand and said, "That's one question I'm *well* prepared to answer, Dan. Spent most of last night in our law library looking it up. The legal basis goes something like this: If a hospital disciplinary committee fails to discharge its responsibility, a member of the public at risk can bring a class-action lawsuit against its membership to compel them to do their job, thereby preventing an incompetent doctor from doing further injury to his patients. However, if proof exists that this same doctor has already been brought before the committee on similar charges and they failed to take appropriate action, then the plaintiff can include that committee, and any higher authority that approves its transactions, in the lawsuit he files and ask for damages. Unfortunately, Gormann has been up before the Bradford surgical conduct-and-review committee on the charge of performing unnecessary surgery twice, and even more unfortunately, Sprague's found this out. So naturally he's bringing suit against them for a bundle!"

Dan stared at Josephson, fascinated and appalled. "How big a bundle?"

"A cool two million dollars!"

Dan whistled softly. "That's a pretty *big* bundle. If Sprague wins, how good are his chances of getting the full amount?"

"Are you kidding?" Josephson exclaimed. "A black nurse, one of Bradford's own, is fatally poisoned. Her husband drops dead at the funeral. Their only son goes berserk. It's pure Greek tragedy, or daytime soap opera. If Sprague can prove negligence on Gormann's part, the jury will award the Harrison boy the moon! That you can be sure of. And you know why? Because each member of that jury will be thinking, Jesus, if we don't do something to make these doctors more accountable, the same thing could happen to me! Don't get me wrong, Dan, I'm not saying Gormann's guilty. He claims it was the nurse on duty's fault, not his, that Delia Harrison got the fatal dose of tetracycline, and as his lawyer I choose to believe him. What I *am* saying is that if Sprague gets a favorable verdict from the jury on this one, the practice of medicine in this state will never be the same."

"That has implications," said Dan softly.

"It sure does," Andrews joined in. "The implications, in fact, are staggering. A two-million-dollar judgment will practically bankrupt the medical society's malpractice fund overnight, and no commercial insurance carrier will touch the doctors here. So that leaves them only one recourse: to go begging to the legislature for relief. And you know as well as I do that along with state moneys comes state control. Before you know it, you'll be up to your eyeballs in regulations."

Grimly Dan nodded. "I can easily see how Sprague's suit against the Bradford hierarchy creates a problem. Even a disaster in the making. And I certainly appreciate your taking the time to drop by and tell me. But exactly what do you expect me to do about it?"

Andrews looked at Josephson as if cuing him in. "Dan," he began, "the executive committee of the county society met here earlier this morning and decided it's got to do a lot more than it's been doing to defuse this crisis. They want *you* to chair a special committee."

"To do what?"

"Whatever's necessary to fight Charles Sprague and lawyers like him. Will you do it?"

Dan pretended to ponder the proposal, though he had already made up his mind. "No," he said with finality.

"I really think you ought to consider it carefully, Dan," Josephson told him.

"Under different circumstances I would. But you've picked the wrong battleground."

"What's that supposed to mean?"

"Look, Ned, I don't want to prejudge this Carl Gormann, but if he did what he's accused of, he ought to be made to pay."

"Even if it brings Bradford Medical Center down with him?"

Dan shrugged. "Sorry, but after my disillusioning experience at the Dubic trial, I'm a little gun-shy. After all, this is Boston. A lot of very famous doctors live here. I'm sure you can find one who believes Gormann's worth defending more than I do."

"Gormann's defense is Ned's responsibility," Andrews said. "Mine is to make sure that the other doctors in this state aren't on trial with him. So I wish you'd think it over some more before giving us your answer. We still feel you're the best man for the job."

"I appreciate your confidence in me, Craig. But unless I miss my guess, it's going to be a dirty job. The newspapers are going to have a field day with the Gormann trial, right, Jimmy?"

Jimmy nodded vigorously.

"So that means a lot of mudslinging between lawyers and doctors. More specifically between Charles Sprague and whoever chairs your committee. Look, I know some of my colleagues think I'm a maverick. But the truth is, I've been a pretty good ol' boy as far as the profession's concerned. And you know why? Because ninety percent of the doctors I know, I'm proud to be associated with. But I'm rapidly running out of patience with the others. Carl Gormann once applied for staff privileges here, you know? But after sizing him up carefully, Gundersen turned him down flat. So even though I'm willing to do all I can to help good doctors, I'm simply not going to head any crusade to save Carl Gormann's ass. Sorry, gentlemen, but that's final."

After Josephson and Andrews had left the office, Dan asked Jimmy, "Well, did I do the right thing or not?"

Jimmy yawned, stretched his arms, and said, "Time will tell. As far as refusing to chair a committee whose main purpose would be to feud with lawyers, you did the right thing. That's politics, not medicine. But you might not be out of it yet. What if Sprague asks *you* to testify on behalf of his client?"

Dan's face mirrored his surprise. "You can't be serious?"

"Why not? He and Angela Adams already know how conscientious and competent you are. It's certainly within the realm of possibility that they'll ask you."

"God!" Dan groaned. "That's got to be the most unnerving thought of the day. But you don't really think they'd ask, do you?"

"Would you turn them down if they did?"

Dan gave Jimmy a cross look. "Probably. I'm no medical Don Quixote, for Chrissake! Now, if you'll excuse me, I'm running way behind schedule."

Jimmy rose abruptly. "Appreciate your time, Doctor," he said with phony formality. "You medical men certainly do a wonderful job. Wunnerful! I just know you'll cure everything someday."

"Yeah, including wise-assery. Now, will you please leave! Go mix a metaphor or something. I'll call you in a couple of days."

At seven A.M., Dr. Sam Biggs briefed his replacement on the handful of patients still in the emergency room and went off duty. Back in his room in the intern quarters, he gobbled two doughnuts and a sleeping pill and climbed into bed. He fell asleep almost immediately. After what seemed like only a few minutes but actually was several hours, his phone woke him. Sam groped for the receiver and drew it to his ear. "Biggs," he mumbled.

"Sam!" a voice boomed. "This is Irv Franklin, your old medical school buddy. How're you?"

"Half-asleep and wishing I was still all the way. Worked the graveyard shift in the ER last night and was really swamped."

"I know," said Franklin. "That's the reason I'm calling. I'm working the ER, too. At Boston City Hospital. And I just finished seeing a patient who says he saw you last night. Remember a guy named Edgar Emmonds?"

"Emmonds?" Biggs repeated, more alert now. "Yeah —vaguely. What's wrong with him?"

"Chest pain. The police picked him up on the West

Side after he'd tied one on and smashed up some bar. Then, on the ride to the station, he complained of severe chest pain, so they took him to your place to be checked. Remember him now?"

"Yeah," Biggs acknowledged. "Yeah, I'll say I do! Obnoxious little guy. Drunk as a skunk."

"Did you run an EKG on him?"

"Tried. But he wouldn't hold still for one. Why?"

"Well, the police had barely locked him in a cell when he vomited, turned blue, and collapsed. So this time they brought him here. I just took a cardiogram on him, and it looks to me like an acute inferior wall myocardial infarct. I was hoping you'd have a tracing I could compare it with. But it doesn't matter. I've admitted him to our coronary care unit anyway. Thought I'd let you know."

Taken aback, Biggs asked, "Think he'll make it?"

"Hope so. His vitals are okay. Besides, it's just as hard to kill drunks in Boston as it was in Baltimore. So go on back to sleep, Sam. I'll ring you again in a few days, and maybe we can get together for a few brews. I'll give you a follow-up on Emmonds then."

"Yeah, Irv. Fine. I'd like that. G'bye."

Hanging up the phone, Sam Biggs sat staring into the grayness of his room. He was no longer sleepy; he was frightened, haunted by self-doubt. He'd made his first serious misdiagnosis, he brooded; others were sure to follow. He looked at the luminous dial on his watch. In three hours he would be back on duty in the ER, and he dreaded it.

# 11

Predictably the newspapers were filled with stories, editorials, and letters to the editor about the *Harrison* v. *Gormann* trial for the next several days. Bostonians, Dan knew, were a diverse and disputatious lot, who liked nothing better than reading about a good, long-running medical controversy. From the mad-scientist types in Cambridge determined to do God's work with gene-transplant experiments to the abortionists at Boston City Hospital determined to do the devil's, tension ran high between its world-famous medical establishment and its politically powerful Catholic majority, sometimes culminating in criminal indictments, always selling newspapers.

Just as urban renewal was changing Boston's venerable face, so these tensions were changing its scientific reputation. From being the nation's fount of medical knowledge, it was becoming its medicolegal storm center.

In the parlance of the motion picture industry, the Gormann case had "legs": word-of-mouth staying power and popular appeal that kept it before the public long after the story first broke. It had all the necessary ingredients: mysterious Charles Sprague with his brooding, Moses-like countenance and his adamant refusal to grant personal interviews on one side; and rich, avaricious Dr. Carl Gormann and the most prominent members of Boston's largest private hospital on the other.

Beneath the surface of the sensationalism lurked fear. Corrupt politicians, shyster lawyers, and crooked businessmen could all be dealt with in time by our democratic system. But there was no defense against bad doctors preying on helpless patients, and this potential personal threat was intolerable.

Indignant letters poured into newspaper and medical society offices throughout the state complaining of every thing from medical school admission policies to licensing for life of physicians. A popular morning TV talk show devoted a week's programs to the malpractice issue. Its guest experts comprised an array of erudite doctors and lawyers, most from the Boston area but also some national figures such as Melvin Belli, a pioneer in personal injury litigation and a seasoned television performer. Belli confided that he was in town to seek Charles Sprague's advice on a malpractice case of his own and would try to get him to come on the show himself. But despite Belli's urging, and all the publicity and suspense, Sprague never deigned to appear.

Dan followed the public controversy with mixed feelings—satisfaction at having had the good sense to stay out of it, concern for some of its spillover effects. On the plus side, it kept the doctors at his hospital on their best behavior. Even Peter Trombley became more receptive to house staff suggestions and ordered more consultations on his patients. Yet almost without exception those physicians who carried out-of-state malpractice insurance were being notified that their policies were unlikely to be renewed. The biggest problem facing Dan was where to find the extra million dollars it would cost Commonwealth General to maintain its liability insurance in its already strained budget. He had heard of hospitals in California refusing to pay such exorbitant premiums and going "bare." But Dan's board of directors would never risk that—not with Sprague the Plague in the vicinity and public awareness what it was.

As he had promised, Jimmy Dallesio did not write a column on the Gormann trial. Not yet, anyway. Gordon Donnelly also delivered on a promise, successfully petitioning the court to compel Jonathan Hale's wife to consent to further diagnostic tests on him and corrective surgery, if indicated. As a result Hale was transferred to Palmer Memorial Hospital, where isotope and X-ray studies confirmed Sloan's diagnosis of low-pressure hydrocephalus. He was taken directly to surgery and underwent a shunt placement procedure to bypass the blockage and reduce the damaging pressure on his brain. The operation went smoothly, and the next morning Sloan called Dan with the good news.

"That's great!" Dan exulted. "How's he doing post-op?"

"Fine, so far. It'll probably be several weeks before we can tell if it'll affect his dementia. But his tremor's already diminished, so I'm cautiously optimistic. And very grateful for the help I got from you and your lawyer-friend."

"You're welcome. But it doesn't come free, you know."

"Oh?" Sloan uttered. "What kind of payment do you have in mind?"

"My medical staff could use a good lecture on dementia. How about presenting Hale's case at our next grand rounds?"

"With the reputation your grand rounds have around town, I'd have to *be* demented, not just able to talk about it, to agree to that."

Dan chuckled. "They do get a bit rowdy, if that's what you mean. And there's one nitpicking neurologist named Brodny that you'll have to watch out for."

"Look," Sloan pleaded, "isn't there some other way I can pay you back?"

"Can't think of any. Will you do it?"

"On one condition. I'll meet your challenge if you'll meet mine."

"Which is?"

"A handball match. I'll give you as much time to prepare as you're giving me. Tonight will be fine."

"Hmm," Dan mused. "I could use the exercise. But I haven't played for a couple of weeks and I'm bound to be rusty. Don't know how good a game I could give you."

"Don't worry about it. I haven't played in three weeks and still have a bruised middle finger from a wall shot."

"All right," Dan said. "I get the message: Never hustle a hustler. Meet you at the Weston YMCA at seven sharp. Loser pays for drinks and dinner."

"You're on!" Sloan agreed.

Dan was first on their assigned court and limbered up by swinging his arms and doing deep knee bends. Sloan joined him shortly and tested the court out by tossing the ball against its front wall at various angles and studying the rebounds. Finally he began hitting the ball on his side of the court, and Dan did the same, watching Sloan out of the corner of his eye to gauge how good he was with his weaker, or "off," hand. Being right-handed, Dan used his left almost exclusively for defensive shots. But Sloan appeared equally adept with either hand, making Dan suspect he was up against a very tough opponent.

Sloan won the serve and sent a Z-shaped shot deep to Dan's left side. Playing it off the back wall, Dan lofted a ceiling shot, expertly aimed and hugging the side wall on the rebound, an exceedingly difficult return for a right-handed opponent. But Sloan did return it—left-handed—confirming Dan's suspicion that he was ambidextrous. With each playing cautiously, return followed return until Sloan attempted and missed a kill shot in the lower left corner, surrendering the serve.

The first match was a clean, hard-fought contest

which Sloan, with his superior left hand, barely managed to win.

During the rest period Dan slumped in a corner, embarrassingly winded, and tried to analyze his mistakes. Somehow it seemed important, even crucial, that he beat Sloan at least one game. Dan did not remember being so competitive as a child, always running a contented second to his older, smarter, more popular brother, Pete. But all that changed when their parents died in an automobile accident when Dan was eleven and they moved in with their Uncle Woody. Woodrow McKinley Brock, a professor of political science at Williams College and a superb athlete in his youth, had taught Dan to box and play handball as well as any boy his age. But only when Dan played Woody did he push himself to his physical limit, since that seemed the one sure way to gain his uncle's respect. Was something like that happening again? Had his brief exposure to Nicholas Sloan, first as an impressive bedside clinician and now as a tough handball opponent, kindled similar feelings?

Dan abandoned such introspection as his breathing eased. The pressing question was not why but *how* to beat Sloan. In reviewing their recent game, Dan realized that he had won most of his points after long rallies, when Sloan, growing leg-weary and impatient, had tried to put the ball away with a low-percentage kill shot. So Dan resolved to play more ceiling shots, make him run.

The strategy worked. Sloan slapped his gloved hands together in frustration as yet another unsuccessful kill shot skipped up to the front wall, giving Dan the second game 21–18.

Squatting beside him, Sloan said accusingly, "You've got me playing your game, haven't you?"

"Yup," Dan admitted, trying to suppress a satisfied smile.

"Well," Sloan said, "I'll either have to figure out what that is, or hope the restaurant we go to takes credit cards."

The third and deciding game was the most grueling either had played in years. Dan took an early lead as Sloan struggled to adjust his strategy. Only his accurate left-hand shots and Dan's occasional overconfidence kept him as close as 11–16 at midgame. Time after time Dan's return hit the ceiling, took a short skip to the front wall, spun to its first bounce on the floor, then rebounded in a steep, sailing arc toward the back wall, where Sloan had to stretch high for it before it plunged to its second bounce on the floor. To Dan's surprise, Sloan let the next such shot hit the back wall and fall to within a few inches of the floor before reaching low and in a windmill whip drilling it toward the front wall, barely missing its lower border. A few returns later Dan lofted another ceiling shot, and again Sloan defied the odds and conventional caution by attempting the same risky back-wall kill. This time the ball reached the front wall, about four feet up, and bounced feebly off, giving Dan an easy put-away and an 11–18 score.

Dan felt a bit guilty serving up another ceiling shot but not guilty enough to relent. This time, however, Sloan caught the ball square with his windmill whip and smashed it dead into the right front corner. To the veteran handballer the thwacking sound had an almost sensual quality.

Dan whistled in admiration at the spectacular shot, but reckoning it was as much luck as skill was not particularly perturbed—not until Sloan clicked off the next six points with similar shots, tying the score at 18–18.

It took Sloan another half hour to win 24–22, and the two left the court amid a loud round of applause from the spectators who had collected.

"Nice game," said Dan sincerely as they entered the locker room. Once the score had reached 20–20 in the final game, it had not mattered much to him who won; he had enjoyed being forced to play at top form.

"There'll be others," Sloan said, grinning.

"Maybe." Dan removed his sweat-soaked gloves and

rubbed his swollen right hand. "If I ever recover from this one!"

Standing at the sink, soaking his hand in cold water, Dan stared at Sloan's image in the mirror. His impressive comeback proved the man to be a cool gambler— an essential quality in a good doctor. Just as he had gambled and beaten Dan in handball, so he had gambled and won with his patient, Jonathan Hale. Mentally Dan filed away that insight about Sloan, suspecting it might prove useful in future dealings with him.

Dan took Nick Sloan to dinner at Vittorio's, a small cafe owned by Jimmy Dallesio's uncle.

"I really shouldn't let you pay for this," Sloan said while pouring himself a glass of vintage wine.

"Why not?" Dan replied. "You won fair and square."

"I know. But I've been trying to think of some way to repay you for your help with Jonathan Hale. And since I can't split my fee with you, at least let me buy dinner."

"Ut uh," Dan said firmly. "Besides, I may even charge it to the hospital. They usually pay for recruitment expenses."

Sloan looked puzzled. "I don't follow you."

"Well, I've been thinking of starting a geriatric unit at Commonwealth General for some time now, and you'd be the ideal person to head it up. Interested?"

Sloan smiled. "Flattered. But I'm afraid I'll have to pass. I'm seriously considering a chief-of-medicine job in Miami right now. That's confidential, by the way. The people at Palmer Memorial don't know it yet."

"Aren't you happy there?"

"The clinical material's great. So's the house staff . . ."

"But?" Dan anticipated.

"But I get weary of the politics. Especially when I'm the sole stationary target for the medical entrepreneurs and empire builders who bitch like hell when their services aren't covered by house staff. Ever hear of Kaplan's rule of the instrument?"

Dan shook his head.

"Well, it goes something like this: Give a small boy a hammer and suddenly everything he encounters needs pounding."

Dan laughed. "In other words, give a doctor a gastroscope and suddenly every patient is a potential candidate for carcinoma of the stomach."

"Or give him a kidney machine and a hospital franchise and watch it grow. Worse yet, good business for the specialist means good business for the hospital, so nobody in the front offices is going to object too strongly."

Dan saw the glint of anger in Sloan's eyes and welcomed it, since it freed him to express his own frustration. "Think doctors make too much money?" he asked.

"Some do." Sloan paused to reflect. "I don't really care how much money they make as long as the country can afford it. But it doesn't look as if it can."

"So what do you recommend?"

"For starters, the Canadian system of putting all hospital-based doctors with gimmicks on salary."

"Oh, I agree," Dan said. "In fact, I'm trying like hell to sell that concept to my hospital board. Come their next meeting I'm giving them an ultimatum: either go to full-time, paid subspecialty chiefs or find a new general director."

"Good luck!" Sloan said sincerely.

"It'll take more than luck. It'll take another million or so dollars for salaries. And with the steep rise in malpractice liability premiums, money's harder to find than a cure for baldness. Speaking of malpractice," Dan added, "what do you think of Charles R. Sprague?"

"I *try* not to think of him at all. But I do read the newspapers."

"Ever been sued?" Dan asked.

Sloan did not immediately reply. "For malpractice?" he finally said. "No, not so far, thank God. But what're the latest figures: one in twenty doctors are being sued nationwide; one in twelve here in Massachusetts? So maybe it's only a matter of time."

The waiter served their main course, and Dan dug into his veal with gusto. Between bites he mused, "I'm convinced the worst thing about being divorced is the evening meal. And I say that with the full realization that my ex-wife ranked as one of the world's worst cooks. You married?"

"No," Sloan said.

"Ever been?"

Sloan finished chewing and said, "No. Came close a few times, but backed off. I suppose that requires an explanation these days."

"Not to me," Dan said hastily. "Not if you don't care to talk about it. My marital scorecard shows loses one, wins zero."

"At least you chose to play."

"Sure," Dan said with a trace of bitterness. "At the end of a long, hard residency. One day Gundersen looked at me and said, 'Lassiter, you ought to get married,' in the same authoritative voice he'd order a patient digitalized. So I got married. Then, a few years later, Gundersen said, 'Lassiter, I'm recommending you for a job at Holmes Memorial Hospital in Springfield.' Since it was go or else, I didn't have any choice. But my wife did, and she decided not to go to Springfield. So I got unmarried. Now, for being such an obedient disciple, I've got Gundersen's job, his throne room, and lonesome dinners."

"I have lonely moments too," Sloan admitted. "Especially the first few hours after leaving the hospital at night. But I guess I'm scared of marriage. My parents were divorced when I was barely a year old. My mother married twice more before she decided she could do better on her own." Sloan sighed. "So part of it is her influence. Anyway, her last husband was Swiss, which is one reason I went to medical school there. The University of Lausanne."

Dan lifted his wineglass and studied Sloan's distorted image through it. His hunch about the man had been right: he and Sloan shared much more than their dedication to medicine. They were both loners, rootless men whose hospitals were their havens by day, but whose nights were often barren and empty.

"Where did you train after Lausanne?" he asked.

"I did my internship in Madison, Wisconsin. Cold winters, warm women."

"Is there a connection?"

Sloan smiled. "I suppose. Anyway, it was Gundersen who got me interested in neurology when he spent three months as acting chief of medicine there. What a superb clinician he was! I was really shocked by his suicide."

"I was even more shocked," Dan stated. "I found his body."

"Why'd he do it? Do you know?"

"Not really. He had polycythemia. Whether it had turned into myelofibrosis or acute leukemia, I don't know."

As they ate, they reminisced about Gundersen and other medical mentors they had known. Over coffee and cognac, however, Dan returned to the malpractice crisis, confiding his refusal to chair a special committee of the medical society to oppose Charles Sprague and his less scrupulous imitators. "I suppose I would've done it," Dan continued, "if it hadn't involved defending Carl Gormann. Or if we could prove that Sprague isn't the public protector he's made out to be. *Or* if there were some way other than malpractice suits to keep doctors in line."

"Is there?" Sloan asked.

"Hell, they test airline pilots every six months! If five percent of pilots were incompetent, nobody would ever fly again. But even that's not a fair comparison."

Sloan gave him a quizzical look.

"People don't need to fly. There are alternate means of transportation. But there's no alternative to doctors. So if you want to compare the medical profession with another, I'd pick the military. A combat officer is pretty much on a par with a busy doctor when it comes to

being responsible for mass lives." Dan smiled ruefully.
"I ought to know. I was one of the greenest shavetails
in Korea once. But I learned fast. My platoon wouldn't
have tolerated an incompetent CO for an instant.
They'd report him, or threaten to frag him—even
though we didn't call it that at the time—or make him
eligible for the Purple Heart by putting a bullet in his
ass. Which, in a long-winded way, brings me to my
point: The military figured out long ago that they
needed their own system of justice—one that was fair,
fast, and frightening! So instead of jury trials they use
court-martials."

"A far cry from our conduct-and-review committees."

"That's for sure! If the patient lives, they shrug and
say, why make a fuss? If the patient dies, they don't
want to get involved. Either way, they're ineffectual."

"I agree. But what do you propose in their place?"

"What I'm proposing—and right now very quietly
and confidentially—is that we seriously consider going
the way of the military to insure discipline and competency. Set up our own version of military courts and,
publicly or privately, court-martial bad doctors. If
they're guilty, sentence them appropriately and in a
way that counts: suspension of hospital privileges, a
probationary period under strict supervision, or just
drum them the hell out of the profession!" Dan sighed
deeply. "Maybe that sounds a bit extreme, but it's the
best *I* can come up with."

"Well, it's novel," Sloan remarked. "I've read a fair
amount about malpractice, but I haven't come across
anybody advocating that approach. Have you?"

"No. I don't know if it's original or not, but I hope
not. I'd much rather somebody else takes the blame if
it ever comes to pass. In fact, you're the first person
I've even broached it to. I don't dare mention it to
Gordon Donnelly. He just might take me seriously and
run with it."

"You are serious, aren't you?"

Solemnly Dan nodded. "I'm pretty fed up with bad

doctors. As fed up as I am with all the talk about the malpractice crisis and Charles Sprague."

As Dan sipped the last of his cognac, Sloan had a look of deep preoccupation on his face. Finally he said, "This may sound crazy, Dan, but why don't you pick up the phone and arrange a meeting with Charles Sprague? Just the two of you."

Dan half-laughed. "What for?"

"Well, meeting Sprague face-to-face might serve two purposes. First, to satisfy your curiosity about him. Second, to relate your concept of medical tribunals and court-martials to him, and if he likes it, gift him with the idea. Let Sprague be the one to propose it to the medical profession. That way it would have maximum impact, and they might just buy it. Especially if he promises to lay off doctors for a while and give us one last chance to clean house."

"Would he, though?" Dan wondered.

"Your guess is as good as mine. But it's worth a try, don't you think?"

"Maybe," Dan conceded. "But it'll take some thought. And I already have enough on my mind. Mainly, how to beat you the next time we play handball."

# 12

Dr. John Reaves, assistant professor of psychiatry at Harvard Medical School, sat in his small, cluttered office overlooking Huntington Avenue writing a progress note in a patient's chart and smoking a cigarette. It was almost seven P.M., and he was worn out from six straight hours of patient interviews, the other frustrations of his day, and his profession generally.

Snuffing out the butt of his cigarette, he lit another while mentally bracing himself for his last patient of the day. Ordinarily he might have succumbed somewhat to his mind-numbing fatigue and the late hour and not concentrated so intently on all the patient said, but he did not dare do that with Darryl Harrison. Unlike most doctors who dealt mainly with disease, with God's inhumanity to man, Reaves also dealt with man's inhumanity to man, of which Darryl Harrison was a prime example.

Before Reaves sent Darryl to see Charles Sprague, he had been dangerous only to himself. Now he was like a live hand grenade, capable of blowing up anyone at any moment, and Reaves only hoped that he could get through the upcoming trial without any of its revelations pulling his pin.

John Reaves was a rarity. He was one of fewer than a hundred American-trained, board-certified black psychiatrists in the country, and one of only a handful of these on the paid faculty of Harvard Medical School. He was as good at "conceptualizing" a patient's problem and helping him deal with it as any psychiatrist in Boston. The results he obtained with his patients, black or white, confirmed this and comforted him. What gave him qualms, however, was the strong suspicion that his talent derived from being on the edge of madness himself.

His own psychiatrist did nothing to discourage him in this disquieting belief. If anything, she helped foster it. The edge gave him the vantage point he needed to see into the psychic abyss of the human unconscious.

Reaves was not only on the edge now, but edgy as well. He knew he could not afford to relax or tune out a single second with Darryl Harrison in his office; couldn't even smoke, since Darryl, a former athlete, hated the smell of tobacco smoke. Sighing, he rose, aired out his office by turning up the air conditioner, and summoned Darryl from the waiting room.

At six foot four, Darryl Harrison was a half-foot taller than Reaves and as lean, light-skinned, and handsome as the psychiatrist was stocky, ebony black, and disproportionately large-headed and long-browed. Once in the office Darryl remained standing after he sat at his desk. Swiveling around, Reaves glanced up at him, saw the scrutinizing look on his face, and asked, "What?"

"Just thinking."

"Mind telling me *what?*"

"Pretty dinky office for such a hotshot nigger psychiatrist."

Reaves sighed. "Make you feel crowded?"

"Naw . . . Just don't feel like talkin' today."

"What do you feel, Darryl?"

"Nothin'."

Reaves nodded, and slipping into the same vernacular, said, "The sky ain't what it seems, either. Ain't blue at all. That's just an optical illusion. It's black."

Harrison gave him a quizzical look. "What you mean by that?"

"Sit down!" Reaves said firmly. "I'm getting a crick in my neck. Sit down and I'll tell you."

Reluctantly Darryl Harrison slumped into the chair opposite Reaves and stretched out his long legs. "Okay, man. The sky ain't blue, it's black. So what? What you mention it for?"

"Some people prefer the truth, others the illusion. Like you telling me you don't feel anything. That's bullshit! You're feeling too much."

Darryl hesitated, his mouth twisting uncertainly. Then he blurted, "Ever since this trial business started, I can't think. Can't function. My dreams scare me. I scare myself."

"How do you scare yourself?"

"I want Gormann. I want him like a bug killer wants a bug. That man don't deserve to live. Not after what he done to my ma and pa."

"And you don't deserve to spend the rest of your life in jail for murdering him. Let the court decide his punishment."

"Look!" Darryl Harrison said accusingly, "you were the one who first told me what he done. Who sent me to see Sprague. I thought they'd put Gormann on trial for murder, not malpractice. Malpractice!" he spat. "That ain't nothin'! You don't even get sent to jail for that. All you lose is money. Well, I don't want no million dollars. I want my folks back!" Blinking, he fought back tears.

Reaves sighed deeply. "I know, Darryl. They were good people."

"Yeah," he said tonelessly. Then his face contorted with rage. "But that Gormann—he ain't good people! And I want to pay him back for what he done. Gonna, too. Bet your ass!"

"Even if what happened to your mother really wasn't his fault?"

"What you mean?" Harrison shouted, pounding his fists on his thighs. "He poisoned her! That honkie doctor pumped so much poison in her veins that it made her puke for days. Puke and bleed!"

"Maybe so. But he didn't do it on purpose, Darryl. He didn't mean to hurt your mother. Somebody made a mistake—either Gormann or the nurse who took his telephone order. It's up to the court to decide exactly who."

"It weren't no nurse! It was Gormann! I just know that's true. My ma and pa keep telling me."

"How do they tell you?"

"How?" Darryl's face turned cautiously cunning. "Oh, no! You ain't gonna trap me there. I'm no schizo. Don't hear no voices tellin' me do this and that. So stop tryin' to trick me. Ain't no way you're gettin' me back on that psycho ward!"

"Answer my question!" Reaves demanded. "How do they tell you?"

"In dreams—that's how! They keep comin' to me in dreams. They're running and I got to run after them."

"Why are they running?"

" 'Cause something horrible's chasing them."

"What?"

Harrison started to speak, faltered, and dropped his head.

"Look at me!"

When he finally obeyed, Reaves was startled to see his eyes wide with hatred and loathing. "By this big hairy bug. Big as a tank. Only it ain't exactly covered with hair, but stickers. Like a porcupine. Long poisonous stickers."

"Like hypodermic needles?"

"Yeah, like them."

"Does the bug have a face?"

Harrison smiled slyly. "You *know* it does. And you know who it looks like, too."

Reaves nodded. "What do you do in this dream?"

"I run—run as fast as I can to catch up with my ma and pa, only I never can. They go through this gate in a stone wall and I can't ever find it. I throw myself at this wall, try to climb over it, but no matter how hard I claw and scrape, I can't get more'n halfway up."

"What happens next in this dream?"

"Then I look down and that bug's right below me, twitching and squirming and making funny cricket noises. It's twice my size, but it's the bug that's scared. Oozing sweat and stinkin' with fear. Like it knows I'm goin' to jump down from that wall and squash it."

"And in this dream, do you?"

Darryl's throat contracted. "Yeah," he admitted. "Once, one time I did."

"How did it feel?"

"It . . . it felt soft and slimy. Boneless. Like it had no spine at all. Made me sick to my stomach. But I was glad I did it."

"Why?"

"So it couldn't scare my folks no more."

Maintaining eye contact with him, Reaves ignored the Kafkaesque aspect of the dream to concentrate on its key revelation: he jumped. Disregarding his own safety, his fear and loathing of the ugly creature below him, Darryl Harrison jumped; he squashed the bug.

"All right," Reaves finally said. "What else do you remember about this dream? Was smashing the bug the scariest part?"

Initially Harrison looked blank. Then, recapturing more of the memory, he suddenly shuddered. Gripping the arms of the chair, he half-rose, as if wanting to run out of the office, before slumping back down. "Naw," he mumbled. "That wasn't the scariest part. The really scary part came later. But I ain't goin' to tell you that. No way, man! I ain't goin' back to that padded palace."

"The hospital, you mean?"

"Yeah. That's 'xactly what I mean."

"It's important that I know, Darryl. Trust me."

"I do—much as anybody. But I still ain't tellin'!"

Reaves reflected a moment before responding. Speaking slowly, he said, "Then I'll tell you. After you killed the bug you felt desolate, dead, devoid of feeling—the emptiest you've ever felt. That was the scariest part, wasn't it?"

Numbly Harrison nodded.

"So you panicked. You threw yourself against that wall and this time you made it to the top. Then you jumped—right?"

Looking dumbfounded, Darryl Harrison rasped, "How you know all this?"

"What made you jump, Darryl? What?"

"No, no more!" Harrison shouted. "I ain't sayin' no more. You tryin' to trick me." Suddenly his eyes welled with tears. Slumping back in his chair, he covered his face with his hands and emitted a shrill, muffled wail. "Don't put me back, Doc. It was just a dream. That's all! Just a dream. I ain't crazy."

Gently Reaves pried Harrison's hands from his face and held them in his own. "Hey, brother," he said soothingly, "why you talkin' such nonsense? I'm the shrink who got you released from that hospital—remember? Got you sprung. So keep your appointments with me, keep sharing your feelings, and I'll do my best to keep you out."

"So you say," said Harrison skeptically, "only why should you care?"

"Why?" Reaves broke into a grin. "Money, man."

"What you mean, money? The thirty dollars a crack you make seeing me ain't goin' to buy you much."

"Well, look at it like this," said Reaves, trying a different tack to ease the tension. "If Sprague wins your trial—which seems like a pretty safe bet—you're going to be a millionaire—right? Now, if I have to commit you again, all that money goes into a trust and you can't give me any. And I sure can't afford that flashy English sports car I got my eye on from what I make seeing you in the hospital. Now you dig?"

Harrison smiled sardonically. "I dig. I don't believe a

word of it, but it ain't a bad con. Okay, Doc, I'll do my best to stay cool till after the trial just so you can get your sports car. When you want to see me again?"

"Thursday. Same time. And daily during the trial."

"Daily!" Harrison exclaimed. "It's goin' to be that rough?"

"For Gormann, it is. For you, I don't know. We'll see."

"Okay, Thursday it is," sighed Harrison. He slapped hands with the psychiatrist and ambled out of the office.

Ah, dreams, thought Reaves morosely as he lit a cigarette and dragged deeply on it—the nightly entertainment by those marvelous filmmakers of the unconscious, Limbic System Studios. Re-runs on request. So how do you handle it, Reaves? Phone the district attorney to tell him that Darryl Harrison might well make an attempt on Dr. Carl Gormann's life, and be told that he ought to be put back in a padded cell? Actually recommit Harrison; doom him to suicide or lifelong institutionalization?

No, Reaves decided. He would simply have to wait and with all his skill determine Darryl Harrison's mental state day by day during the Gormann trial. He would also have to cancel three weeks of patient appointments out of his schedule.

Having already agreed to testify for the plaintiff, Reaves had planned to attend as many of the trial sessions as his time allowed. Now, with Darryl Harrison at the breaking point, it had become a life-or-death necessity that he attend them all.

With Gormann, Harrison, himself, and innumerable others out there, the edge was certainly crowded these days.

# 13

The month of August was sweltering, but Dan hardly noticed it since he seldom ventured outside the air-conditioned hospital during the day. The heat he did feel was generated by medical politics, not the midsummer sun. The stickiest issue arose from his push for full-time, paid subspecialty chiefs in every department. As anticipated, it met an equally forceful counterpush by Peter Trombley and certain influential old-timers on the hospital staff. The battleground was the boardroom, the objective the backing and votes of a majority of Commonwealth General's eleven board members.

Committee meeting followed committee meeting, usually at mealtimes, until Dan almost forgot what it was like to eat without his briefcase by his side and a stack of papers beside his plate. Finally at the board meeting in early September, the issue was decided. Dan had a letter of resignation in his pocket in case the vote went against him, but his side won handily.

His triumph was marred only by a late-night phone call from Nicholas Sloan informing him of Jonathan Hale's death. A week before, Sloan had told him that

Hale's dementia was improving rapidly but that he had developed a phlebitis in his left leg and wondered if he should anticoagulate him. Dan advised against it— it was extremely risky to anticoagulate anyone who had undergone recent brain surgery—unless there was evidence that the blood clot in Hale's leg vein was fragmenting and lodging in his lungs. Two days later, Hale complained of sudden breathlessness and chest pain. A lung scan suggested he had suffered a large pulmonary embolism, and pulmonary arteriography confirmed it. This forced Sloan's hand. He immediately started Hale on heparin and spent much of the next twenty-four hours at his bedside watching for any signs of a cerebral bleed. Hale seemed to breathe easier over the next few days and so did his doctors. However, on the night of Dan's board meeting, he suddenly collapsed in the bathroom of his room and died within minutes.

An autopsy would be performed the next morning, Sloan informed Dan, but he was pretty sure that Hale had died of a massive intracranial hemorrhage. Dan tried to console him; the heparin was a calculated risk and he had really had no choice in using it. Nonetheless, he shared Sloan's deep disappointment over the outcome.

Dan spent most of the next two weeks traveling— four days in Chicago, where he served on the AMA-sponsored National Commission on the Cost of Health Care, and four days in Washington, D.C., testifying before a House of Representatives subcommittee on health. When he returned to Boston, his desk was piled so high with paperwork that he wished he had never left. Before the day ended, though, he would wish with equal fervor that he had never returned.

In the morning Jason Whitlow, the hospital attorney, dropped by to see him. Whitlow was a man in his early sixties, the scion of a wealthy shipbuilding family and a true Boston Brahmin who practiced law more as a hobby than as a profession. Although his outward appearance was as starchy as the shirt collars he wore, he had a dry sense of humor that Dan always enjoyed.

"Been away, I understand," Whitlow began in his laconic New England twang.

"That's right," Dan said.

"Don't travel much myself," Whitlow informed him. "Don't enjoy it. Neither does the missus."

"So you've told me," Dan said curtly, wishing the lawyer would come to the point. "What can I do for you, Jason?"

Whitlow gave him a doleful look. "Remember a patient named Emmonds? Edgar Emmonds?"

"Emmonds?" Dan repeated, looking puzzled. "I don't recall anybody by that name."

"Didn't think you would. He was treated in your emergency room a couple of months ago. Treated and released."

"So?" Dan inquired. "You didn't come over here to tell me a grateful patient remembered us in his will."

"Nooo," Whitlow drawled, "I came to tell you he's suing you."

"Me?" Dan emitted a startled little laugh. "What for?"

"Well, he was recently released from Boston City Hospital after spending a month there recovering from a coronary. Apparently the night before they admitted him he had been brought here by the police when he complained of chest pain after they arrested him on a drunk-and-disorderly charge. Raised quite a ruckus in your emergency room, I understand. So one of your interns, name of Biggs, gave him a quick going-over and released him."

"Wait a second," said Dan, rubbing his chin. "I remember the guy. He was dead drunk, running around looking for booze. I was just coming into the hospital when he burst out of an examining room, and I grabbed him long enough for the cops to get handcuffs on him. Is *that* what this is all about? He claims I injured him in some way? That's unbelievable!" Dan laughed at the absurdity of it.

Whitlow remained unsmiling. "No, Dan, that's not what it's about. This fellow Emmonds claims he should have been kept here—that by letting the police take him to jail you endangered his life."

"Oh, for Chrissake!" Dan exploded. "He was so smashed the intern couldn't even take an EKG on him. And what does that have to do with me? I didn't treat him."

"I know, Dan, I know. And I tried to get Archie Cogswell to see it that way. Cogswell of Cogswell and Smith is his attorney, you understand. But Archie's got a bit of rascal in him, too, and he wouldn't. Evidently Emmonds has sworn off the booze and wants cash for a business venture, so he decided to sue. Cogswell explained that Commonwealth General's a government-supported hospital, hence immune from malpractice suits. But he also told Emmonds that there was another way to go: sue the intern and the doctor legally responsible for the emergency room—you."

Dan stared hard at Whitlow, less upset than ironically amused. "I don't want to tell you your business, Jason, but that sounds like the stupidest lawsuit I've ever heard of."

"Oh, we'll win it, I'm not worried about that. But it's going to take some of your time and, as always, it's going to cost."

Dan shook his head disgustedly. "If you're so sure we'll win, why don't you try to persuade Cogswell to drop it?"

"I did try, Dan. But he's hoping we'll settle, so he wouldn't listen. Besides," Whitlow added consolingly, "it could be worse."

"How?"

"Instead of Cogswell, Emmonds could have gotten Charles Sprague to represent him."

"Sprague, huh?" mused Dan, his curiosity aroused. "Why didn't he?"

"Oh, he tried. That greedy little man certainly tried. But Sprague turned him down flat. At least that's the story I got."

"Hmmm. I suppose I should be flattered. I now have the Sprague Good Doctor Stamp of Approval."

"I'm not so sure that distinction means much anymore."

"What do you mean?"

"Well, while you were away I got a call from Ned Josephson. Ned used to think that about Sprague, too, but he doesn't now. In fact, Ned sounded plenty upset. Sprague's suing a young doctor who's built quite a reputation for excellence in this town. I understand he's a friend of yours."

"Mind telling me who?" Dan said impatiently.

"Dr. Nicholas Sloan."

"What?" gasped Dan, struggling to surmount the shocks of incredulity set off in his brain.

"You wouldn't call him one of the bad ones, would you?"

"Hell, no! He's top-notch. Why would Sprague want to sue him?"

"You know about a patient of Sloan's named Jonathan Hale?"

"Sure," said Dan. "I know the whole story. I was one of the consultants on the case. What about Hale?"

"Well, the way I understand it, Sloan went to court to get permission to operate on him."

"That's right! And he was one-hundred-percent correct."

"I guess his widow disagrees. So, apparently, does Charles Sprague."

"Look," fumed Dan, making a visible effort to control his anger, "I don't give a damn what they think. Hale had an operable condition. It was nobody's fault that he developed a post-op phlebitis and pulmonary embolism. Sloan had to anticoagulate him or he would have died."

"He *did* die, Dan," Whitlow said softly.

"I know that! But not before Nick Sloan did everything humanly possible to save him. Absolutely everything! He went out of his way to give Hale one last chance at a normal life and he damned near brought off a miracle."

"Oh, I believe you, Dan. But Hale's wife claims he'd still be alive if it weren't for Sloan's treatment."

"A turnip's alive, but I wouldn't want to be married to one!" Dan sighed exasperatedly. "Any more bad news in your briefcase, Jason?"

"No, that's it. You've had more than your share for one day. Sorry I had to be the one to tell you, but that's what you pay me for. I'll keep you informed."

"Yeah, thanks." Dan stood up to hasten Whitlow's departure from his office, wanting solitude in which to ponder these stunning developments before calling Nicholas Sloan to offer his moral support and any assistance he could provide. Sprague! thought Dan, his anger mounting at the man for the chaos he was creating within the medical profession and at himself for not doing more to stop him. But even as he pondered, a cautionary instinct warned him against involving himself in Sloan's battles. He knew too well the dangers of yielding to his more adventuresome impulses, of meddling in another's life.

More than twenty years earlier, as a death-haunted medical student he had relentlessly dissected a human corpse by day, down to the last spicule of bone and strand of muscle, while at night he had obsessively tried to piece together the man's former life. As Dan's mind flashed back to the episode, he saw lower Washington Street, a squalid section of Boston long buried under by urban renewal. He saw himself staggering painfully away from a flaming car crash and the burning body of the man trapped inside. That was where his obsession with his cadaver—his almost mystical sense of kinship with the young man who in life had been named Rick Ferrar—had led; into a netherworld where murder was as commonplace as seedy bars and littered streets. The fiery automobile collision was no accident; Dan had caused it. He felt horror, looking back, but no guilt. The man riding with him was a hired killer, one of the murderers of Rick Ferrar, and he and his partner had meant to harm, possibly kill, Dan, too, to insure his silence. Instead Dan had done the killing, incinerating one man in the car crash and setting up the other so that Rick's big, black boyhood friend, Lem Harper, could kill him—thereby avenging Rick's death.

That had been the climax, though not the end, of the most bizarre interlude in Dan's life. The end had come a month later, when the medical school buried the year's collection of cadavers. At the cemetery, in the midst of the burial services, Dan had realized the full, frightening extent of his personal hatred of death —a hatred begun at age eleven with the loss of both his parents and intensified by the slaughter of his comrades in Korea. It was the driving force behind his becoming a doctor and his rapid rise within the profession; for his war against death, he had needed to arm himself with all the medical knowledge there was.

Dan rarely let himself dwell on that morbid episode. When he did it was usually for the purpose of reminding himself of the perils of being drawn into another obsession. Let somebody else worry about Charles Sprague, he told himself.

But from the time he tried to phone Nicholas Sloan a little before noon until Sloan finally returned his call at two o'clock, he continued to brood over the injustice done his friend. Oddly, Sloan sounded far less upset over the malpractice suit brought against him by Hale's widow than Dan was. At least twice he repeated that since he had treated Hale properly, he felt certain the court would exonerate him. Yes, he knew all about Sprague's almost perfect record of convictions, yet he remained confident that justice would prevail. Having seen Sprague and Angela Adams in action in a courtroom, Dan was not nearly so sanguine, but he didn't say so to Sloan.

After hanging up the phone, Dan paced the floor restlessly, grappling with indecision, until one compelling conclusion emerged: Nicholas Sloan was a dedicated physician. By bringing suit against him, Sprague had finally and forever dispelled the myth that he only went after bad doctors—and with that barrier out of the way, Dan was ready to act.

# 14

The darkening sky made Dan wish for his raincoat as he hurried toward the Suffolk County Superior Courthouse to meet Ned Josephson for lunch. He was late, but Ned was even later. Twenty minutes passed before he came striding breathlessly through the huge, cathedrallike foyer of the courthouse to join Dan at the base of the Rufus Choate statue. "Sorry to be so late," he panted, thrusting out his hand.

"Rough morning?"

"Jury selections are always rough. But there's more wrangling over this one than I've seen in a long time."

Knowing he meant the Gormann trial, Dan did not question him further. "Where do you want to eat?" he said.

Josephson glanced at his watch. "Somewhere close by. I don't have much time."

They settled for a small Chinese restaurant a few blocks away. The petite hostess seated them in a booth, brought them appetizers and tea, and left them deep in conversation.

"Okay, Ned," Dan began, "you've convinced me.

Something has to be done about Charles Sprague. If he's got no compunctions about suing doctors like Nick Sloan, I've got none about trying to stop him. But I'm still not interested in testifying for Carl Gormann, so just forget it."

"What *are* you interested in?" asked Josephson.

"Stopping Sprague!" Dan said forcefully. "Doctors in this state are in trouble and Sprague's the reason."

"Other lawyers try malpractice cases," Josephson pointed out.

"Sure, and they win some and lose some. Look at the statistics. Eighty percent of the verdicts favor the doctor. Well, Sprague's turned that upside down. He doesn't lose—mainly, I suppose, because his medical spy system helps him pick his shots carefully. But by suing Nick Sloan he's gone too far. He's either been badly misinformed or, more likely, the guy simply hates doctors—all doctors! The question is, why?"

Josephson studied him intently for a moment. "I'm not sure I follow you. You seem more spooked by Sprague than I am, and I have to face him in court. What's your stake in this?"

It was a question Dan disliked trying to answer. Evasively he said, "Look, *you* came to *me*. You asked my help on the malpractice crisis. Well, there wouldn't be a crisis if it weren't for Sprague—at least not on the scale of this one. So Sprague's the instigator, and there are some questions about him I want answered."

"Like what?"

"Like why he came out of retirement seven or eight years ago and started trying malpractice cases. Why he moves east every few years—from Los Angeles to Denver to wherever. Now here. Why he bears such a grudge against doctors. Any theories, Ned?"

Josephson shook his head. "No, not really. Not even his fellow lawyers know the answers. What do you suggest we do—hire a detective?"

"If necessary. Hell, you guys hire them all the time to investigate claimants, witnesses, prospective jurors, don't you? So why not now? Maybe the nickname

Sprague the Plague is appropriate. Know how we handle an epidemic, Ned? First we isolate and identify the virulent organism. Then we locate its source. Finally we try to figure out a way to stop its spread. The same principles hold here. All we have to do is apply them."

Josephson nodded. "Okay, you've convinced me. What do we do next?"

"I don't know," Dan admitted. "I'll have to think about it."

"Well," said Josephson after glancing at his watch, "if you want to take a look at your specimen, he's in the courtroom. Care to observe him in action for a while?"

Dan hesitated, trying to remember if he had any office appointments for that afternoon. "Let me call my secretary first to let her know where I'll be."

"How's the Gormann trial shaping up?" Dan asked Josephson on their walk back to the courthouse.

"Too early to tell. The key issue is whether Gormann ordered the IV tetracycline given four times a day, as it was, or once a day, as he claims. So a lot depends on the testimony of the nurse who transcribed his telephone order. Took me awhile to track her down—she's working in New York now—but I finally did."

"Will she own up to the mistake—if it was a mistake?"

"I don't know. I haven't really talked to her about it. Hammond has."

"Who's Hammond?"

Josephson turned to him with wide-eyed wonder. "You mean to tell me you've never heard of Sidney Hammond?"

"I *am* telling you."

"Well, Sidney Hammond is a malpractice specialist from Los Angeles. Very successful and *very* expensive. Gormann's hired him for his personal counsel while I look after the insurance fund's interests. From a batting-average point of view, Hammond's right up there with Sprague. In fact, he's only lost one malpractice case in the last few years and that, interestingly enough, was to Sprague. So it's going to be a shoot-out between two top guns, and I'll be happy to stay out of the line of fire."

"How can the medical society's malpractice fund afford a hotshot lawyer like Hammond?"

"They can't. Gormann's paying Hammond himself —which, believe me, will run into six figures."

"If Hammond's from Los Angeles and has faced Sprague in court before, do you think he knows him well enough to tell us something about his personal life?"

"I don't know," Josephson replied. "Ask him yourself when we get to the courtroom. He's champing at the bit to make his opening statement, but I doubt if we'll get to it today."

"What's taking so long?"

"Well, this is a big one for Sprague. Second-biggest award for damages he's ever asked for. And a jury trial begins with a search for jurors who tend to buy the version of the truth you're trying to sell. So their selection is just as important to a case as any trial tactics."

Dan followed Ned Josephson through the doors of Courtroom 229, the domain of Justice Jacob Richman, and down the aisle of the large, uncarpeted, sparsely furnished room to the spectator seats in front. It was a little before two P.M., and the jury box was empty.

"Sidney," Josephson said to the man seated at the defense table reading through a stack of juror questionnaires, "I'd like you to meet Dr. Daniel Lassiter, director of Commonwealth General Hospital."

Hammond put down his reading glasses, rose, and extended his hand. "Nice to meet you, Dr. Lassiter. Don't tell me you've decided to testify for us after all?"

"Afraid not," Dan said. "But perhaps I can help in other ways."

"Good," Hammond replied and to Dan's relief did not ask him to elaborate. The man had more than the

California look. With his wavy gray hair, white at the temples, tanned face, gold-rimmed glasses, impeccably tailored pinstripe suit, and manicured fingernails, Hammond looked as if he had been sent straight from central casting to play the quintessential trial lawyer.

In the short time they had to talk, Hammond admitted he had been beaten rather handily by Sprague in their previous courtroom battle and hoped to even the score. But except for telling Dan something about the innovative work Sprague had done with the California Trial Lawyers' Association back in the early 1950s, he knew nothing of the man's personal life and asked Dan to please share with him anything pertinent he might uncover.

When jury selection resumed, Charles Sprague, to the defense lawyers' surprise and Dan's disappointment, did not appear. Angela Adams took over the courtroom duties. Simply but stylishly dressed, she looked more rested and even more attractive than Dan remembered her. As before, her manner was poised, assured, and thoroughly professional.

The presiding justice began the session by signaling the courtroom clerk to call the final prospective juror—traditionally the hardest spot to fill.

The clerk rose and said, "Mrs. Madge Higby, please take a seat in the jury box."

A portly woman in her fifties rose, stepped forward, and fumbled briefly with the jury box gate latch before settling into the seat nearest the judge's platform. She crossed her legs, adjusted her skirt, and looked up expectantly.

"You were here this morning when we started the trial?" Justice Richman asked.

"Yes, yes, I was, Judge."

"Then you understand in general terms the type of case we have here before us?"

"Yes, I do."

"Have you heard or read anything about this case or the circumstances out of which it arises?"

Mrs. Higby hesitated, looking flustered. "Well, I *have* read about it. I mean, you know, there's been a lot about it in the newspapers and on TV."

"Have you formed any opinion on this case from anything you have heard or read thus far?"

"Oh, no!" Mrs. Higby exclaimed, her hand flying to her mouth.

Richman nodded and then ran through a long list of questions pertaining to her occupation, religion, medical history, and professional acquaintances. Satisfied with her answers, he concluded with the standard, all-encompassing query: "Do you feel that if you remain a juror in this case you can return and will return a fair, just, and impartial verdict based solely on the law and the evidence presented here?"

"I do," Mrs. Higby stated as solemnly as if making a marriage vow.

Turning toward Angela Adams, Justice Richman asked, "Does plaintiff's counsel have any questions for this prospective juror?"

She rose gracefully and said, "I *would* like to ask Mrs. Higby a few questions, Your Honor."

"Proceed."

Taking a step toward the jury box, Angela Adams made direct eye contact with the woman and smiled. Mrs. Higby responded with a twitchy smile of her own and averted her gaze.

"You listed under occupation that you are a housewife. Have you been employed in any other capacity in the past?"

"Well, I did work before I got married and for a couple of years after that."

"And what did you do, Mrs. Higby?"

"I was in the restaurant business."

"You ran a restaurant?"

"No. I didn't *run* a restaurant," Mrs. Higby replied, sounding a bit miffed. "I just waited tables. Things like that."

"Did the restaurant you worked in serve liquor?"

"Well, yes. There was a bar."

"And did you work the bar?"

"Well . . ." Mrs. Higby faltered, as if unsure where the questions might be leading. "I guess you could say that, since I helped out there from time to time. Once I had to work it a solid month when one of the barmaids quit without notice."

"I see," Angela Adams said curtly and returned to the defense table to consult her notes.

Leaning forward, Dan whispered to Ned Josephson, "What the hell's going on?"

"Waitresses are usually pretty tough cookies," Josephson explained, "but barmaids are rock-hard. Not too generous when it comes to handing out large sums of money in damages. My hunch is that Angela will turn this one down cold."

Josephson was right. When the time came, Angela Adams dismissed Mrs. Higby with a peremptory challenge and a polite smile. Shortly thereafter the judge declared a ten-minute recess.

As Dan strolled out into the corridor with Ned Josephson, a sudden clap of thunder made him hunch his shoulders and shiver. "How long's this going to go on?" he asked Ned.

"Oh, the rest of the afternoon and well into tomorrow, I'd imagine. But there's no reason for you to stay."

"Maybe there is," Dan ventured.

"Oh?" Josephson eyed him quizzically. "Tell me."

"Angela Adams," Dan said. "I'd like to meet her. Maybe get to know her."

Josephson's eyebrows lifted. "Do you mean to tell me you'd actually date Angela Adams just to help our cause. How self-sacrificing can you be?"

Dan grinned. "Desperate situations require desperate remedies."

Josephson pondered. "Think your ego can take a hard put-down? Chances are that's what you'll get."

Dan shrugged. "It's worth a try, don't you think?"

"Maybe so," Josephson conceded. "I learned a long

time ago there's no predicting the whims of a woman
or a jury. But I wouldn't rush into it without some sort
of game plan."

"I'll leave that to you," said Dan. "It'll be my neck,
your plan."

"I still can't believe you're serious. But if you are,
stick around. I'll give it some thought." Josephson took
a step toward the courtroom and then swung around.
"You sure don't look like a male Mata Hari to me."

"Mata Hari never claimed she didn't like her work."

"Yeah, well just don't go liking it too much. I don't
want the judge to get wind of it and declare a mistrial."

Back in the courtroom, the search for the elusive
eighth juror droned on. Although increasingly aware
of glances Angela Adams kept sending in his direction,
Dan could not be sure they were aimed at him. When
the court session adjourned at five P.M., she was immediately besieged by reporters.

"Well?" Dan faced Josephson. "I obviously can't get
to her through that mob. Any ideas?"

"Follow me." Josephson led him down a back staircase, past a security guard at ground level, to a delivery
dock in the courthouse rear. "Wait here," he told
Dan.

"For what?"

"Well, unless I miss my guess, Angela will leave the
building this way to escape the crowd. Sprague usually
does. Give her at least fifteen, twenty minutes to show.
If she doesn't, you can bill me for your time."

Dan took up a position in front of the window overlooking the rain-drenched driveway. While he waited,
idle thoughts and speculations flitted through his mind
until one dominated: was it Angela Adams the woman
or the law partner and possible paramour of Charles
Sprague who interested him most?

Twenty minutes passed. Dan was about to leave
when he suddenly heard the click of high heels behind
him. Turning, he saw her approach, carrying a bulging
briefcase but no raincoat or umbrella.

"Hello," Dan said casually. "I don't know whether to introduce myself or not."

Taken aback, Angela Adams replied, "I know who you are, Dr. Lassiter. What I don't know is what you're doing here."

"Waiting for the rain to let up." Dan glanced toward the window behind him.

Angela eyed him skeptically. "There is a front door, you know."

"And too many reporters around it."

"Oh? Are you in the news?"

"No," said Dan, matching her even stare, "you are. I tried to speak to you in the courtroom, but the lineup was three-deep in every direction. So Ned Josephson suggested I wait for you here."

"Ned did?" Angela looked confused. "Why would Ned do that?"

"He figured this would be the best place to intercept you."

"All right," Angela said, "you've intercepted me. Now what?"

Her amused look stung Dan. He was seldom intimidated by women, particularly career women, and hadn't expected to be now. But there was something about Angela Adams, perhaps the mingled feeling of lure and entrapment she roused in him, that momentarily shook his poise. Recovering quickly, he decided to be outrageous, hoping she would play along. "Well," he began gravely, "I was watching you in the courtroom. The way you walk, the way you move. I don't know any easy way to tell you this, but I think you're in the early stages of *neurotrophica gravidarum*."

"Really?" Angela exclaimed, eyes glittering. "I've suspected something like that for a long time, but I could never get a doctor to take me seriously."

"I'm not surprised. It's a very rare condition. The worst part is that it usually strikes its victim in the bloom of womanhood."

"How awful!" said Angela, raising her hand to her

heart. "But how did you know I was pregnant? You see, Dr. Lassiter, a working knowledge of Latin is essential to my profession, too. *Gravidarum* does mean pregnant, doesn't it?"

"Uh . . . yes. And *neuro* means nerves—which I seem to have a bad case of right now. Since the phony disease ploy didn't work, how about letting me off the hook and agreeing to have a drink with me?"

"I might," Angela considered, "on one condition: that you state clearly and concisely what you have in mind."

Dan exhaled audibly. "Okay. The simple truth is that I'm curious about you—have been ever since you cross-examined me at the Dubic trial. I'm also curious about your senior partner."

Angela's smile faded and her eyes bore into him. "Would you waylay Charles Sprague like this?"

Dan did not reply.

"I see," she replied, "—quite possibly more than I want to. If Charles Sprague interests you so much, why don't you just make an appointment to talk to him?"

"You know, you're the second person to suggest that to me lately."

"Who was the first?"

"A doctor-friend of mine. He thought Mr. Sprague might be interested in some of my ideas on how to deal with bad doctors."

Angela shrugged noncommittally. "He might. So might I, if you'd approached me differently." Abruptly she picked up her briefcase. "Now, if you'll please excuse me, Doctor," she said curtly and swept past him.

# 15

Angela flung open the dock door only to be driven back by a dense sheet of rain. Muttering a sibilant "Shit" under her breath, she turned to Dan, the defiant look on her face softening. "Oh well," she said sheepishly, "that's one grand exit that didn't come off. This is an expensive dress."

She brushed a wisp of hair from her eyes, and they exchanged stares. Finally Dan said, "I learned in the army never to volunteer, but . . . Here, hold my jacket."

"What for?"

Patiently he explained, "If you'll kindly take my jacket, I'll make a dash for my car, pick you up, and drive you to yours."

"You don't have to do that," she protested. "It's bound to let up soon."

In reply, Dan half-opened the door to let the rain splatter at their feet. "It's about three hundred yards to my car. If I don't drown, I'll be back in a few minutes. You'll wait, won't you?" he added with a trace of sarcasm.

"I'll wait," Angela said meekly. "Pass me your jacket."

Dan handed it to her, opened the door, squinted at the downpour, and with a grimace plunged into it.

Soon he drove up in his Datsun and beckoned. Climbing in beside him, Angela stared. From matted hair to waterlogged shoes, Dan was thoroughly drenched. Watching the droplets run down his forehead, she compressed her lips but couldn't keep from laughing. "You look a sight!"

"Never mind that! Do you _have_ a handkerchief I can borrow?"

She shook her head. "Just Kleenex."

"Oh, great!" Dan groaned. "Would you believe my heater doesn't work? Just the air conditioner."

"Mine does. Drive to my car and you can warm up there."

Following her directions, Dan pulled up beside a silver Mercedes coupe, and they nimbly changed cars in the rain.

"Between my Datsun and your Mercedes, makes you wonder who won World War Two," he remarked.

"Mine's rented," Angela informed him, "but it's friendly enough." After a minute or two of letting the engine warm up, she turned the heater on and directed the stream at Dan.

"Want a cigarette?" she offered, reaching into her purse for a pack.

Hugging himself to keep from shivering, Dan shook his head. "No thanks. Gave them up a few years ago and went back to nail-biting. Jesus, I'm cold!" he blurted through chattering teeth. "If only I knew you better, I'd—"

"You'd what?"

"I'd hug you—for warmth."

"Sorry." Angela pointed to her dress. "It's silk and it stains."

"Ah, well," Dan sighed resignedly. "What's a little pneumonia between friends?"

"I know a good doctor."

"That's news!"

"Why?"

"I thought the only doctors you knew were played by Bela Lugosi."

"Oh, come on!" she protested. "Let's not get into that. Besides, I have more important things on my mind right now."

"Like what?"

"Like whether to take pity on you and invite you up to my apartment for a drink. It's only a mile or so from here."

"Hmm," Dan murmured. "The least you can do for a shivering victim of the storm."

Dan followed Angela's car down Cambridge Street to the parking ramp of a modern, thirty-story apartment building overlooking the Charles River.

"Still raining, Miss Adams?" asked the young, uniformed elevator operator as he whisked them to the top floor.

"It's letting up, George," Angela replied. "I expect a rainbow to break out over Dr. Lassiter any minute now."

Dan smiled tolerantly.

"You a medical doctor?" the elevator operator asked.

Dan nodded. "When I'm not scuba diving through parking lots with my clothes on."

"You taking any new patients?" George rubbed his flank and grimaced. "Got a bad back."

"I might," Dan considered, "if you can afford me."

"How much do you charge?"

"I'm on the barter system."

"The what?" George looked puzzled. "I don't get it."

"Well, you look about my size. Loan me a T-shirt and a pair of pants and I'll see you for free."

George turned to Angela. "Is he on the level?"

"He'd better be," she said. "I'm a witness."

George's face brightened and he rubbed his hands with glee. "You got a deal, Doc. I'll bring 'em up soon as I go off duty in half an hour."

Dan followed Angela out of the elevator and down

the hallway to her front door. From its furnishing, a rich mix of traditional and antique pieces on obviously expensive Oriental rugs, to its walk-around garden terrace, her apartment was impressive.

"Mind if I use your bathroom to dry off a bit?" asked Dan after taking a quick look around.

Angela pointed to the connecting corridor between living room and bedroom. "Second door on the right. But first tell me what you want to drink."

"Whiskey and water's fine," he said and headed down the corridor.

Drying himself off with a bath towel before Angela's Jacuzzi, Dan marveled at its intricate tubes and timers and drains. Having seen them before in hospitals but never in homes, he was tempted to try it out. Maybe next time, he mused—if there was a next time.

Returning to the living room, Dan accepted with thanks the drink Angela had fixed for him.

"Now, Dr. Lassiter," she said in the distinctive way lawyers said it, implying that whatever followed would be businesslike and to the point, "you went to a lot of trouble to get me alone. Forgive my bluntness, but what the hell do you want?"

Dan took a long swallow of whiskey, sighed contentedly, and said, "Answers to a few questions. One in particular."

"All right. Ask."

"What's your relationship with Charles Sprague?"

Angela shrugged. "Friend. Partner."

"That's all?"

Her face hardened. "We're not lovers, if that's what you mean."

"I know it's pedestrian to ask, but what's he really like?"

"You said one question—remember?"

"I'll answer any one for you in return."

Angela hesitated, as if groping for words. "I hate to disappoint you, Dr. Lassiter, but Charles is one of the dearest, kindest men I've ever known."

"Okay," said Dan, "your turn."

Angela gave him an enigmatic little smile. "Are you married?"

He shook his head. "Divorced. And you—married or divorced?"

"Why does it have to be one or the other?"

"I can't imagine anyone with your looks going five years past puberty without getting married."

"You're wrong. I went seven. But I'm divorced too. Have been for years."

"Where'd you go to law school?"

Angela looked amused. "Why do you ask that?"

"It's called getting acquainted. Is it a prerequisite of your law firm to be mysterious?"

"What does that mean?"

"Well, compared to Charles Sprague, Howard Hughes was a publicity hound. What's this crusade of his all about?"

"I don't know anything about a crusade," she said firmly. "Charles is just a very good, very conscientious lawyer. That's all."

"And the captain of the *Titanic* told the passengers they were just stopping for ice."

Angela couldn't help smiling, and Dan took quick advantage. Extending his glass, he said, "How about a refill? In return, I promise not to ask any more questions about Charles Sprague. Just you."

Angela gazed penetratingly at him as she took the glass. "Somehow I don't quite trust you. I can't help feeling you're angling for something more than the usual male-female relationship."

"If that's in the offing, I'll settle," Dan said hastily. "But I'd still like to know more about you."

"It goes down easier with another drink." Angela went back into the kitchen to fix them. "All right," she began after they were once again seated on the couch facing the night sky. "The short and simple annals of Angela Adams, eh? I grew up in Portland, Oregon, and lost my virginity in the Pine Room of the Beta House at Oregon State when I was nineteen. It was neither the best nor worst thing that ever happened to me. I married the guy after I graduated from college and divorced him shortly after we both graduated from law school. I never married again, nor am I seeing anyone special at the moment. Any more questions?"

Innocently Dan said, "Can't think of a one."

"See? Your imagined mysteries can turn out to be rather humdrum once the truth is known."

Before Dan could reply, the doorbell rang and George delivered the promised loan of clothes. A few minutes later Dan emerged from the bathroom in a gray cotton jersey and pair of tight-fitting jeans. "Well," he said, his hands plunged deep into the pants pockets to stretch the crotch, "how do I look?"

Angela fought back a giggle. "Just . . . far out! How about a ride on your Honda?"

"Sorry. It's in the shop for repairs. How about going to a concert with me tonight?"

"They'd never let you in Symphony Hall dressed like that."

"It's not that kind of concert. So happens I have two tickets for the Emerson, Lake, Palmer bash at the Garden—for which I'm suitably, if not stylishly, attired. Care to join me?"

Angela stared. "Ordinarily, no. I barely know you. But I'm astounded. Don't tell me you're into rock?"

"Hardly," admitted Dan. "In fact, I've never been to a rock concert before. I got tickets to this one to hear Carl Palmer. I played drums in college—not great but not badly—and I want to see if Palmer really is the world's best."

Angela hesitated. "I'm tempted. I tried to get a ticket for that concert myself, only it's been sold out for weeks. But you said you had *two* tickets. Who's the other one for?"

Dan's brow furrowed. "Oh, I almost forgot! For someone very close to me. Not exactly intimate, but close. Someone you know, too."

"Who?" she demanded.

Dan paused for effect. "Gordon Donnelly. He's my neighbor."

Angela broke into a grin. "But Gordon detests rock! I know. I tried to take him to an Allman Brothers concert in Miami and he flatly refused. Said the rock scene was nothing more than a return to the womb and the mother's heartbeat pounding through the fetal sac."

Dan nodded knowingly. "That sounds like Gordon. The only way I could get him to go was to tell him this was a program of twelve-tone polyphonics by Schoenberg. Now that you know, will you go?"

Angela smiled acquiescingly. "To spare Gordon, I'll do it. Call him and tell him he's off the hook."

Boston Garden was transformed. Forty huge loudspeaker enclosures capable of delivering 72,000 watts of amplification hung from the ceiling; a fifty-eight member orchestra and chorus filled the three-tiered stage. As the hands of the Garden clock edged past the scheduled starting time of eight o'clock, the eager crowd began a rhythmic clapping and chanting, then roared approval when the houselights finally dimmed.

Suddenly the clamor eased as the conductor rose several feet in the air atop a hydraulic podium and gave the downbeat. A short silence heightened anticipation and then, from the constellation of loudspeakers, rolled the thunder of "Abaddon's Bolero." Simultaneously a cone of bright light flooded the stage to reveal Keith Emerson scampering between a Hammond organ and a Moog synthesizer, Greg Lake adroitly picking at a bass guitar, and in a cockpit among kettles, snares, gongs, and tubular bells, Carl Palmer beating a pulsating rhythm on drums.

The music grew progressively louder until it felt to Dan as if it were approaching the pain threshold of 130 decibels, eased temporarily, and then climaxed with a Palmer drum solo. The solo went on and on. Just when Dan expected him to slow down from sheer muscular exhaustion, Palmer quickened the beat, bringing the crowd to its feet with screams of praise.

Two hours and two encores later the concert concluded with Palmer featured in a tumultuous and primitive piece called "Tank."

"We're lucky to escape with our hearing—or our lives!" Angela said as the thunderous applause diminished and Dan signaled he was ready to leave.

Preceding him up the congested aisle, Angela turned to comment again when Dan suddenly arched his spine and grunted sharply as if stabbed. "Jesus Christ!" he roared and swung around to glare murderously up at a girl riding on her boyfriend's shoulders who had just spilled a container of beer down his back.

"Oh, hey, mister. I'm sorry," she stammered. "Honest!"

Seething, Dan put Angela behind him and bulled a path up the crowded aisle to the outer lobby.

It was raining when they reached the street. Declining Angela's offer to share her umbrella with him, Dan was almost grateful to the rain for washing some of the sticky beer residue from his shirt as they walked to his car.

Driving back, they talked about the concert until Angela said, "It's been a marvelous evening, Dan. The most relaxing I've spent in weeks. But you were a bit calculating in the way you set it up. I still can't shake off the suspicion you're more interested in Charles Sprague than in me."

"If that were true, I would've asked *him* to the concert."

"Be serious for a minute," she urged. "I am!"

"You sure you want to get into this?"

"No, I'm not sure. But we *are* into it. So level."

"All right," Dan said reluctantly. "I am interested in Charles Sprague. Or *was*. The malpractice crisis he's caused could topple the entire medical structure in this state. I've even been sued myself, did you know?"

"No," Angela said, surprised. "I didn't know!"

"By some drunk I never even treated who claims one of my interns endangered his life by missing the fact

154

that he'd suffered a coronary. Hell, after the ruckus he raised in our emergency room, the intern might've missed anything on him, including smallpox! So I am concerned. I'm also wet, hungry, and—if you must know—feeling a bit amorous."

"Oh, dear!" In a gesture of feigned innocence, Angela's hand flew to her breast. "Are you always this blunt in expressing your feelings?"

Dan shrugged. "I try to be. How about you?"

"I go more by intuition."

"And what does your intuition tell you?"

"That you're still not dealing from the top of the deck."

Dan fell silent while carefully choosing his next words. He couldn't confide the whole truth to her— whatever that was—but maybe he could allay her suspicions by confiding part. "All right," he finally said, "there is someone we should talk about . . . Dr. Nicholas Sloan."

Angela drew back, an odd, almost wincing expression on her face. "Why him?"

"Because Nick's a good doctor and a good friend. And it makes me mad as hell that your law firm is suing him. Especially on behalf of a heartless bitch like Mavis Hale! I was involved in the Hale case as a consultant. If Sloan made any fatal mistakes—which I doubt— then I'm as much to blame for them as he is." The expression on Angela's face warned him to curb his anger. "So if you want to talk about what's bothering me," he continued in a calmer voice, "let's talk about that."

"Do you plan to testify for Dr. Sloan?"

"Damned right. Along with every other name doctor in town."

"Then we're on opposite sides, Dan, and there's nothing we *can* talk about. You ought to know that."

In the ensuing silence Dan could feel the sexual tension that had been building between them all evening begin to dissipate. He tried to recoup by making amusing small talk, but she remained moody and withdrawn as if his championship of Sloan had made her retreat behind some impenetrable barrier.

Back at her apartment, Angela announced, "Look, Dan, it's late. If you don't mind, I'd just as soon skip the nightcap. Why don't you take a Jacuzzi while I put your wet clothes in the dryer? It buzzes when the cycle's finished. I presume you can manage the rest—including pouring your own drink if you want one—without me. Just make sure the front door locks behind you when you let yourself out."

Dan clenched his teeth to keep from wincing at her abrupt dismissal. "Where will you be while I'm doing all this?"

"In bed. I've a long day ahead of me in court and I'll have to get up at dawn to do the preparing I should've done tonight."

Her words hardly explained her rudeness, but Dan did not directly challenge her on these grounds. Instead he said lightly, "Sure you trust me wandering around your apartment alone?"

"I trust you," Angela said flatly. "You're an unlikely rapist and we're both responsible adults."

"That's not the issue."

"Perhaps not. But we'll have to discuss *that* some other time. Follow me and I'll get you a fresh towel."

Alone in Angela's guest bathroom, a beach-size towel in one hand, a stiff whiskey in the other, Dan gave his reflected image in the mirror a baffled look and then wearily shed his sodden clothes, wrapping them in a towel from the rack and leaving them outside the door for Angela to put in the dryer. That done, he turned his attention to the set of printed instructions on the wall above the Jacuzzi.

Turning on the faucets, Dan sipped most of his drink while waiting for the tub to half-fill with water. Then, after checking the instructions again, he adjusted the inflow knobs, set the wall timer for fifteen minutes, tested the temperature of the water to make sure it was tepid, and climbed in.

For the time it took him to finish his whiskey, Dan sat up in the tub, trying to make sense out of the bewildering upheavals of the night. But he could deduce no plausible explanation for Angela's behavior. There were so many loose ends, such large gaps in his personal knowledge of her, that he could probably do as well reciting "She loves me, she loves me not" while plucking the petals from a daisy. Finally he gave up and slid down in the tub to enjoy the whirling caress of water currents against his body. With the combination of alcohol and exhaustion clouding his mind, he inadvertently dozed off.

Moments later, the click of the door latch woke him. Looking up, he caught a brief glimpse of Angela's nude profile before she shut off the light. He sprang up to help her safely into the tub. "Careful," he warned, lowering her gently.

"No, care*less*," she corrected. "Very careless. But I don't care. I'm tired of waiting. Is this what you had in mind before your indignant outburst over your friend Sloan?"

"Not exactly." Dan had not dared imagine anything so erotic. "But it'll do."

"It should! I hope aggressive women don't turn you off."

"Let the facts speak for themselves."

"*Let* them," Angela purred, stretching out on top of him.

Their lovemaking was intense, uninhibited, and progressively more satisfying as they learned each other's special likes and ways. The move from bathroom to bedroom permitted Dan to see as well as feel Angela. Firm-breasted and flat-stomached, she was in superb shape for a woman near or possibly past forty. Yet the extent of her sensuality surprised him. Their first coupling in the Jacuzzi had been frantic and utterly unrestrained; at its height Angela had locked her legs around his waist, allowing him no room to withdraw. Each subsequent climax had ended the same way, as if they left her so open and vulnerable she could not bear to be unfilled.

She gave no indication of being protected from pregnancy, and he could not bring himself to ask. To his professional eye, the brownish pigment surrounding her nipples and the few stretch marks on her abdomen suggested she had borne one or more children. But his instincts warned him against asking about that, too. Clearly she had acted impulsively, out of overwhelming need, but whether the need was primarily psychic or physical, he could not guess. Lying beside her in bed after promising to leave shortly, entranced by the serene composure of her face, his mind grappled with these and other unanswered questions. Would she want to see him, go to bed with him, again? Or was this merely a glorious one-night stand? After all, as she had pointedly reminded him earlier, they were on opposite sides in an impending war.

# 16

Though short on sleep, Dan was suffused with energy when he arrived at Commonwealth General Hospital the next morning. But by five P.M., after putting in a grueling day of rounds, meetings, interviews, and consultations, his eyes burned with fatigue and his yawning became embarrassingly irrepressible. Moreover, doubt weighed heavily on his mind. He longed to phone Angela and see her that evening, but he wondered if it might not be wiser to wait a day or two, give her a chance to recover from last night.

Weary as he was, Dan knew he wanted to be with her again, the sooner, the better; but he was less certain why she held such a strong lure for him. His sexual needs had been met for the time being, so that wasn't the reason. An element of fantasy fulfillment contributed mightily to his feelings, he realized, but beyond that what was there? The possibility of an enduring relationship? Maybe past experience had made him too cynical, or maybe there were too many imponderables, but love between man and woman, he believed, was as elusive as smoke.

Shortly after six, Angela solved the dilemma for him by phoning to invite him to dinner. He appeared at her apartment an hour later, bearing the latest Emerson, Lake, and Palmer tapes as gifts.

"Well," Angela began brightly, once they were seated on the couch in her living room, drinks in hand, "who goes first? Do you want to tell me about your day at the hospital or hear about my day in court?"

"You," Dan said without hesitation. "It's bound to be more interesting."

"It wasn't. But tomorrow will be. Both sides make their opening statements to the jury."

"Good," he said, but did not pursue it. If he'd learned anything from last night, it was to stay clear of the subject of malpractice trials.

"I hope you like Spanish-style cooking," Angela said, "because that's what you're getting. *Arroz con pollo.* My part-time housekeeper is Puerto Rican, and that's her specialty. The sangria I concocted myself."

They were barely through the main course when the telephone rang. Angela answered it and told Dan the call was for him.

"Dr. Lassiter," began the now familiar voice of Jim Hermanson, "I hate to disturb you, but I've got a tough case here and I need help."

"All right," Dan said supportively, "tell me."

"What makes the case touchy as well as tough," Hermanson continued, "is that he's a private patient of Peter Trombley's, and I can't reach him. He's out sailing somewhere."

"How nice," Dan said dryly.

"Yeah. Anyway, he admitted a seventy-year-old man named Hedberg two days ago 'cause of chest pain and elevated enzyme levels. Looked like a coronary at first, but his EKG and cardiac scan are only mildly abnormal, so I'm not so sure."

"What's his problem now?" asked Dan to orient his thinking.

"Right after supper tonight the old guy complained of

heaviness in his chest, and the nurse gave him a slug of morphine."

"On whose orders?"

Hermanson sighed. "You're not going to like this, but Trombley's. He left a standing order."

"A *standing* narcotic order?"

"That's what he wrote. A quarter grain every four hours as necessary."

Dan grimaced at this blatant disregard for medical department recommendations but withheld comment. "Go on," he said tightly.

"Well, within minutes the guy stopped complaining of chest pain or anything else. He also stopped breathing. Right now, he's comatose, shocky, and on a respirator. I gave him a stat dose of Narcan to counteract the morphine, but it hasn't helped worth a damn. I've also done all the routine things—blood gases, repeat EKG, chest X ray—and frankly, Dr. Lassiter, I still don't know what's going on, except that he doesn't look long for this world."

"Okay," Dan said, "I'll be right over to see him. Meet you on the intensive care unit in fifteen minutes."

"Right," said Hermanson, sounding relieved. "Thanks."

Hanging up the phone, Dan turned to Angela, gestured futilely, and said, "Sorry, but I've an emergency at the hospital and have to go."

"Damn!" Angela muttered, unable to hide her disappointment.

Impulsively Dan said, "Come with me?"

"Me? Why?"

"I'm just not ready for our evening to end."

"Hmm," Angela considered. "I don't like hospitals any better than you said you liked courtrooms. But maybe I will, since it's the one sure way to get you back here."

"My thoughts exactly," said Dan, feeling his sensuality stir.

On the drive to the hospital, Dan told Angela what

little he knew about Trombley's patient. When he finished, she asked, "Why couldn't it just be a coronary?"

"Oh, it could, only somehow I don't think so. According to Hermanson, he suffered a respiratory arrest, not a cardiac one, which is pretty unusual for an acute coronary. Makes me suspect his heart's not the main culprit."

"What then?"

"Well, remember the old axiom of French mystery writers, *'Cherchez la femme'*? The modern medical equivalent of that is *Cherchez la drug.*"

"The morphine?"

"Very good!" Dan winked at her. "Your legal training's taught you not to overlook any possibilities, however remote, either—and you're right. Morphine certainly could produce respiratory arrest in someone with chronic lung disease. But since he doesn't have that, I'll have to consider other causes."

"Like what?" Angela asked curiously.

"Let me examine him first. Then I'll let you know."

At the hospital Dan used his master key to enter the nursing supervisor's office and borrow a white coat and stethoscope for Angela to wear.

"Do doctors dress up impostors very often?" she asked as they headed for the elevators.

"All the time," Dan replied.

"Hmm," she mused. "That makes me wonder about all those young doctors who came around to stare at my appendectomy scar."

"I'll give odds there was a tire salesman in the group," Dan said confidently.

Angela looked at him askance for a moment before declaring, "You're making it up!"

In the ICU Dan introduced Jim Hermanson to Angela, took the patient's chart from his hands, and then went with Jim to the bedside while Angela watched from outside the glass-walled cubicle.

Mr. Miles Hedberg was tube-laden from throat to

groin, making examination difficult. After listening to his chest, Dan detached his endotracheal tube from the bellowslike apparatus forcing a mixture of compressed air and oxygen into his lungs to see if the patient could now breathe on his own. But his motionless rib cage and silent lungs made it quickly apparent he could not, and Dan reattached him to the mechanical ventilator.

"All right," he said to Hermanson, "let's go discuss it in the conference room."

Out in the corridor he took Angela's arm and led her to the room where Hedberg's chest X ray was mounted on the fluorescent-lit viewing box embedded in the wall. Dan studied it while sipping coffee. "Heart size's pretty big, even for a seventy-year-old," he remarked.

"I noticed," said Hermanson. "But the echo study doesn't show any significant effusion."

Taking a seat at the conference table, Dan waved Hermanson to a chair opposite him and passed him the patient's chart. "All right, Jim," he said, "let's talk. What do you think's going on?"

Intentionally or not, Hermanson ducked the question and spent the next several minutes reviewing the results of numerous laboratory tests. Annoyed, Dan snapped, "Enough! We have computers to analyze lab data. I expect you to use your own computer," he said, pointing to his head, "and tell me what's really wrong. So far you've spent all your time treating the complications of some disease—morphine shock, respiratory arrest, coma—without taking the trouble to figure out what that disease might be! That's simply not acceptable, Jim. Not for a chief resident."

Hermanson flushed but took the criticism without flinching. "I'm well aware of that, Dr. Lassiter. I suppose I could alibi by claiming I've been too busy the last couple of hours keeping the guy alive to have time to think, but the truth is, I simply don't know."

"Look, Jim," Dan said in a more conciliatory voice, "I respect your honesty *and* your ability. But all the reams of lab data you've collected have told you so far is what the underlying disease *isn't!* To find out what it *is* you've got to use your head. Use logic!"

"Gladly!" said Hermanson, "if you'll guide me."

"Well, I'm obviously not going to let the patient die to prove a point. But before I tell you what I think the diagnosis is, I want to give you a fair crack at coming up with it yourself. What you do first is break the case down into its four essential parts: symptoms, signs, lab data, and clinical course. Then you isolate the most distinctive features of each and use them to formulate your differential diagnosis. Now, as far as Mr. Hedberg is concerned, his main symptoms are chest pain and narcotic intolerance. His main signs are a big heart and hypothermia—or haven't you noticed the rectal temperature of ninety-six degrees?"

Chagrined, Hermanson admitted he had, but in view of the other complications, had not considered it significant.

"Well," Dan said, eyeing him critically, "we'll get back to that. Let's finish our case analysis first. The most striking lab abnormality is his elevated enzyme levels, both liver and muscle, and the most unusual aspect of his clinical course is morphine-induced respiratory arrest. Follow me so far?"

The chief resident nodded.

"Okay, the next thing you do is try to think of one disease that produces the entire picture. In other words, use Occam's razor."

Angela asked, "What's that?"

"A rule of logic that's damned useful in making medical diagnoses. It's always better to consider one cause for two or more seemingly related events than multiple causes. Getting back to Mr. Hedberg, he's an unusual case, so he might well be suffering from some unusual condition, either an uncommon manifestation of a common disease or a common manifestation of a rare one. Now, using that rule of logic, Jim, what comes to mind?"

Under Dan's unyielding stare Hermanson felt as uneasy as a freshman medical student taking an oral exam. "Well," he began hesitantly, "as you pointed out, he does have mild hypothermia, and that should always make you consider hypothyroidism."

Expressionless, Dan said, "All right. Let's consider it. Can thyroid failure explain all his main features?"

Hermanson knitted his brow and then slowly, embarrassedly, grinned. "Christ, yes! Of course, it can."

"All right," Dan said. "So we have a tentative diagnosis. Now what?"

"Treat him for it!" Hermanson declared enthusiastically. "But before or after checking with Trombley?"

"After, if possible. But the fact that the shock didn't respond to the morphine antagonist you gave is ominous, so I wouldn't wait too long. When did Trombley's answering service say he'd be back from his sail?"

"Around midnight." Hermanson glanced at his watch. "Three hours from now. *Can* we wait?"

"Can the *patient* wait, you mean? The longer he stays shocky, the greater the damage to his vital organs. So go ahead and draw your baseline thyroid function tests and inject four-tenths milligram of sodium thyroxine in him now. On my orders!"

Hermanson nodded but still looked faintly troubled. "For Chrissake, Jim, go ahead!" Dan exclaimed. "Never mind Trombley. Let me worry about him, as I usually do. It's the patient you have to worry about. Besides, the hospital rule covering emergency care when the private doc's temporarily unavailable is clear. So go ahead and shoot him full of thyroid hormone now. If Trombley disagrees with the treatment, he can always get a nephrologist to put the patient on an artificial kidney and dialyze it out! Now can we go?"

Hermanson rose abruptly. "Thanks for your help, Dr. Lassiter. And your moral support, Miss Adams."

"Well," Dan said to Angela in the car, "what do you think of hospital life?"

"I'm impressed. It's nice to watch a real pro in action."

"Yeah," Dan agreed. "I watched one at the Dubic trial. I'm sure glad we're on the same side now."

"I hope so," she said softly. "I really do."

The moment they entered her apartment, Angela was in his arms. Again their lovemaking was intense. Again Angela's legs kept him locked tightly for several minutes after they'd climaxed.

# 17

At eight the next morning Dan met Jimmy Dallesio for breakfast, choosing a coffee shop near the Suffolk County Courthouse so that they could attend the Gormann trial later on.

"All right, Jimmy," said Dan, "what can you tell me about Charles Sprague?"

Jimmy reached into his briefcase and removed a bulky manila envelope. "Here's my file on him—mostly newspaper clips, but also a biographical sketch I wrote out. Let me read it to you."

"Maybe you'd better," Dan said, remembering Jimmy's handwriting.

Jimmy began: "Charles Roland Sprague. Born December 18,1914, in Pasadena, California, the only child of John and Etta Sprague. Father a citrus grower and amateur botanist; mother a schoolteacher. According to high school yearbook, a smart kid, a good athlete, and a private pilot who flew his own crop-dusting plane. Graduated from Yale University magna cum laude with a B.S. in anthropology in 1935. Got his master's degree in paleontology there in 1936. Taught vertebrate paleontology at Yale for one year and then got tired of fossils and switched to law. Entered the University of Michigan Law School in 1938 and once again did damned well. Associate editor of the *Michigan Law Review* and Order of the Coif—their honor society. Practiced general law in Escanaba, Michigan, a town of around 15,000 in the upper part of the state, until the outbreak of World War Two. Then he did something pretty romantic. Obviously he could've landed a good job with the Judge Advocate General's Corps if he'd wanted one, but he got himself an aviation cadet appointment. Moreover, they put him in fighter planes, which means he must have been a real hotshot in flying school. From February 1943 to March 1944, he flew with the 422nd Heavy Bomber Wing out of Peterborough, England—"

"Peterborough!" Dan exclaimed. "Huh! My Uncle Woody flew out of there for a while, too. Wonder if the two of them knew each other?" He made a mental note to call Woody that evening and ask. "Go on."

"Got shot down over France in April 1944 and was imprisoned in a POW camp run by the SS near Calais. He tried to escape, was recaptured and severely beaten, sustaining a hearing loss in his right ear. His camp was liberated shortly after the Normandy invasion, but because of his physical disability Sprague's fly-boy days were over. So he requested and got transferred to the Judge Advocate General's Corps. Now this next part is a bit unusual, Dan. Might give you a real clue to his character. Instead of rotating home as a disabled POW, certain of early discharge, damned if he didn't accept a job as chief assistant prosecutor at the Nuremberg war crime trials."

"That *is* interesting," Dan agreed. "What do you make of it?"

"One of two things. Either he hated the Nazis enough to want to make damned sure they got the kind of justice they deserved. Or else he wanted to take advantage of the excellent experience the Nuremberg trials offered young lawyers. Anyway, he resigned from the JAGC in 1948 with the rank of lieutenant colonel and was admitted to the State Bar of California in 1950. Practiced general law in Chula Vista, California, until 1953, then moved on. Admitted to the Colorado State Bar that year and practiced in Greeley, Colorado, another small town, until 1956."

"Moved around a lot, didn't he?"

"Yeah, and for no apparent reason. No swindles, scandals, or black marks on his record. Maybe he liked to fish and hunt. Or maybe he just liked the pace of a small town. But éventually he tired of that, too, 'cause his next move was to a big city and a more lucrative type of practice. In 1959 he was admitted to the Connecticut Bar Association. He practiced both general and corporate law in Hartford for the next four years. Made a bundle apparently and in 1963 sort of retired. Simply dropped out of sight for a while. Then he pulled the biggest switch of all."

"Tell me," Dan said impatiently.

"Well, in the spring of 1964 he left Hartford and the United States and joined the faculty of the Max Planck Institute in Munich, Germany. Even more puzzling, after a year he transferred from its International Law Division to its Human Biophysics Division and did outstanding work there. Published several papers on human stress tolerance during simulated space travel and other feats of endurance."

"Any idea why?"

"Not exactly. But my lawyer-friends tell me that estimates or actual measurements of that kind can play a decisive role in certain personal-injury cases. And with the kind of experience Sprague picked up there, he's probably as expert on that subject as any doctor."

"Interesting," Dan murmured. "Then what?"

"Well, either he'd been planning it all along—which is why he worked in the Max Planck's Human Biophysics Division—or something pretty traumatic happened to him, 'cause doctors' foibles suddenly became his main interest. In 1968 he returned home, joined a

Detroit law firm specializing in malpractice cases, and took on most of their clients suffering orthopedic-type injuries. Then in 1970 he moved back to California to start his own law firm. The rest you know."

"Yeah," Dan said gloomily, "the rest I know—but not why. The guy's led a strange enough life as it is, but what the hell could've happened to him in Germany, or before, to turn him against doctors? Or maybe I'm making it too complicated. Maybe he's just in it for the money."

"Maybe. But you don't sound too convinced."

"I'm not! Was Sprague ever married, do you know?"

"I didn't come across any mention of a wife. Why?"

"What I'm really trying to track down is whether Sprague was ever married, a widower, a mistreated patient in a military or civilian hospital, even a mental institution—anything that might provide a rational basis for his grudge against doctors."

"Assuming that he bears one?"

"That's right. But it sure looks like it to me. Why else would he suddenly come out of retirement to specialize in malpractice cases? Why would he refuse to settle cases out of court? Even you suspect he's set up some sort of spy system in the medical profession. Why go to *that* extreme, if he wasn't driven by something personal?"

Jimmy gestured futilely. "I wish I could tell you. It'd make a hell of a story. Or book. Speaking of motivation, though, why your intense interest in this guy?"

Dan hesitated, wanting to be truthful to himself as well as to Jimmy. "Initially, curiosity," he said. "And concern for what Sprague's doing to the practice of medicine in this state. Now, though, it's gotten more complicated. You see, Jimmy . . ." He paused to measure his next words. "I'm involved with Angela Adams."

Jimmy's eyes widened behind his thick-lensed spectacles. "You're, ah, what?"

"Involved. Which is to say we have what's known nowadays as a relationship."

"How did all *this* come about?"

"Part design, part accident. I wanted to crack the mystery of Charles Sprague and figured I could possibly get her to spill some revealing stuff. But she got wise to that fast, so now we hardly ever discuss Sprague. That's why I need your help."

"I'll do whatever I can." Jimmy glanced at his watch. "Well, we'd better get a move on if we want to hear Sprague's opening statement."

At ten minutes to nine Courtroom 229 was packed to capacity. Without Jimmy's intercession Dan never would have got past the security guard at the door and been allowed to stand at the back. Ned Josephson, Sidney Hammond, and Dr. Carl Gormann, a fleshy-faced man in his late fifties, sat at the defense table. Angela Adams and Charles Sprague flanked a handsome but sullen-looking black youth, presumably Darryl Harrison, at the plaintiff's table.

Promptly at nine, Justice Richman convened the court and called on Charles Sprague to make his statement to the jury. Dan, standing diagonally across the room from him, saw Sprague rise, suddenly sway sideways, and slump back in his chair. "Excuse me a moment, Your Honor," he rasped and reached into a vest pocket. Again, as at the Dubic trial, Dan observed him take a pill from a box and either swallow it dry or put it under his tongue to dissolve.

When Sprague rose again, the audience held its collective breath. He gave Angela a reassuring nod and shuffled slowly forward to greet the judge and jury. For a long while he stood, hands gripping the lectern, gazing down at it, gathering his thoughts, or else waiting for his head to clear. "This morning . . . ," he finally began, ". . . this morning it is my responsibility to make a statement to you as to why the defendant doctor in this case—all the defendant doctors—should be held liable to young Darryl Harrison for the damages he has suffered through their negligence. This statement can be short or long, concise or excruciatingly detailed." He smiled fleetingly. "I promise you it will *not* be long." Then his face turned somber. "I also promise you it will not be pleasant. In fact, it will likely make you exceedingly uncomfortable—as uncomfortable as I've been, living with the facts in this case for the last several months. I am not by nature an emotional man. But as I stand before you now, I cannot help being overcome by anger. We are asking damages, monetary recompense, for our client, but money is not what he wants. Darryl Harrison wants what he cannot have—his loving parents back. Short of this—far short—he wishes to see justice done. As his counsel, it is my sworn duty to present the proofs in this case so that you, the jury, can provide that justice.

"Let the facts speak for themselves, you've all heard —and, indeed, the facts will speak. Harshly! But before they do, I would like to add a personal perspective. It is not my custom to make inflammatory statements to a jury, and I hope you will not perceive this as one. But I want you to know," Sprague said in a low, compelling voice, "that I speak from the heart when I tell you this is the most flagrant, most tragic case of medical malpractice I have ever brought before the bar in all my years of practice. A patient has not merely been maimed or killed. No! A family—an entire family—has nearly been wiped out! And if that were not enough, the physician whose irresponsible actions brought about this tragedy has been whitewashed by his equally irresponsible peers. Death, of course, awaits all of us, but Delia Harrison was not meant to die at age thirty-eight. Delia Harrison *would not* have died at such a young age were it not for a long and shocking series of mistakes perpetrated on her by the defendant. By the physician to whom she entrusted her life. *By Dr. Carl Gormann.*" Sprague pivoted slowly toward the defense table and fixed his gaze on Gormann until the man uncomfortably looked away.

"Yes, Dr. Carl Gormann," Sprague repeated with distaste. "Not once, not twice, but on at least *five separate occasions,* Dr. Gormann could have prevented this needless tragedy from happening, and *each time* he failed!"

At a gentle tap on his shoulder, Dan turned to find Craig Andrews standing beside him. "Sprague's in fine, fire-breathing form this morning," he whispered.

"But what's with the pill bit?"

"I don't know," Dan whispered back. "I'll see what I can find out."

"The meeting's still on for tomorrow night. Can you make it?"

"I'll try," said Dan and turned back to listen.

"Five times he failed!" Sprague was saying, his voice strident with indignation. "Yes, to err is human. And yes, God gives most of us a second chance to make amends. He gave Carl Gormann *five* chances, and each went for naught. Be assured, I will make crystal-clear to you when and how he failed, but I cannot tell you why. Only the defendant himself can tell you that, and will be given ample opportunity to do so when his time comes.

"To begin: two summers ago Delia Harrison, a respected nurse on the staff of Bradford Medical Center, consulted Dr. Carl Gormann because of excessive menstrual flow. His office record reveals Dr. Gormann examined her, made a tentative diagnosis of 'dysfunctional uterine bleeding'—a condition we will have experts explain to you in full—and recommended hysterectomy. Through testimony of her friends we will show that Mrs. Harrison became very upset over the prospect of such surgery and requested a second opinion. But Dr. Gormann discouraged her from this; in fact, told her it would be a waste of another doctor's time." Again Sprague turned to stare accusingly at Gormann before rasping, "His *first* mistake!

"So Mrs. Harrison consented to the surgery—unnecessary surgery, as the pathologist's report will prove —and when she began running a fever postoperatively, what did Dr. Gormann do? Journey back to the hospital that night to examine her, try to discover the source of her fever? He did not!" Sprague barked. "His *second* mistake! Did he obtain a medical consultation, as good medical practice might dictate? No! He chose not to do that. Then what did he do? He treated her by telephone! His *third* mistake!"

Dan almost winced as Sprague once again turned to stare at Gormann, imagining the terrible toll this form of conditioning must be taking on Gormann's nerves.

"Even then," Sprague continued, "disaster might've been averted if only Dr. Gormann had taken the time to look up and verify the proper dosage of IV tetracycline before ordering it given. We will show that Dr. Gormann did not do this. We will, in fact, prove that he behaved even more irresponsibly than that when he made *his fourth mistake!*"

As Sprague again turned from the jury box to the defense table, he suddenly swayed in a half-circle and stumbled, barely managing to grab the lectern to keep from falling. Angela sprang up and rushed to his side.

As they exchanged whispers, Justice Richman asked, "Does counsel for the plaintiff wish a recess?"

Sprague looked up at him and smiled. "A glass of water will do fine, Your Honor."

"Are you sure, Mr. Sprague?" Richman said with concern.

"Quite sure, Your Honor."

Observing the vertiginous attack from across the room, Dan wondered about its cause. Was Sprague experiencing chest pain, an irregular heartbeat, an intermittently insufficient blood supply to his brain? The man *was* ill, perhaps seriously, Dan decided. His pill-popping was not a dramatic device at all.

"And so," Sprague began, then paused to clear phlegm from his throat, ". . . and so, because of a series of decisions—wrong or self-serving on the defendant's part—Delia Harrison is dead at the age of thirty-eight. Dead, buried, and doomed to be forgotten by all but close friends and a surviving son, if it were not for this trial. But if these proceedings accomplish anything, it will be to rectify Dr. Gormann's *fifth* mistake—his fifth and most reprehensible!"

As the elderly lawyer sipped water, the crowd stirred and Dan could almost sense their mounting indignation. Sprague had prepared them for this climactic accusation masterfully.

"I repeat," he said at last, "because of a long list of grievous mistakes on the defendant's part, Mrs. Delia Harrison, an exceptional wife and mother, is dead at thirty-eight. This court cannot bring her back. Nor can it bring back Morris Harrison, her loving husband, whose grief proved too great for his ailing heart and who dropped dead at her funeral. But there is still one more victim to be considered, a seventeen-year-old boy who until just recently was never told the true facts of his mother's death; who was literally driven crazy wondering what terrible outrage he had committed against God that He would punish him by the loss of his parents. Ladies and gentlemen of the jury, this is why we are in this courtroom today: to tell Darryl Harrison that it was *not God,* but the negligence and misdeeds of a man, that orphaned him—Dr. Gormann . . . Dr. Carl Gormann!" And once more the slow, dramatic turn toward the defense table.

A dead silence followed Sprague's last declaration. Dan glanced around. Gormann, eyes glazed and fists clenched, looked severely shaken; Josephson looked pained; Hammond grim. But it was the expression on the Harrison boy's face, the implacable hatred hinting he would destroy the world if the choice were only his, that made Dan shudder with the realization that malpractice, like murder, was no abstraction to the victims it created.

Sprague paused to give the audience time to stare with loathing at Gormann before going on. "We also want to make clear to the medical profession that when we entrust our health, our very lives, to their care, it is with the understanding that *they repay our trust with truth!* Our military leaders hold the heavy responsibility for mass lives, too. They demote incompetents and discharge mental and physical misfits. So must the medical profession if we are to continue to trust and tolerate them. So must we *make* them—for their salvation as well as our own!"

After this preface, Sprague spent the next several minutes giving his reasons, along with their legal basis, for including Bradford Medical Center's disciplinary committees in his suit on behalf of the Harrison youth, and then he wearily sat down.

Looking up at the courtroom clock, Dan was surprised to see that Sprague's emotion-charged statement had taken only thirty minutes. It had seemed far longer to him and most likely an eternity to Gormann. After a brief recess, Justice Richman called on Sidney Hammond to speak for the defense.

Hammond's opening statement was skillfully constructed, reasoned, and delivered, but it lacked the theme and gut impact of Sprague's "five mistakes" oration. Delia Harrison, he pointed out, had chosen Gormann for her personal physician because she worked at the same hospital as he did, respected his ability, and observed his kindness and concern for his patients. Despite the negative pathology report, the hysterectomy she underwent *was* necessary—as expert witnesses would testify. The fatal dose of tetracycline she received was, indeed, a tragic error—though not Carl Gormann's. Despite its length and occasional flashes of eloquence, Hammond's statement did little to blunt Sprague's slashing accusations, and Dan noticed, as he was sure the members of the jury had, that never once did Hammond look at the Harrison boy.

At noon Dan left the courthouse and walked slowly, pensively, to his car, emotionally spent and vaguely troubled. Sprague's allusion to the military toward the end of his statement intrigued him. Apparently they had both reached the same conclusions independently and ought to sit down and discuss them. But that thought was peripheral to his troubled mind. The question was, Did Sprague really have to be stopped and did

Dan have to take the lead in stopping him? At times the lawyer's face and manner had been almost those of a wrathful Old Testament God. Was that what made Dan want to challenge him? He seemed to have a penchant for defying and trying to outdo strong authoritarian figures. A psychiatrist-friend had once tried to explain this by speculating that Dan was still locked in adolescent rebellion because of conflicts left unresolved by the premature deaths of his father and older brother. But Dan rejected that reasoning regarding Sprague. The man was simply the greatest trial lawyer he had ever seen—explanation enough for his string of courtroom successes, but not for the mystifying paradoxes in his personal life. It was the need to solve this mystery that drove Dan. Just as he could never give up on an obscure medical case until he'd made the diagnosis, he couldn't give up on Sprague, especially now when some clues to the man were beginning to emerge.

"That was some oration your senior partner gave in court today," said Dan shortly after arriving at Angela's apartment that evening. "I'm damned glad I'm not Carl Gormann—or what's left of him."

"It's far from over," Angela cautioned. "Gormann's side has plenty of fight—and God knows what else— left in them. Sidney Hammond's as egotistical as he is rich. He doesn't take cases unless he thinks he can win. But let's talk about something else, if you don't mind. How's your patient, Mr. Hedberg, doing?"

"Much better. He's awake, off the respirator, and raising hell with the nurses. Even Peter Trombley's impressed, at least to the extent of claiming he considered the diagnosis of hypothyroidism all along. Especially— and get this!—since Hedberg had been on thyroid pills in the past. Of course Trombley didn't bother to tell anybody that, nor mention it in his admitting note. Now, if someone wanted to sue *him* for malpractice, or even for impersonating a doctor, I wouldn't raise much of a fuss."

"I don't want to sue *anybody* right now," Angela

said wearily. "So finish your drink and let's go out for dinner. Or better yet, let's eat here. I'll order up a pizza—okay?"

"Sounds very domestic," Dan said.

"Well, that's the way I feel. Any objections?"

"None . . . well, one. No anchovies."

The pizza arrived and they consumed it, along with two bottles of red wine. Afterward, Angela nestled contentedly on the couch in Dan's arms. "What brought you to the courthouse today?" she asked almost absently.

"I was having breakfast nearby with another of our mutual friends, Jimmy Dallesio, and decided to tag along."

"That's all?"

"Well, I'd never seen Charles Sprague in action and I wondered if he was as good as you are."

"I learned almost everything I know about trial tactics from Charles. He's a marvelous teacher . . . a marvelous man, despite what you doctors think of him."

"I've nothing personal against him. What's that genteel British saying? 'Ideas contend; gentlemen do not.' But there must be ways of dealing with bad doctors so that the good ones aren't made to suffer too."

"Maybe, but so far your profession hasn't come up with any. Take the way you talked about Peter Trombley earlier. Here you are, head of a major hospital, and yet you can't get one of your doctors to adhere to the most basic principles of good medical practice. If it weren't for a gutsy resident like Jim Hermanson calling you in last night, that man would've died, wouldn't he?"

"Probably," Dan admitted.

"And yet in almost the same breath you're ready to condemn Charles Sprague's method of dealing with the Carl Gormanns of your profession. Can't you see the inconsistency in that?"

Dan pondered the point but did not respond to it

directly. Instead he asked, "Is it true Sprague never settles any of his malpractice cases out of court?"

Angela disentangled herself and sat up. "Why do you ask that?"

"Because you put me on the spot with your question, and I need that information to answer."

"All right," she said reluctantly, "it's true Charles rarely settles out of court. There's a reason, but it's *his* reason and I don't feel I can divulge it. Now, tell me—"

"Well, to quote Camus, 'I am against anybody who believes in anything absolutely.' "

"I see. I didn't realize doctors were so well read."

"Bachelor doctors, mostly."

"Well, I haven't read enough Camus to argue his meaning, but if you're implying Charles is a fanatic—"

"I'm not," Dan said hastily.

"Then what *are* you implying?"

"That we're treading on dangerous ground."

"All right," Angela agreed with outward calm. "I'll change the records, you change the subject."

When she returned to him on the couch, Dan noticed a subtle transformation in her eyes, a guarded look that had not been there before but that persisted even after their ardent lovemaking.

Later, lying quietly in bed, Dan invited her to drive up to the Berkshire Hills that weekend to meet his Uncle Woody and was a little put out when Angela told him she had commitments for the weekend she couldn't break, but not what they were.

At six A.M. Dan woke and tried to slip out of bed without disturbing Angela's sleep. But she sat up abruptly and seized him, and in the eerie dawn light their lovemaking transcended anything he had ever experienced before. It was a fierce, clawing, thrusting act of passion whose impetus totally mystified Dan and left him vaguely apprehensive.

What he never could have imagined was that Angela, her fertile period for the month over, intended this to be their last time in bed together.

# 18

The next morning Nicholas Sloan telephoned Dan at his office to ask his confidential opinion of Ned Josephson. Should he retain Josephson to defend him in the suit brought by Hale's widow or should he engage the services of an outside malpractice specialist?

Dan gave him a frank and favorable appraisal of Josephson and went on to describe to Sloan some of the activities of the group Josephson and Craig Andrews had collected to combat Charles Sprague's threat to the medical community.

"But I thought you refused to go along with them?"

"I did, since their main function was to try to save Carl Gormann's ass. But I changed my mind. In fact, you changed it for me."

"Me?" said Sloan. "How?"

"When Sprague sued you, I decided he had to be stopped. Hell, Nick, if the way you treated Jonathan Hale is grounds for malpractice, so's everything I do."

"I appreciate your support, Dan. I really do. But don't get involved in anything potentially messy on my account."

"Oh, I don't think it'll come to that. So far all the group's done is raise an emergency fund to lobby legislators and encourage doctors to countersue. On my suggestion they're also trying to learn all they can about Charles Sprague. That guy's led a pretty strange life, you know. Even spent several years studying biophysics at the Max Planck Institute. With all the moving around and career-switching he's done, I've a hunch he's got a few skeletons tucked away in closets here and there, and I'd sure like to uncover them."

"To blackmail him?" said Sloan incredulously.

"No, to understand him! I'll only resort to blackmail if he won't drop his suit against you."

Sloan laughed. "You *are* a friend. Look, I'm leaving town for the weekend. Want to get off by myself and do some serious thinking. Especially about the job offer in Miami. But I'll be back late Sunday. So how about a handball match and dinner Monday night? I'll pay."

"You'll have to! Losers do," Dan reminded him. "But you're on. See you Monday, seven P.M."

At Anthony's Pier Four that evening, Dan joined Ned Josephson's group in a private dining room. In addition to Ned and Craig Andrews, Henry Deckert, administrator of the state society's mutual malpractice fund, and John Wilson, president of the county society, were there. The sixth member, Dr. William Schramm, a prominent neurosurgeon, did not arrive until after dinner. Having come directly from ten straight hours of surgery, he looked haggard and incensed. "Put Charles Sprague and a sharp scalpel in the same room with me and I could easily slit his throat!" he snarled, taking the seat beside Dan.

"Sounds like you could use a drink, Bill," Dan said sympathetically.

"I could use several!" Schramm declared. "But one will have to do." He made a wry face. "I'm still on call. In fact, I'm on call the whole damned weekend. Thanks to Charles R. Sprague!"

"Sprague?" Dan's mind flashed back to the attack the lawyer had suffered in the courtroom yesterday. "Don't tell me he's a patient of yours?"

"Mine? God forbid!" Schramm exclaimed in mock horror. "As a good Catholic I'm opposed to euthanasia, but I'd petition the Pope to make an exception in his case. No, it's not Sprague personally, but what he's done to the practice of neurosurgery in this town, that's got me working my ass off. Know how many neurosurgeons he's sued in the last eight years? Sixteen! Three here in town. And won every damned suit that went to trial. Sure, that back-surgeon butcher in California deserved to be nailed. Psychopath that he was, he crippled more patients than a polio epidemic! And there *is* too much disk surgery done in this state—or was. But Jesus Christ Almighty, Sprague's driven half the neurosurgeons out of town and got the other half scared to do more than burr holes."

"That bad, huh?" remarked Dan.

"Bad! I'll tell you how bad. We used to have an association. Twenty-eight of us neurosurgeons got together and worked out a schedule so that four took night call once a week—one for each section of town. Well, that worked fine when we had our full group. Now only half of us are left and we keep dwindling all the time. Worse yet, we're doing lousy work. Shit! We've gotten cautious as bankers. But what can we do? With this malpractice threat hanging over us, walking into an emergency room at night is about as safe for a neurosurgeon as walking through the combat zone is for a stacked blond."

The waitress brought Schramm's drink, and as he gulped it down, John Wilson, a urologist, said, "The situation's not quite that bad in urology, but bad enough. So what do we do?"

"Raise hell, that's what!" Schramm growled. "Get our side of the story in the papers and on the air. Make clear to the public that we're hurting now but *they're* going to hurt even worse later on. Sure, Sprague and his malpractice crusade has put the fear of God into a lot of crummy doctors. But no matter how many lives that's saving by making them shape up, it's going to cost even more in the long run by preventing doctors, particularly surgeons, from undertaking risky procedures when, in their judgment, it's the only way to keep the patient alive! Hell, we can't send all our high-risk patients to Canada or the Mayo Clinic! We've got to keep doing some surgery just to earn the ten or twenty thousand dollars we're shelling out for malpractice insurance premiums!"

"Well, as you know, Bill," Dan said, "at my hospital we've switched to full-time staff, and we pay their malpractice coverage. You're welcome to join us."

"Thanks, Dan," Schramm said with a trace of sarcasm. "I could also go back in the army and be a dashing major again. But I'm not ready to go on salary yet. Besides, I've got a little fight still left in me." He scanned the group. "So thanks for letting me bitch, and let's get down to business."

Business consisted primarily of an analysis, presented by Henry Deckert, of the distribution and type of malpractice cases pending in the Massachusetts courts. The list was long and discouraging. Although Sprague's firm represented less than a tenth of them, the rate at which doctors were being sued had tripled since he began to operate in the state.

The meeting broke up around ten. Out in the parking lot Schramm said to Dan, "Shit! What a day! I operated on a sweet old lady, a prize-winning horticulturist, for what I was almost sure was a benign tumor sitting on top of her motor strip. The scan suggested a meningioma, and the arteriogram was textbook-typical for one. So I crack open her skull and get ready to shell it out; only it's soft as mush and malignant as hell." He sighed deeply. "At least you internists win more than you lose."

Dan nodded sympathetically.

"Look, Dan," Schramm continued earnestly, "I know I'm a loudmouth. I've made a few derogatory cracks to the press about lawyers that I probably shouldn't have.

But I get so damned discouraged at times. You would, too, if all you dealt with was brain tumors and gorks. And if that weren't bad enough, along comes an asshole like Sprague who tells me I'd better be infallible or else! So I think your plan to dig into his background is a good one. The guy has *got* to be vulnerable somewhere! So keep it up and let me know what you find. I could sure use a little light at the end of this tunnel."

# 19

On his drive across the state to Williamstown the next morning, Dan thought longingly of Angela. He wished he had spent the night with her, wished even more that she had been free to spend this weekend with him.

Williamstown, Massachusetts, that steepled college town deep in the Berkshire Hills, would always be home. Dan had been born and raised there. His Uncle Woody still lived in the old three-story Cape Cod house at the edge of the Williams College campus that Dan's maternal grandfather had built and that his father, an electrical engineer, had modernized. It was a spacious, comfortable old place.

Woodrow McKinley Brock, a middleweight boxing champion in college, a B-17 bomber pilot in the war, now a professor of political science who wrote popular biographies of presidents and remained to this day a redoubtable lover and leaver of women, had been Dan's idol as a youth—an idol with feet of steel. His bachelor uncle baffled him in many ways but had never once disillusioned him.

Woody was on the front stoop when Dan drove up.

"Well," he said, after a hearty hug, "what brings you to the sticks?"

"A mystery," Dan replied.

"Then stop right there," Woody ordered. "I never discuss mysteries cold sober. Make yourself comfortable inside while I fix us a drink."

When his uncle joined Dan in the den, he asked, "Now what's this mystery?"

"Name of Charles Sprague."

"Ah, Charlie Sprague," Woody said. "Been meaning to look him up next time I'm in Boston. I never dreamed he'd end up being the scourge of the medical profession."

"How well did you know him during the war?"

"As well as I wanted to—or he wanted to know me. You know from Korea what I mean, though it's worse for fly-boys than for infantry."

"How so?"

"Charlie flew a P-38 interceptor, which wasn't much of a match for the souped-up Messerschmitts the Germans were sending against us. So I never knew from one day to the next if he'd still be around. But being the only lawyer in the outfit made him conspicuous. Guys would bring their legal problems to him."

"Any idea why he passed up the JAGC for wings?"

"Nothing fancy. No hero complex or death wish, believe me. He just loved to fly!"

"What else can you tell me about him?"

"Hmm." Pensively Woody rubbed his jaw. "Let me hunt up a photo of our old outfit."

He returned a few minutes later and showed Dan a framed photograph of the Peterborough-based wing. "Lieutenant Charles Sprague," he said, pointing at the third figure from the right in the front row.

Dan took the photograph from Woody and studied it intently. Although it was a depiction of Sprague as a young man and too tiny to show details, Dan had the curious feeling that he had seen the same face, or one closely resembling it, before. Yet how could that be?

"You wouldn't have a magnifying glass handy, would you?" he asked.

"Sure," said Woody. "What respectable bibliophile and biographer wouldn't? Reach behind you. It's in the top drawer of my desk."

Under magnification the face looked even more tantalizingly familiar, but Dan still could not place it.

Observing his odd expression, Woody asked about it.

Dan turned to him with a perplexed look. "I've seen this same face somewhere before, but for the life of me can't figure where."

"Charles Lindbergh," Woody volunteered.

"What?"

"Sprague looked a little like Lindbergh in those days. In fact, some of the guys even nicknamed him Lindy, so maybe that's it."

"Maybe," granted Dan, though far from convinced. He finished his drink and handed Woody a typescript of Jimmy Dallesio's biographical sketch of Sprague. "Tell me what you make of this."

Woody put on his bifocals and read it. When he finished he shook his head and said, "Wow! No wonder you're so mystified. I never realized Charlie was such a dilettante."

"In some areas, maybe. But he's no dilettante when it comes to malpractice law. He's the reigning master. The question is, Why?"

Woody said, "Beats me! Nothing I remember about him from the war years sheds any light on that."

"Know why he switched to the JAGC after the war instead of getting discharged?"

"Yes!" Woody declared emphatically. "He hated Germans. Nazi Germans. We bumped into each other in London one night shortly after V-E Day and he made that clear. If it'd been up to him, he'd have dropped the first atomic bomb on the Krauts, not Hiroshima, even though they'd already surrendered." Woody paused thoughtfully. "Which makes it damned hard to understand why he'd go back to Germany to live. The Max Planck Institute's outstanding, but even so . . ."

"Or why he'd switch from its international law to its biophysics division."

"Well, I have a tentative explanation for that. Wouldn't matter if you were King Solomon and drew up the greatest code of international law ever. There'd still be no way you could enforce it except with guns—making it a pretty frustrating field for a man like Charlie Sprague to work in. Its biophysics division, however, is reputedly the world's best."

"So I understand. What's driving me nuts, though, is what came first. Did Sprague switch to human biophysics 'cause he'd already decided to specialize in malpractice? Or did he decide that after switching?"

Woody gestured futilely. "Your guess is as good as mine. Maybe I can find out, though, by looking him up and asking him."

"That'd sure be helpful."

"Anything more I can do?"

"Tell me whatever you can about Sprague as a person. Anything at all."

"Well, it's over thirty years ago, but I do retain certain impressions. He was a two-fisted drinker and brawler but not much of a womanizer. At least he turned me down the few times I tried to get him to double-date. I can't recall for sure if Charlie was married at the time, but I tend to think he was."

"There's no mention of a wife in any of his news clips."

"Well, it'd be easy enough to find out," Woody said. "Just have somebody dig out his air force 201 file."

"You're a retired bird colonel," Dan reminded him. "Have one of your high-level Pentagon buddies do it."

"Those records are buried in St. Louis, not Washington."

"Then have one of your high-level Pentagon buddies get one of his high-level St. Louis buddies to do it."

"That's illegal," Woody protested.

"It's also important."

"It's *important* that you know whether Charlie Sprague's ever been married? Why?"

"Right now it's just a hunch. But I'm a hunch player. Learned that from you. And if I'm right, it could be crucial."

"All right." Woody gestured accommodatingly. "I'll do what I can."

# 20

Monday morning Dan received a phone call from Ned Josephson informing him that the Gormann trial had been postponed for two days because of the unavailability of the judge. Ned then asked what he had learned about Sprague.

"Bits and pieces," Dan replied. "Nothing substantial." But he promised Ned he'd stick with the search.

That evening he met Nicholas Sloan at the Y for their handball match. "How was your weekend?" Dan asked as they changed into gym togs.

"So-so," Sloan said. "I drove up the coast to Lewiston and holed up there."

"The lawsuit worrying you?"

"It brings a lot of things into focus, I guess."

"Well, don't take your frustration out on me. I intend to beat you this time."

Their first game was almost a replay of the last one they had played. Dan pulled ahead, but Sloan caught up with a series of spectacular wall shots and won by two points. After that he seemed to tire, and although pushed to the limit of his skill and endurance, Dan took the next two games and the match.

They went to Vittorio's again for dinner afterward. Though gracious in defeat, Sloan seemed preoccupied, and their table conversation was broken by long silences. Dan, still suspecting the impending malpractice suit was weighing heavily on his mind, tried to draw Sloan out on the subject, but he minimized his concern over it.

"Even though I'm one of the unlucky ones being sued," he told Dan, "I still can't help feeling that the malpractice crisis is just a big smoke screen covering the real problems facing medicine today."

What troubled him far more, Sloan confided, was the seemingly endless array of problems he had to cope with at the hospital: a house staff becoming ever more concerned with disease and laboratory tests than with their patients as human beings; the cost-be-damned-the-other-hospitals-have-it mentality of Palmer Memorial's administrative staff; worst of all, the behavior of his fellow doctors, who, like small animals before an impending storm, sensed that the era of free-enterprise medicine and governmental largess was ending and so scurried about frantically feathering their nests.

Though somewhat surprised by the vehemence behind Sloan's assessment, Dan gloomily agreed with it. He, too, feared he was witnessing something akin to the last days of the Roman Empire insofar as American medicine was concerned and said so.

"Then what the hell's wrong with our leaders!" Sloan retorted. "If they know the system's on its last legs, why not try to save it, or at least prop it up, instead of shoving it over the brink? What's happened to them—to all of us?"

"Change!" Dan declared with conviction. "Human beings have only a limited capacity to adapt to change, and we've been hit by too much, too soon; the Vietnam war, the disintegration of the family, the decay of our cities, Watergate! But those are just the social upheavals. The biggest, fastest changes of all have come in medicine. Medical knowledge is doubling every three years now, and most doctors can't absorb even a small fraction of it. So, human nature being what it is, they revert. Instead of yearning for more disease-fighting facts, for medical mastery, doctors yearn for money! Look at the flurry of excitement that followed the invention of the artificial kidney. For the first time, we could offer our renal-failure patients a fighting chance. So what happened? Kidney patients, no matter how mild their disease, were placed on dialysis indiscriminately, and the government's going broke paying for it. But ever since I put the nephrologists at my hospital on fixed salaries, they've become a lot more choosy about whom they dialyze. So it's not totally hopeless, Nick."

"No, I suppose not. But yours is only one of eighty hospitals in the Boston area. The move to paid staff hasn't made much headway at Palmer Memorial and isn't likely to . . . which is one of the reasons I plan to resign my job there soon and take the one in Miami."

Dan looked surprised. "Sure the situation's any better down there?"

"No, but I don't have to be."

Dan gave him a questioning look.

"One of the advantages of bachelorhood," Sloan said cryptically.

"Meaning what?"

"Meaning if I don't like it. I can always move on."

Dan studied him for a moment. "Look, Nick, forgive me if I seem out of line, but it sounds to me like you're running from something. It's none of my business, I know, but if you want to talk about it, I'm willing to listen."

"That's decent of you, Dan. But the truth is, I don't. Not yet, anyway. I *will* take your advice on one thing, though. I'm making a return visit to Miami at the end of the week, and I intend to take a good, hard look at where they're at before committing myself to the hospital there."

"Well, that's encouraging," Dan said. "After all, good handball players aren't easy to find."

For two days Dan tried repeatedly but unsuccessfully to phone Angela. Nor did she make any attempt to contact him. Hurt and puzzled, he went to the Suffolk County Courthouse Wednesday afternoon and sat through the last hour of the Gormann trial session, hoping to find out why. With mounting impatience, he stood on the fringe of the mob of reporters surrounding her and Sprague outside the courtroom and tried to catch her eye. Failing that, he followed the handful who tagged along with them on their way out of the building, and finally got a moment alone with her.

"Hello," he began and got a cordial nod in return. "Mind if I walk you to your car?"

Angela shrugged.

"Have a nice weekend?" he asked.

"Not particularly," she replied. "Did you?"

"So-so. Have you gotten my phone messages?"

"Yes. Six of them, I believe."

"Then why haven't you answered any?"

"That should be obvious, Dr. Lassiter. I don't wish to talk to you. Or see you again."

The finality of her words stunned Dan. "For God's sake, why?"

Angela shifted her feet as if tempted to walk away. Then she said accusingly, "What harm has Charles Sprague ever done you?"

"Me personally? None. That's not the point."

"No," she sighed, "I suppose you wouldn't think so. Politicians, even doctor-politicians, never see the principles involved in any issue, only the points—for or against them. Well, *the point,* as far as I'm concerned, is this: Charles Sprague is a highly respected and respectable attorney. He is also my law partner and dear friend. Whatever he does, he does openly and within the law. So if you want to fight him, even destroy him, go right ahead. But do it openly—in the newspapers, the courtroom, the Bar Association's Ethics Committee

—not through some secret, dirt-digging cabal. Oh, I know all about that! It's beneath you, Dan. I don't sleep around; you must know that. And I felt some very strong emotions for you. But as long as you persist in such detestable tactics, I never want to see you again. Good-bye!"

Dan was struck dumb. How could Angela possibly have learned about Josephson's group? Who could have told her? Jimmy had warned him this might happen, but he was above suspicion. Nobody could be as close-mouthed about a confidence as Jimmy. Wordless and wounded, knowing he would miss the companionship as much as the sex they had shared, he watched Angela get into her Mercedes and start the engine. Finally regaining his voice, he cried out for her to wait, but she drove off.

Deeply distraught over his breakup with Angela, lonelier than ever in his empty house, Dan left gladly for Los Angeles and the annual session of the American Association of Medical Colleges on Friday.

On his last day in Los Angeles Dan went out to dinner with an old friend, Dr. Edward Moorhead, a witty, competent, chain-smoking cancer specialist. Ed began dinner by toasting Dan's appointment as general director of Boston's Commonwealth General and asked about the malpractice crisis there. Dan described it honestly, seeking comparisons with the one suffered a few years before in California, and told Ed he was particularly upset because a fine physician and close friend named Nicholas Sloan was being sued, too.

"Nick Sloan!" exclaimed Ed. "I know him. And you're right, he's a hell of a doctor." Ed went on to explain that he'd known Nick since he was senior medical resident at UCLA Medical Center and Ed was taking a cancer-chemotherapy fellowship there. Subsequently they had both settled in Los Angeles, Sloan as director of medical education at Harbor General Hospital, and Ed in private practice.

"A funny guy," Ed reflected. "Great to spend an

evening with away from the hospital, but basically a loner. Real quiet, too, until one of the profs asked him a question and it became apparent he ate, drank, and breathed medicine. Would've been the top internist in Los Angeles if he'd remained."

After Dan confided that Sloan was building a similar reputation in Boston but did not plan to stay there either, the two fell into a discussion of their friend's peripatetic career. Dan was startled when Ed mentioned that Sloan had been sued for malpractice once before, quite possibly by Sprague's firm.

"Are you sure?" he asked sharply.

"Reasonably sure," Ed affirmed. "The story I got was that Sloan was so disgusted when the hospital attorney insisted they settle the case out of court that he just up and resigned. Next I heard he landed a job in Denver, and now you say he's at Palmer Memorial in Boston."

"That's not so unusual," Dan pointed out. "The director of medical education and the hospital administrator are as naturally enemies as the mongoose and the snake, so there's always been a rapid turnover in DME jobs. The average length of stay is around two years."

"Even so," Ed mused, "what does strike me as unusual is for a doctor like Sloan to be sued for malpractice by the *same* lawyer twice at opposite ends of the country. Like lightning striking the same place twice."

"Damned unusual," muttered Dan, deeply troubled by the coincidence, if coincidence it was.

# 21

Before leaving Los Angeles, Dan put through a phone
call to Henry Deckert requesting the loan of certain
documents he had accumulated, and Henry promised
to have them waiting for him on his arrival at Logan
Airport. Despite several drinks to temper his restless-
ness, Dan kept pondering three questions on the long
flight home: Why would Nick Sloan conceal the fact
that he had been sued for malpractice before, particularly if Sprague's law firm had been the one bringing
suit against him? How had Angela learned of Josephson's group and from whom? Most puzzling of all, why
—as Woody had recently informed him—was the military record on Lieutenant Colonel Charles R. Sprague
missing from air force files, voiding any future claims
he might ever make for veterans' benefits, along with
any written proof for five years of his life? Using the
same inductive reasoning that had served him so well
in making medical diagnoses, Dan could not help con-
cluding that they were all pieces of the same puzzle,
but he needed more information to fit them together.
Broodingly aware that he had passed the point where

he could quell his compelling curiosity, he was determined to do just that, even though more than a little fearful of what he might find. It was, he realized morosely, much like tracking down a cancer in a patient long suspected of harboring one, only to have the satisfaction of discovery give way to despair once the cancer's incurability became known.

Henry Deckert was at the airport with a complete list of all the malpractice actions Sprague's firm had initiated, along with complete transcripts of several of them in a large carton. Dan placated Deckert's curiosity as to why he wanted them by pledging to reveal all when the time came, and went straight home, where he sat up reading all night long. With each added fact disclosed by the documents, a clearer picture emerged. The first was that Dr. Nicholas Sloan had, indeed, been sued for malpractice in Los Angeles by Neil Rosensweig, then as now a partner in Sprague's law firm. The second, as Ned Josephson and other defense lawyers had learned to their sorrow, was that Sprague did have an uncanny talent for pulling legal rabbits, and with them favorable verdicts, out of his hat with crucial, last-minute courtroom disclosures. Dan could understand this happening occasionally, as in the Dubic trial; what was much harder to explain was how Sprague managed it so consistently.

After reading a few trial transcripts and several more closing arguments, Dan reluctantly concluded that Gordon Donnelly's theory was correct: Sprague went after bad doctors only—Nicholas Sloan being the sole exception. Or was he?

Toward dawn, while shaving and showering, Dan was suddenly struck by an unnerving possibility. Drying himself hastily, he rushed back to his den to recheck the summary list of Sprague's malpractice cases that Deckert had compiled. Although the law firm of Sprague, Adams, Rosensweig and Cane had been involved in malpractice actions in widely scattered areas, those Sprague had handled himself clustered in four geographical areas—Los Angeles, Denver, Detroit, Boston—the very same cities, except for Detroit, where Dr. Nicholas Sloan had worked as a hospital-based educator.

At eight A.M. Dan phoned the County Medical Society's office and asked Craig Andrews's secretary to dig out Sloan's curriculum vitae and read it to him. His hunch paid off: Nicholas Sloan had been full-time chief of medicine at a Detroit hospital for two years before coming to Boston. Dan next phoned Jimmy Dallesio, promising him breakfast and an intellectual exercise if he drove out to his place right away.

Jimmy agreed and over a plate of bacon and eggs listened raptly while Dan described his findings.

*"Marrone!"* Jimmy exclaimed at the end. "That's quite a plot you've woven! Pure Agatha Christie. But what the hell's it all mean?"

Soberly Dan replied, "I don't know, and I'm not so sure I want to know. Nick Sloan is one of the most dedicated doctors I've ever met. You ought to see some of the nearly miraculous cures he's pulled off with old people. Charles Sprague, whatever his motivation, is not only making a fortune off the medical profession but wreaking havoc with the way medicine's practiced. Hard as hell to believe the two of them would team up, but possible, even explainable."

"How?"

"I'm sick and tired of bad doctors, too," Dan said grimly, "and how they victimize their patients. Gordon Donnelly thinks some of them should be tried for manslaughter, not malpractice, and I tend to agree. Look at Dubic and Gormann. Or an egomaniac at Commonwealth General named Trombley who drives me up the wall with his supposed infallibility. Maybe Sloan just couldn't stomach them anymore. Maybe he tried to work within the rules, the disciplinary committees, to get rid of them and found out how futile that was. So along comes Sprague and suggests a vigilante approach, and Sloan agrees, providing he, not Sprague, picks the doctors they go after. I know that sounds pretty far-fetched, but it makes a crazy kind of sense, particularly if you postulate that Charles Sprague isn't the medical nemesis he's made out to be—Nick Sloan is!"

"Then why get Sprague to sue him—twice?"

"To throw suspicion off him as Sprague's source of cases. Just like you, a lot of doctors suspected Sprague had some inside source, and sooner or later, as he and Sloan moved their base of operations around, somebody'd put two and two together. Ed Moorhead almost did. There might also be another reason . . ."

"What?"

"Well, with the medical community here in such an uproar over Sprague and lawyers like him, all the big-name doctors, particularly the ones being sued, are organizing to strike back. What better way to know their plans than for Sloan to join them?"

"Makes sense," Jimmy agreed.

Too much sense, thought Dan, suddenly and sickeningly realizing who probably told Angela about Ned Josephson's group.

Seeing the anguished look on his face, Jimmy asked about it. But Dan answered evasively and fell silent as an even more monstrous suspicion took root in his mind.

"So what do you plan to do about it?" Jimmy prompted.

"Do?" Dan repeated distractedly. "First of all, swear you to secrecy for the time being."

Jimmy nodded. "Then what?"

"Then have a little talk with Dr. Nicholas Sloan. Give him a chance to confirm or deny what I suspect, and if he confirms it, make him stop. But before I do that, there're a few more mysteries I'd like to clear up with your help."

"Okay. How?"

"I want to know for sure if Sprague was ever married. Never mind why for now. Just get on the phone to newspaper pals of yours in Pasadena, New Haven, and Ann Arbor and find out if a marriage license was issued to him in any of those places. If Sprague did marry before World War Two, it was probably in one of those towns. In the meanwhile, I'm going to try to track down another bit of information through a friend of mine on the State Board of Pharmacy. I know Sprague takes nitroglycerin. What I don't know, and intend to find out, is the doctor who's prescribing it."

"Sloan?" ventured Jimmy, and when Dan nodded, he whistled admiringly. "I'm supposed to be the investigative sleuth, not you. Only now you've got a real-life mystery, not just a medical one, on your hands, so go at it easy."

"What do you mean?"

"I've heard you accuse Sprague of being a fanatic. But if you're right, it's Sloan, not Sprague, who's the fanatic."

"So?"

"So be careful."

"Oh, come on!" Dan growled. "I hope you're not trying to warn me I might be in some danger. The guy's a doctor, for Chrissake!"

"I'm not worried about you being in any physical danger at all. Just the opposite."

"Then what?" asked Dan exasperatedly.

"Look, Dan, how long have I known you—fifteen, sixteen years? How many nights' sleep have you lost in that time trying to undo the damage some quack doctor did to a patient? A lot, right? I've heard you complain about it enough. So you and Sloan might not be so far apart in your feelings, after all. In which case you're going to have one hell of a time bringing yourself to blow the whistle on him."

"I might," Dan agreed. "All depends on why he's doing it."

"What if he's doing it for the very reason he should be doing it? To protect the public against bad doctors. Then what're you going to do?"

# 22

Jimmy succeeded in discovering that Charles Sprague had married a Margaret Sanborn in New Haven, Connecticut, in 1936. But where or from whom Sprague got his nitroglycerin tablets, Dan was unable to learn. Nor, working quietly and alone, could he uncover any solid proof that Dr. Nicholas Sloan and Sprague were in collusion—leaving Dan in a quandary. Should he confront Sloan with his suspicions or not? A comic interlude decided the issue for him.

Edgar Emmonds, falling off the wagon and off a twenty-foot dry dock, was taken by police ambulance to Commonwealth General. Regaining consciousness in the emergency room, Emmonds was horrified to find himself in the very hospital he was suing and fuzzily concluded they would never let him leave it alive. The ER intern tried to calm him with an ounce of paraldehyde. But Emmonds, growing more and more agitated by the prospect of his imminent demise, kept bellowing, "Get me out of here or I'm a goner! Lassiter, the grand Pooh-Bah, is going to kill me!" In desperation, the intern gave him a shot of Thorazine, which promptly lowered Emmonds's blood pressure but not his voice. Frantically, the intern consulted Dr. Hirsh, the willowy, attractive medical resident, who telephoned Dan even though it was two in the morning. Dan was little concerned about Emmonds's fractured wrist and ribs, but his paranoiac ravings and the ruckus he was causing annoyed him.

"Do I *have* to admit him?" asked the medical resident in a voice that clearly conveyed the hope that she did not.

"You do," Dan reluctantly replied, well aware of the danger of occult spinal cord damage and resultant paraplegia developing overnight in such patients.

"Where? Orthopedics or psychiatry?"

Sighing, Dan told her he would come in and evaluate the patient himself before deciding where to send him.

On the drive to the hospital Dan was struck by an intriguing thought: Edgar Emmonds might just possibly turn out to be something more than a nuisance.

In the emergency room, Dr. Hirsh took him to the cubicle where Emmonds had been temporarily sequestered and restrained.

"Mr. Emmonds!" she shouted to rouse him from torpor. "Mr. Emmonds, this is Dr. Lassiter."

"Lassiter!" gasped Emmonds, eyes bulging in horror. "You're Lassiter?"

"Okay, just take it easy," Dan urged.

"Please—please don't hurt me, Doctor," Emmonds pleaded, cowering at the far side of the bed.

"Look" Dan said sternly, "just shut up and lie still, so I can examine you."

"Doc, I'm sorry. I didn't want to sue you. Honest, I didn't! But I needed the money and that shyster lawyer told me I had to."

"What shyster lawyer?" asked Dan.

"You know, that Dorchester dandy, Cogswell. He talked me into it."

Suddenly Dan remembered something Jason Whitlow had told him and paused thoughtfully. "Yeah? Well, if Cogswell made you do it, how come you went to Charles Sprague first and told *him* how we mistreated you?"

Emmonds looked startled. "Sprague!" He rubbed his brow as if to clear his bleary mind. "Who told you that?"

"There's a war on, don't you know? We've got spies who tell us everything. So let's have the truth!"

"Okay, okay," Emmonds whined. "I did go to see Sprague. He listened to me, but he didn't act the least bit interested until I mentioned that you were my doctor."

"Your doctor!" Dan exploded, leaning menacingly over him. "Dammit, Emmonds, I am *not your doctor*. I never have been. Will you get that *straight!*"

"Uh—yessir," Emmonds answered anxiously.

"I'm just the poor slob you're *suing!*"

"Yeah, well, I guess you're right. But the truth is, I'd like you for my doctor. If you're willing to let bygones be bygones, I'll drop the suit and everything!"

Ignoring Emmonds's proposal, Dan asked, "So then what happened between you and Sprague?"

"He tells me to wait in his outer office while he makes a phone call."

"To whom?"

"Beats me! I seen him write your name down, so I figure he was checking up on you."

"You *sure* you don't know whom he called?"

"Naw, I really don't. Didn't hear a thing."

"Okay," Dan said impatiently. "What next?"

"Well, after a few minutes he calls me back in to tell me he can't take my case. That got my Irish up, and we exchanged a few words. Then something real funny happens. Sprague grabs his head like it's splitting, gags a few times, and starts to head for his bathroom, but staggers all over the place like he's really tied one on. I was scared he was having a stroke or something and helped him back to his desk. He grabs some pills from the drawer, swallows them down, and after a couple of minutes seems okay. Then he thanks me for my help and tells me to go see Cogswell. He'll put in a good word on my behalf. That's it, I swear! That's all that happened."

"You sure?" Dan persisted. "You absolutely sure he didn't say or do anything else?"

"Like what?"

"Like call his doctor?"

"Oh, yeah!" recalled Emmonds. "Now that you mention it, I think he did."

Dan stared at him intensely. *"What doctor?"*

"He never said. As I was leaving the office, though, I heard him tell his secretary to get Palmer Memorial Hospital on the phone. Honest, Doc, that's all I can tell you. Now, you going to be my doctor or ain't you?"

Abstractedly, Dan nodded.

"Well, then!" Emmonds said, brightening. "In that case, how 'bout another shot of paraldehyde?"

The next morning Dan phoned Dr. Nicholas Sloan's office to arrange a meeting with him, only to learn from his secretary that Sloan was still in Miami and would not be returning until the beginning of the following week. Though hardly looking forward to a showdown between them, Dan felt frustrated by the delay. Later that morning Ned Josephson dropped by to see him. Henry Deckert had told him about the documents Dan borrowed, and he was curious to find out what, if anything, Dan had learned from them.

"I think I'm on to something," Dan replied cautiously, "but it's still too early to be sure. Why?"

The Gormann trial was now in its second week and going badly, Josephson explained. Doubtless Dan had seen the new flurry of stories and editorials in the newspapers, avoiding mention of the trial itself but condemning the medical profession's apparent laxity in policing itself. "So if Sprague wins big," Josephson warned, "you can kiss any chance of the legislature modifying the existing malpractice statutes good-bye. The public won't let them. And the most important bills are scheduled to be voted on soon. So if you can come up with anything to counteract the bad press we're getting, we can sure use it."

In their ensuing discussion, Dan was surprised to learn that Charles Sprague had not appeared at the Gormann trial all week, leaving the courtroom work to Angela. "Any idea why?" he asked.

Josephson shook his head. "He's not on vacation, that's for sure. The guy doesn't take vacations. Maybe he's still sick, only I'm not counting on it. More likely, he's hard at work putting together a big surprise to counter our surprise."

Dan asked what that was, and Josephson revealed that Hammond had succeeded in persuading Joanne Lorris, the former Bradford Medical Center nurse who had transcribed Gormann's IV tetracycline order for Delia Harrison, to admit she'd made a mistake.

"Doesn't that make her liable for damages, too?"

"Yes. But under the captain-of-the-ship doctrine the hospital's malpractice policy covers her."

"Even so," Dan argued, "nursing errors in transcribing telephone orders or dispensing meds aren't all that uncommon. In fact, one study showed they happened one-sixth of the time. And Gormann *did* countersign the order the next day."

"True—which makes him guilty of negligence but not gross misconduct. More important, it helps get the hospital's conduct-and-review committees off the hook. Gormann is a busy doctor, seeing on the average ten to fifteen hospital patients and forty to fifty office patients a day. Also, he's always accepted Medicaid patients when a lot of other GPs wouldn't. So despite the type of assembly-line medicine he practices and the amount of questionable surgery he does, he must make a lot of sick people better."

"I see your point," Dan grudgingly admitted. "It doesn't take another Sir William Osler to cure pelvic inflammatory disease with penicillin. We can't all be purists."

"That's right. And if that nurse can convince the

jury that she, not Gormann, was initially responsible for screwing up the tetracycline order, they might just find in our favor. I'd almost bet on it if we were up against any other lawyer than Sprague. But with him in the picture, the most I can realistically hope for is to win a no-cause verdict for the hospital committees he's included in his action."

Dan nodded sympathetically.

"One thing's sure," Josephson went on. "Even if he has to drag himself out of his deathbed, Sprague's going to be in court to cross-examine that nurse. Angela Adams is good, very good, but she simply can't intimidate a witness the way Sprague can. So he'll be there, all right. I'd bet my life's savings on it!"

"When's that likely to be?"

"Middle of next week. So if you come up with anything we can use against Sprague before then, I'd sure appreciate knowing it. I'll tell you the truth, Dan; I'm scared. Not for me—I can always practice general law. But you guys don't stand a prayer of getting the legislative relief you need if Sprague wins this one!"

# 23

Long after Josephson left his office, Dan stood by the windows staring into cloudless space and brooding over the implications of the lawyer's parting admonition. He well knew how important the pending legislative changes were to the orderly practice of medicine in the state. Yet what could *he* do to halt the drift toward their defeat? Something, he felt sure, for he alone had the knowledge, and quite possibly the power, to persuade Sloan and Sprague to dissolve their misalliance, if not actual collusion. What could have possibly possessed Nick Sloan to enter into such an irresponsible arrangement with Sprague in the first place? If only Dan knew the answer to that, he might be better able to deal with him. But with Sloan out of town and Sprague unlikely to enlighten or even meet with him, he was stymied.

Picking up the telephone, Dan was about to book passage on the next flight to Miami when another approach, a potentially embarrassing but promising one, suddenly occurred to him.

That afternoon Dan made the now familiar trek to

the Suffolk County Courthouse and listened to Angela's scathing cross-examination of the chairman of Bradford's medical conduct-and-review committee. Dan had no way of knowing what testimony the elderly internist had already given, but he couldn't help admiring the way Angela had him stammering out admissions to every conceivable laxity. The younger, more self-assured chairman of their surgery committee fared no better as she cut him down to size with frequent reminders of the penalty for perjury. After the court session ended, Dan waited in his car for Angela to leave the courthouse parking lot in her Mercedes and then followed her to her apartment building.

Ten minutes later, a cake box in hand, Dan strode down the hallway to Angela's apartment and pushed the buzzer.

Opening the door, Angela appeared startled to see him. "You—?" she exclaimed. "How did you get up here? The security—"

Dan smiled sardonically. "George is a patient of mine, remember? Told him it was your birthday and I wanted to surprise you with a cake. Here," he said, handing her the cardboard box. "German chocolate. Hope you like it."

Nonplussed, Angela hesitated and then took the box, "All right, Dan," she said, her look turning stern and intimidating, "what do you want?"

"Two things. A drink, preferably a stiff one, and to talk. Not about us—that still stings, but it's no longer the main issue. I need answers to a few questions and I'm not leaving until I get them."

"I'll have you evicted."

"By George? He has a bad back. By the police? On what grounds? Breaking and entering? Attempted rape?" The edge to Dan's voice surprised even him and made Angela wince.

"I know the law!" she snapped. Then, sighing deeply and rubbing her hand over her eyes, she said, "Look, Dan, I've put in a long, tiring day and I'm not up to this. I know you're too responsible a person to just barge in here on a whim. Your pride wouldn't let you. So you must have a good reason . . ."

"I do."

"Then *please* tell me, and no more games."

Dan walked past her into the kitchen, where he poured them drinks. "Here," he said, "take a few swallows of this first. I'll get to the point soon enough, I promise."

"Okay." Angela smiled thinly. "I can certainly use it. How've you been?"

"Busy—in a strange, sleuthlike sort of way. Which is not to say I haven't missed you. I'm human."

"I'm human too."

"I know. But being female, you're evidently more changeable."

"Perhaps. But what happened between us came about more or less by accident. It certainly wasn't planned."

"How do you know? I lead a rich fantasy life."

"And I'm impulsive. So it happened and it's over. Accept it."

Dan shrugged. "If you say it's over, then it is. But I don't like to make the same mistake twice—with patients or women. Also, I've a bit of a personality quirk. I'm obsessive. Not obsessive compulsive—just obsessive. Once, in my first year of medical school, I became obsessed with my anatomy lab cadaver; had to know who he was, how he lived, and especially how he died. But that's too long a story to go into now."

Angela stared penetratingly at him. "What are you trying to say, Dan? That you're obsessed with me? I simply don't believe it."

"And you're right. You're only a part, albeit an important one, of a mystery I've been trying to solve. But before I get to that, I'd still like to know why you chose me for a lover; why so intense, and why the abrupt kiss-off? And don't tell me it had to do with my delving into the life of Charles Sprague. He's exactly what you said he was—a damned good lawyer. He didn't instigate the present malpractice crisis; somebody else did. And we *both* know who that is."

Angela drained her drink and rose to fix them both another, needing time to think. "Look," she said finally, "I have a feeling—an unnerving one—that what's been obsessing you and why I went to bed with you are all of a piece. But I'm not prepared to say more than that until I know exactly what you were hinting at a few moments ago. So suppose you tell me that first. If it's what I think it is, I promise I'll be equally honest with you, though I warn you now it's not going to be painless for either of us. Some of it's going to hurt."

Dan studied her in silence. Once before he had seen the same forlorn and melancholy look on Angela's face, but when? Suddenly it came to him: at the Dubic trial immediately after Dubic had broken down on the witness stand and victory seemed assured. "All right," he began slowly, "you know Nick Sloan, don't you?"

Angela half-laughed and in a tired voice said, "You could say that. I was once married to him."

Her answer hit Dan like a blow to the gut, leaving him stunned and momentarily speechless.

"That's right," Angela went on. "Adams is my maiden name. I was once Mrs. Nicholas Sloan and quite happy to be, for a time. Oh, for God's sake, Dan, don't look so shocked. I don't mean to sound patronizing, but you know the standard warning to children: play with fire and you're likely to get burned. Well, you're not only playing with fire right now but about to ignite a powder keg. Shall I go on?"

Dan drew a deep, calming breath and nodded.

"Nick and I were married in 1959 and divorced in 1963. I'll get to the reason why later—after you've told me what's prompted your interest in us."

"Actually, it wasn't your relationship with Nick that primarily interested me—not until you exploded that bombshell about your marriage, it wasn't. What I was really after was the facts behind his relationship with Charles Sprague. Specifically, how in the world Sprague ever got Nick to feed him the names of bad doctors to sue."

Angela frowned slightly. "You think Charles and Nick are in collusion?"

"I think more than that. I think the two are related, quite possibly father and son."

"Do you?" Angela exclaimed. "Based on what?"

"On a photo I recently saw of Charles Sprague as a young air force lieutenant. It took me awhile to figure out whom the face reminded me of, but the resemblance between the two is quite striking."

"And you deduced he and Nick might be father and son from a photo taken back in the 1940s? Without ever having seen Charles up close? Amazing! But what makes you think the two of them are in cahoots?"

Dan told her, pretending to know that Sprague's two malpractice suits against Sloan were a sham and that Nick was also Sprague's personal doctor.

Angela accepted his point-by-point deductions dispassionately. "It's really very clever of you to figure all that out, Dan," she said. "Very clever, indeed. They've been at it for almost eight years now and nobody's ever done it before. But you're wrong about one thing. Charles Sprague never tried to persuade Nick to do anything underhanded. Quite the contrary."

"Are you sure about that?"

Angela laughed harshly. "Very! How well do you know Nicholas Sloan?"

Dan shrugged. "Evidently not too well. In fact, hardly at all."

"That's right! Do you have any idea what a risk-taker he is?"

Dan thought back fleetingly to their handball matches but shook his head.

"Well, he's quite incredible, believe me. Take the Dubic trial. *He was there!* The same day you were. In fact, you were largely responsible for his presence."

"Me?" Dan cried. "How?"

"Well, Charles could barely speak above a whisper because of a bad cold, and Nick was afraid I might not be able to handle your cross-examination without his medical help. He was determined to nail Dubic and mad as hell that a doctor as reputable as you would agree to defend him. So he showed up. *In disguise.* It was all quite insane, but then, you see, so is Nick. Quite! I can tell from your face that you find that hard to believe. You admire Nick, don't you?"

"Yes," Dan said softly. "In a way."

"So do I—in a way. I only wish I'd never married him, or agreed to take part in his incredible scheme." Angela fell silent for a moment, a remote, almost tearful, look in her eyes. "It was Charles who finally convinced me. Charles is such a dear man."

"Let me freshen your drink," Dan said and took the glass from her hand.

"Oh! Thanks." Then, as an afterthought, "I hope you don't have any sick patients in the hospital."

"No, not really. Why?"

"Well," she sighed, "now that I've told you this much of the story, I suppose I've no choice but to finish it— and that'll take some time."

"I've got time."

"Then I must impose two preconditions on you. First, that you swear to keep all I'm about to reveal in the strictest confidence until tomorrow. That's an absolute must, Dan."

"All right. But why until tomorrow?"

"That's when I want you to go someplace with me to visit somebody. You've Saturday morning free, haven't you?"

"Yes."

"Good! It's not far—less than an hour's drive—but it's quite crucial that you go there with me before you decide what to do with all I'm about to divulge. Is that understood?"

Dan nodded. "It is, providing I know ahead of time where we're going and why."

"You will. You'll know everything there is to know before you leave here tonight. But that part comes later, and I'd rather start at the beginning." For a moment Angela appeared lost in thought. Then she smiled wryly and said, "Ever read any books by Thomas Berger, particularly *Killing Time,* or any Dostoevski?"

"A little Dostoevski, a long time ago. Why?"

"They both use the same theme: the logic of insanity. Ask your psychiatrist-friends about it sometime, especially those who treat a lot of schizophrenics. In most cases only the initial premise of schizophrenics is wrong; from there on, an impeccable logic governs what they do. Their actions are actually more logical and predictable than those of so-called sane people. Unlike schizophrenics, the ones we consider normal suffer not just one, but several, lapses in logical thought. Take you, for example."

"What about me?" asked Dan, intrigued.

"Well, on the surface, you're an eminently sane and sensible man. Yet you've allowed yourself to become obsessed with the lives of people who only marginally touch on your own. Oh, I'm sure you've been able to rationalize it as being for the good of the medical profession, but that's only a half-truth and you know it. You're also driven by deep-seated needs of your own. Nick, on the other hand, knows exactly why he's doing it—the faulty premise again."

"If you have serious doubts about Nick Sloan's mental stability, why do his dirty work for him? Does he have some hold over you?"

"No!" Angela answered. "Nick's never *forced* me to do anything. I got involved of my own free will. Foolishly, perhaps; out of halfhearted conviction in his cause and wholehearted concern for him. But I never thought it would be so all-consuming or go on for so long. I tried to extricate myself several times—once for almost a year. I took a cottage at Malibu; had a series of meaningless affairs . . . I tried again with you, too, only in a much more serious way, as I'll explain later. But there were always the weekends. For almost fifteen straight years I hardly ever missed one. My little insanity, I suppose. My penance for God only knows what . . . Oh, Dan," Angela suddenly wailed. "It's all so sick, so painful to talk about. Nick had Nate Clineman, the psychiatrist, to talk to. I didn't. I kept it all bottled up inside and now it's so hard . . . so hard . . ."

Dan lifted her from the chair and wrapped his arms around her, hugging her tightly until she began to calm down. Then, seating her beside him on the couch, he stroked her hand.

"Nice bedside manner you have, Doctor."

"The story," Dan reminded her.

Bleakly Angela nodded and told it clearly, calmly, and in intense bursts between long sips of Scotch. Only toward the very end did she begin to slur her words, but by then Dan, too, had become quite drunk, hoping to dull the impact of her transmitted pain.

The story of Angela's eighteen-year involvement with Nicholas Sloan was both bizarre and tragic. They first met at Stanford Law School when Angela was a first-year student and Nick was in his second year. Despite his taciturn manner and sense of rootlessness, Nick was the most brilliant and sensitive man Angela had ever dated, and after a three-month courtship they married. A year later Angela gave birth to a boy, whom they named William Charles Sloan in honor of William Sloan, the man who had adopted Nick after his real father, Charles Sprague, had deserted and divorced his mother when Nick was a year old. Angela never knew why Nick insisted on giving their son the middle name of Charles, or how he really felt about his father, since it was the one subject Nick adamantly refused to discuss with her. Little Billy, a contented and adorable baby, soon became the great joy of Nicholas Sloan's life. From the moment he got home from class in the afternoon to the boy's bedtime, the pair were inseparable. When Billy was six months old, Angela weaned him from her breast, hired a teenaged baby-sitter, and returned to law school. At the age of nine months Billy learned to walk, and a month later, during a momentary lapse on the part of the baby-sitter, fell down the cellar stairs. Nick and Angela were summoned at once. Although bleeding from a scalp laceration, Billy was conscious and smiling when they got home. Nonetheless, they rushed him to the nearest emergency room, where skull X rays showed a two-inch, linear, nondisplaced skull fracture behind his right temporal area. On the advice of the ER doctor, Billy was taken to a nearby private pediatrician rather than to the university hospital clinic where he had received his postnatal checkups.

The pediatrician's name was Darren "Duke" Bauman, a huge former USC football player, who was popular with the kiddies and prospering from the busy practice he had built up over the years. He was also getting paunchy, going through a messy divorce, depressed, drinking too much, and feeling so exhausted by late afternoon—the time he saw Billy—that he couldn't think clearly without a pick-me-up drink or amphetamine. Bauman looked at the skull X rays the ER doctor had sent along, acted reassured by the babysitter's report that Billy had not been unconscious for more than a few minutes, and gave him a cursory examination. He then sent the Sloans home with a sheet of instructions concerning the danger signs to watch for following a head injury. What Bauman neglected to do was read the series of reports that had been appearing in the leading pediatric journals for the past year warning of the newly recognized and perilous entity of "growing skull fracture." Thus he lacked the clinical knowledge to suspect it, warn the parents of its possible occurrence, or spot its development in time to prevent its disastrous sequelae.

Though no pediatrician, Dan was familiar with this condition and grimaced at its mention, grimly anticipating what Angela would tell him next.

Because Billy began sleeping more and acting less alert, the Sloans took him back to Bauman's office the following week. The pediatrician checked his eyes and reflexes and commented noncommittally on the persistent swelling behind his right temple, but neglected to get repeat skull X rays or a neurological consultation at that time. He assured the Sloans that Billy seemed fine and admonished them against being overprotective parents. Two weeks later, however, Nick happened to notice the scalp over Billy's healed laceration bulge during a crying spell. Gingerly pressing down on the area, he was aghast to find a hole in the skull big enough to admit the tip of his index finger. This time Bauman was bypassed and Billy was taken to a pediatric neurologist at the Stanford medical school. The neurologist, although outwardly calm, was sufficiently disturbed by the skull separation and its probable cause to admit Billy directly to the hospital. That same day he underwent repeat skull films, a right carotid arteriogram to visualize the cerebral blood vessels beneath the injured area, and a pneumoencephalogram, in which air is injected into the spinal canal to outline the fluid-filled cavities within the brain.

To the neurologist's dismay and the Sloans' horror, a portion of Billy's brain had herniated through the rent in the membranous dura lining the underside of his skull and had become incarcerated, infarcted, destroyed, and absorbed—forming a progressively enlarging cyst that was producing pressure on the rest of his brain. An immediate craniotomy was performed, the rip in the dura repaired, and the cyst fluid drained via a long plastic tube inserted into the infant's abdominal cavity. Afterward, Dr. Fred Sobel, the neurosurgeon who had performed the operation, was cautiously hopeful he had corrected the condition before it produced permanent brain damage. But that hope faded when the left arm and leg weakness that Billy had developed postoperatively worsened over the next two weeks and he regressed to the point where he could no longer utter words, only gurgles.

Sobel, who had taken an intense personal interest in the Sloan infant, next considered a second, more extensive shunting procedure. He obtained a second opinion from his former mentor in Los Angeles, the foremost pediatric neurosurgeon in the country. The consultant flew up to see Billy, but after a painstaking evaluation reluctantly concluded that his brain damage was irreversible and that further surgery would be futile. It fell to Sobel to relay this heartbreaking news to the Sloans, which he did with as much professional detachment as possible. But having grown quite attached to the Sloan infant himself, the look of absolute devastation on his parents' faces brought Sobel's feelings of frustration and futility to a boil. In a serious breach of professional etiquette, he muttered, "Damned dumb pediatrician! If only he knew what he was doing, none of this would've happened."

Nick, though numb with grief at what the neurosurgeon had told him, asked Sobel to repeat the remark.

"Forget it, Mr. Sloan," he advised.

"Repeat it!" Nick ordered harshly.

"Look, Mr. Sloan, I had no business saying what I just did, but I'm human, too. So's the pediatrician who blew the diagnosis in your son's case. You're a lawyer. You can sue if you want to. But that won't help Billy any."

Dan cringed at the mental image he'd formed of the scene.

"Did he sue?" he asked Angela.

"No. Nick was after blood, not money, at the time."

"What *did* he do?"

"Enough, Dan!" Angela implored. "Enough! It's past midnight, and I can't take much more of this self-torture. I'll tell you the rest of the story when we visit Billy tomorrow."

"Is that where we're going?"

"Yes. We keep him in a private home for the mentally retarded outside of Gloucester. So try to hold your curiosity in check until then, and let me get some sleep."

"I'll try," Dan said, "though what you've told me so far raises more questions than it answers."

"Well, suffice it to say that after our talk with the neurosurgeon caring for Billy, Nick drove home in stony silence, dropped me off at the door, and told me he'd be back in an hour. I didn't see him again for *six years*. By then, he had an M.D. degree from Lausanne, an internship certificate from Wisconsin, and was starting a medical residency at UCLA Medical Center."

"Did you hear from him at all during those six years?"

"Not from Nick, but from his father, Charles. Somehow he and Nick had met and decided to make something of their biological connection. Charles was a pretty strange duck himself in those days. The hearing loss he'd suffered in a Nazi POW camp had made him more of a loner than ever. But"—she shrugged—"somehow seeing his only child again after twenty-five years worked a change. Quite a profound change. I adore the man. His ogrelike courtroom demeanor is strictly an act. In private, he is simply the most erudite and endearing man imaginable. I don't think I'd have considered taking part in Nick's preposterous scheme for a minute if it weren't for Charles. He kept working on me, first to join his law firm, then to handle an occasional malpractice case, until I finally gave in—to my ultimate regret. Now, enough, Dan! That outlines the whole picture for you in broad strokes; I'll fill in the details tomorrow—okay?"

Reluctantly Dan rose from the couch, swayed precariously until he managed to steady himself on Angela's shoulders, hugged her briefly, and turned to leave.

"Take a taxi home," she advised. "I wouldn't want you getting in an auto accident."

"Why not? If the smashup proved fatal, that'd dispose of the one person who can blow the whistle on your whole setup."

"True, but I've grown rather fond of you, in and out of bed."

With one hand on the doorknob, Dan paused and turned back to her. "One last question. You said earlier that you had a special reason for going to bed with me. What?"

Angela's initial response was to drop her eyes and shake her head in vigorous refusal. Then, sighing deeply, she said, "Oh, why not? Why not send you on your way with one more mind-blowing surprise? I went to bed with you for one purpose and one only: I wanted to get pregnant."

"You wanted—what?"

"You heard correctly. I wanted you to impregnate me. Unfortunately you didn't, and I don't intend to give you a second chance."

"That's nice to know," Dan said sarcastically. "But if that was your only purpose—which I doubt— shouldn't I, at least, have been consulted? After all, it would've been my kid too."

Angela shrugged. "You never asked."

"No, I just assumed—"

"Assumed that a forty-year-old career woman would know how to protect herself. Well, that's a reasonable enough assumption, I suppose, but an unnecessary one. All you had to do to verify it was to ask. But you didn't," she taunted, "and you happened to be wrong."

"Why, Angela?" demanded Dan, his eyes glinting angrily. "For Nick's sake? To shake him sufficiently so that he might be willing to give up his vendetta and lead a more normal life?"

"No, Dan. Not for Nick—for me! I swear to God, it had nothing whatsoever to do with Nick. He's a lost cause, believe me. Nor could I ever be that ruthless. I did it solely for selfish—and insane—reasons." She shrugged. "My little insanity. I didn't want to marry again, or grow old alone. So, not thinking too clearly, I decided I wanted another child. If I had gotten pregnant, I would've told you."

"Then what?"

"Depends on how much you want a kid with your last name. I would've married you before giving birth and divorced you afterwards, if that's what you wanted."

Dan shook his head in consternation. "I don't believe this. Not you, not this business about your trying to get pregnant, not any of it! Talk about sensory overload, for Chrissake! You're damned right I'm taking a cab home. The way my mind's reeling right now, I couldn't find my way out of the elevator. So good night, Angela. Even if you're really the Queen of Sheba, don't tell me. Not till morning anyway."

# 24

"Whose idea was it to team up—Sprague's or Sloan's?" Dan asked Angela as they drove along the coast road on their way to Gloucester.

"It certainly wasn't Charles's. Good as he was, he'd forsaken trial work years before and only went back to it for Nick's sake. The funny part is, I don't think the idea originated with Nick either."

"Who then?"

"Nick's never come right out and said so, but from little hints he's dropped or let slip over the years, I get the distinct impression it was Nate Clineman's idea."

"Clineman!" Dan almost gasped. "A world-famous psychiatrist like Nate Clineman suggesting something as far out as that! It's almost beyond belief."

"I find most psychiatrists almost beyond belief," Angela said dryly.

"But I know Nate. We've served on various national committees together. He's a brilliant and very methodical man who's done more for the field of psychiatry with his psychotropic drug research than anybody since Freud. Have you met him?"

"A few times. He testified for us once. And you're right. He is an unusual man. But I'm still pretty sure it was Nate who first suggested that Nick and Charles join forces. It's my guess that it was a desperate gamble on Nate's part that paid off. Otherwise he might've had to institutionalize Nick."

"Institutionalize him! Why?"

"Look, Dan, you know only one Nick Sloan—the dedicated doctor he is now. I know at least three more: the young law student I was deeply in love with; the still-young medical resident who used to drop by my Los Angeles apartment for supper occasionally and went with me to visit Billy the weekends he wasn't on call. He was very unstable, very manic-depressive, in those days until Nate managed to regulate him on lithium. There's yet another side to his personality, a volatile and vengeful side; his 'medical avenger' complex is a manifestation of it. Nick's never once been violent with me, never even raised his voice. But something snapped inside him when Fred Sobel told us Billy would never be normal, and I'm almost sure he set out to do, or did, something violent that night. Don't ask me what, since I don't know. But whatever it was, it made it impossible for him to come home again for six years."

"Does anybody know?"

"Charles might or might not. Nate Clineman would, if anybody did, but I've never discussed it with him. Why do *you* want to know?"

"I'm still trying to fit pieces to a puzzle. If enough come together, I might stand a chance of getting Nick to give up his vendetta against bad doctors. So what happened to him the night he left home could be important."

"I only wish I could tell you. The mere thought he might've committed mayhem, even murder, that night makes me shudder."

"Bauman?"

"No, not Bauman. That I'm sure of. Bauman finished himself off a few years later with cirrhosis of the liver."

"Who then?"

Angela shrugged and slowed down as the outer gates of the Munson Home for the Handicapped loomed into view. A ten-foot vine-overgrown wire fence encircled its spacious grounds. Inside the gate, the complex comprised a four-story administration building, several one- and two-story satellite structures, and on its perimeter a series of cottages for the children.

The director of the home seemed delighted to meet a doctor of Dan's renown and, over coffee, told him more about its operation than he cared to know. Finally, the director summoned a cottage master to escort Dan and Angela to the indoor pool where Billy was receiving his daily hydrotherapy.

Entering the humid, plastic-domed structure, they walked to the shallow end of the pool and stopped above a teenaged youth submerged up to his face in two feet of water. "Billy!" the cottage master shouted. "Stand up! Your mother and a doctor-friend are here to see you."

Billy did not so much as blink an eye in response at first. Then, with robotlike slowness and rigidity, he propped himself up on his elbows, drew in his legs, and raised himself to a sitting, then a standing position. Slowly and intently, as if unable to scan, his eyes moved from face to face until he uttered, "Ma—ma," on recognizing Angela.

"Hello, Billy," Angela said cheerfully. "This nice man here is Dr. Lassiter. Las-sit-er. Shake hands with him, Billy."

"H—hand," repeated Billy and tentatively extended his to grasp Dan's.

Dan was not surprised at the strength of his grip. Because of the brain damage produced by the traumatic cyst, Billy's left side was misshapen, his hand twisted and clawlike, and his leg nearly fleshless. But his right arm and leg were powerfully muscled. His face was also asymmetric, fleshed out and animated on the right, drooping and lifeless on the left. Having seen countless such cases before, Dan was not particularly perturbed by his physical deformities. What he found much harder to take, however, was the intense effort Billy put forth to try to comprehend what was said to him and to answer appropriately. It told Dan that Billy had enough residual intelligence to know how hopelessly abnormal he was, and it made him heartsick for the boy. He now understood why Angela had insisted that he accompany her here before daring to pass judgment on her ex-husband's vengeful behavior.

Not surprisingly, Angela seemed quite at ease and accepting of her son's infirmity. During the hour they spent together, she touched and hugged him and made Billy smile a lot.

"There are worse things in life for a woman than a mentally retarded child," she remarked to Dan as they were leaving the grounds. "I don't blame God. He gave me a healthy baby to start with and the capacity to bear more. I don't even blame Bauman. He meant Billy no harm, and his own life must've been sheer hell to put him on the skids."

"Do you blame anybody?" asked Dan.

"Sometimes," she replied softly. "Sometimes I blame Nick. That's the reason we haven't visited Billy together for a long time, even when we both lived in Los Angeles. Now we can't, without running the risk of someone we know, or who knows about us, seeing us together. But don't judge Nick too harshly, Dan. The love he gave Billy in the beginning was something to behold."

"I'm having trouble judging anybody right now."

Angela gave Dan a wry, knowing look. "It isn't easy, is it? One of the reasons I turned down the judgeship offered me a few years ago. But you have to admire Nick in a way for doing it. He really tries to be fair in picking the bad doctors he goes after; hardly ever picking the borderline ones. The logic of insanity again. Once you believe you've been appointed God's avenging angel, you're obliged to be fair. Maybe he really is God's angel. Who knows?"

"I certainly don't," Dan said. "Not after today."

"Hmm," murmured Angela and took his hand. "I actually believe you've become humble. I like that. I like it enough to want to hold hands with you, but that's all for now."

"Meaning there might be more to come later?"

"That depends—"

"On what?"

"On what you decide to do. It wasn't my intention to confuse you, Dan, but maybe I have by some of my remarks about Nick. I can assure you of one thing, though. I won't stand by and let Nick be hurt. If you can convince him to give up his vendetta against bad doctors, fine. But if you try to force him, I'll fight you tooth and nail."

"Why?"

"It would simply be too risky. His anger might be all that's keeping him going. Remove his outlet for it, his safety valve, and there's no telling how he'll hold up."

"No," Dan sighed, "I suppose not. But I don't intend to do anything until after I've talked to him and maybe to Nate Clineman." Dan released Angela's hand to lift the latch on the main gate, then grasped it again as they continued on to her car in the parking lot.

Unobserved by them, a black Dodge Dart sedan had just pulled into a parking space three rows behind Angela's car. Inside it, Nicholas Sloan reacted to the sight of them together with surprise, then with suspicion, finally with jaw-tightening resentment.

Nick had rented the sedan at Logan Airport immediately upon deplaning for the sole purpose of driving up to the Munson Home to meet Angela. He knew when she was likely to be there, and he wanted to tell her about a development of great importance to his future—and hers, too, he hoped—without delay.

Now, watching her and Lassiter stroll hand in hand to her Mercedes, the matter that he could hardly wait to discuss with her seemed to lose most of its significance and all of its urgency. The moment he had boarded his Boston-bound flight that morning, he had resolved to deal fairly and openly and at long last with Angela in hopes of making amends for all the years of heartbreak he had caused her.

But now, before dealing so directly with Angela, he would first have to deal with his erstwhile friend and colleague Daniel Lassiter.

# 25

Dan left Angela at the door of her apartment around four P.M. and drove on to Wayland. As usual, he checked with his answering service and was surprised to learn that a Dr. Nicholas Sloan had phoned twice, requesting that he return the call.

Dan did, and was immediately put at ease by Nick's friendly greeting. "How'd Miami go?" he asked.

"Quite well," Sloan replied. "In fact, much better than expected. They're a pretty progressive bunch down there and heavily into gerontology—which fits my research interests beautifully. Anyway, they made me an offer that I'd really like to talk over with you."

"Fine," said Dan. "There are a few things I'd like to talk to you about, too. How about dinner tonight?"

"You're on! Provided we settle who pays in the usual manner."

"You *are* a fanatic!"

"I'm worse than that. After all the rich food they fed me down there, I'm getting a little paunchy and want to work it off."

"Okay," Dan said. "Usual time and place?"

Sloan hesitated. "Usual time. But you've had the home court advantage twice now. So this time let's try my bailiwick—the Huntington Avenue Y."

"You reserve the court and I'll be there," said Dan, not exactly in the mood for handball after his emotionally trying day, but preferring the informality of a locker room or restaurant to an office setting for confronting Sloan with his findings.

But Sloan was not in the locker room when Dan arrived at the Y shortly before seven to change. Nor was he in the observation gallery. Dan was further surprised to learn from the desk attendant that Sloan had booked their court for eight o'clock, not seven, and was now in the boxing room.

Dan found him there, dressed in his gym togs and expertly punching a light bag. "Hey, Nick!" he shouted above the percussive beat of the bag. "What's going on?"

Sloan lowered his hands immediately and turned to him with an apologetic grin. "Dan, I'm sorry, but I goofed. I didn't realize until after I got here that we usually play at seven, not eight, so I booked the court for the wrong time."

Dan shrugged. "No problem. I can work out in here for a while."

"You used to box in college, didn't you?"

"A little," Dan answered modestly; actually he had fought a great deal in college and beyond, maintaining his prowess in the sport by periodically sparring with the local pros.

"Me, too," Sloan said. "Want to go a few rounds while we're waiting?"

"I'd just as soon talk, Nick."

"Aw, we'll have plenty of time for that later." Sloan patted his middle. "I'm more interested in working off some of this flab. Come on," he urged, "I'll get a couple sets of gloves from the attendant."

Dan hesitated, suddenly made uneasy by the suspicion that, for some unknown reason, Sloan was setting him up for a beating. "All right," he agreed. "Better ask him for some headgear, too."

"Not for me," Sloan said. "I've got a thick skull. But I'll get one for you, if you want."

Dan scrutinized his face for any hint that their sparring might represent no mere whim but something more calculated, even vindictive, on Sloan's part. "No, never mind," he said. "I suppose headgear really isn't needed for a little gentlemanly workout between two aging sluggers. Just let me get my old mouthpiece out of my gym bag and I'll be right with you."

Moments later, Dan tightened the laces on his right-hand glove with his teeth, slipped between the ropes, and squared off against Sloan in the center of the ring. They touched gloves and then began circling each other, looking for an opening.

Dan, still suspicious of Sloan's motive, shuffled forward in a semicrouch, elbows and gloves drawn in close to his body, and threw a lazy left jab to test his response.

Sloan sidestepped it and countered with a hard left hook to the head and a short right cross to the midsection. Gliding inside, Dan deftly deflected the hook with his glove and blocked the cross with his elbow. But the force behind Sloan's blows confirmed his suspicion.

Dan snapped a jab high off Sloan's cheek, and he responded with a roundhouse right that barely missed Dan's jaw.

"Hey—easy!" Dan cautioned.

But the spiteful scowl on Sloan's face told him that his opponent had no intention of taking it easy.

Dan backpedaled, letting Sloan come to him. Finally he did, flicking a pair of jabs at Dan's nose to force his head back and then leaping forward with a flurry of left hooks. As Dan twisted sideways to absorb the hooks on his shoulder, Sloan smashed a solid, scintillating right to his jaw, momentarily stunning him.

Angrily Dan crouched low, bobbing and weaving to

avoid more hooks, feinted with both hands, and then landed a short, vicious uppercut to Sloan's gut, sending him stumbling back against the ropes. Dan did not pursue him to punish him more, as he doubtless would have done had this been a street brawl or a legitimate bout. Still baffled by Sloan's behavior, he held back, allowing him to regain his balance. They had traded hard blows, and maybe that would be enough to satisfy whatever was eating at him, Dan hoped.

But again Sloan came forward scowling. He jabbed at Dan's face twice and then let loose with a vicious right hook. Having anticipated it, Dan blocked it easily and, stepping in close, slammed another short uppercut into Sloan's midsection. As he'd learned long ago, short of a knock-out, facial punches merely made an opponent mad; belly punches made him quit.

Sloan went rubbery-legged and doubled over, turtle-like, to protect his head while trying to catch his breath.

Again Dan took a backward step, giving Sloan a chance to recover, only to realize he was not as badly hurt as he pretended. Suddenly Sloan sprang forward, pummeling Dan with both hands and forcing him back against the ropes. Agilely Dan bounced off them and slipped sideways, trapping Sloan in a corner and dazing him with a right cross to the jaw.

Grunting in pain, Sloan momentarily fell to one knee and then lurched forward to deliver a glancing blow to Dan's forehead.

"Hey, what's going on?" Dan shouted to Sloan as they clinched. "You after blood?"

"Yeah," Sloan growled. "Your blood!"

"Why?" Dan asked, breaking free of his gloved grasp and shoving him back.

For his reply Sloan aimed a savage right at Dan's jaw, which Dan partially blocked, and in the same motion smashed Sloan squarely in the nose.

"I asked why," Dan repeated as Sloan's nostrils gushed blood.

"I thought you were my friend," muttered Sloan, wiping at the blood with his glove.

"I thought so, too."

"Then what the hell were you doing with Angela this afternoon?"

"She took me to see Billy."

"Billy's none of your business!" Charging forward, Sloan shoved Dan off balance with a shoulder butt and then knocked him to his knees with a vicious chop to the head.

Dan jumped to his feet, shaking his head clear, and snarled, "Okay, you asked for it." He circled sideways until Sloan fell a step behind, then reversed direction and connected with a combination left hook and right cross. Sloan staggered back against the ropes, and Dan was immediately upon him, battering his belly until he dropped his guard and then landing a bone-crunching right to the jaw.

Glassy-eyed and slack-jawed, Sloan collapsed against the ropes and slid down into a sitting position.

"*Now* would you rather talk or fight?" Dan demanded.

"Fight! But not with these," Sloan said, starting to pull off his gloves. "Let's see how good you are bare-fisted."

"Oh, shit!" Dan groaned, curious to know what had so angered Sloan but tired of his childish bravado.

Hastily slipping off his gloves, Dan reached behind the ropes for the three-legged stool in the corner and brandished it over Sloan's head. "Okay," he announced. "You want to keep fighting, we'll fight. You with your fists, me with this!"

Sloan half-rose, saw Dan cock his arm to bring the stool crashing down on his head, and slipped back to the canvas. "Okay!" he gestured mollifyingly, "we'll talk."

"Where?"

"The steam room okay?" asked Sloan, struggling shakily to his feet.

"It'll do for starters. But what we've got to say to each other will take a fairly long time. So after that let's go someplace else. Like, maybe, a restaurant?"

"Or like the nearest emergency room?" Sloan said, gingerly rubbing the side of his face. "I think you might've fractured my jaw."

"Now," Dan began once the two of them were alone in the steam room, "do you mind telling me just what the hell that was all about?"

"You may not believe this," Sloan said, "but I'm not really sure. I saw you and Angela leaving the Munson Home together and . . ." He shrugged. "I was really thrown."

"Oh? You the jealous type, Nick?"

"Maybe. Or just plain paranoid—figuring the two of you were ganging up on me."

"I see," Dan said with exaggerated patience. "I don't think that quite describes it."

"But if she took you to see Billy, then she told you everything . . ."

"Yeah, *after* I figured most of it out for myself. Like your relationship with Charles Sprague—personally and professionally. But you couldn't be more wrong about Angela. She insisted I go see Billy so that I might better understand you. And she was right. I do understand— up to a point. But I still don't approve of the way you operate and I wish you'd stop!"

"And if I refuse, what will you do then?"

With sweat smarting his eyes and dripping down his face, Dan gave Sloan a rueful look. "I'd hate to hurt you *or* your career. You're too good a doctor for me to want to do that."

"I appreciate your consideration, Dan, but I'm afraid you're going to have to."

"What do you mean?"

"Simply that I'm not going to stop of my own free will; not as long as the Dubics and the Gormanns are allowed to do anything they damned please with their patients. Somebody's got to put the fear of God, or financial ruin, in them. And I don't see you volunteering for any vigilante brigade. The only volunteering you've done so far is to defend a money-grubbing quack like Emil Dubic. How do you square that with your vaunted conscience?"

Dan looked chagrined. "Not too well. But that still doesn't mean I can condone what you're doing. Jesus, Nick, do you really think it's fair using your hospital position to spy on unsuspecting doctors?"

"And coming up with nothing but admiration for most of them."

"Maybe the others deserve to be treated fairly too?"

"As fairly as they treat their patients?" Sloan challenged. "I'd have no quarrel with a system of justice as equitable as that."

Dan exhaled in frustration. "Dammit, Nick, I don't like bad doctors any better than you do. But I just don't believe your scare tactics can get rid of them without hurting the good ones even more. Why make them suffer just so you can wreak eternal vengeance on one inept pediatrician?"

"You don't really believe I'm still doing that, do you?"

"I don't know what to believe."

"Look, Dan, you're an associate editor of the *New England Journal of Medicine,* so you must've read the Rand Corporation's study of malpractice in California. That certainly debunked a lot of the popular myths perpetuated by the medical profession. 'Good' doctors were *not* sued nearly as often as 'bad' ones. In fact, a mere three-fifths of one percent of the 8,000 doctors in Los Angeles were responsible for ten percent of the claims and thirty percent of the payments to the plaintiffs. But what've the doctors out there done about it? Nothing! They still favor statewide mutual malpractice funds over countywide ones to make sure nobody they know is looking over their shoulders. So if you can't get them to police themselves that way, why not another? By hitting them where it really hurts—in their pocketbooks!"

"Oh, I agree!" Dan said. "Hit them as hard as you can. But do it aboveboard. You know damned well it's unethical for a lawyer to initiate first contact with a potential claimant. It's *inexcusable* for a doctor-lawyer to do it, especially when he uses his hospital teaching post to hunt such cases down. Come on, Nick. You're not so far gone you can't see how unfair that is! So give it up! Give it up before you're caught by someone who doesn't know how much you really love medicine and makes sure you never teach or practice again."

Using his towel to wipe sweat from his eyes, Sloan gazed pensively at Dan a long moment before saying, "Your arguments aren't that convincing, Dan—not from a guy who wrote: 'The only thing worse than a bad doctor is good doctors who let him get away with it.' But you might just be right. Maybe the beating you gave me tonight knocked some sense into me. Or maybe the job offer I had in Miami to be chief of medicine of their new medical school and director of their Gerontology Institute is too tempting to turn down. But to prove how grateful I am for the personal interest you've taken in me, I'm going to let you play a part in helping me decide. What we lawyers call 'shifting the burden.' "

"Me!" Dan exclaimed. "What can I do?"

"Be at the Gormann trial tomorrow, and don't do anything about me until afterwards. That's not asking too much, is it?"

"No," Dan admitted. "But why the Gormann trial?"

"Don't worry. I had nothing to do with that one, outside of giving my father some perfectly proper advice on its medical aspects. There was none of the looking-over-the-shoulder business that seems to bother you so much."

"Then why is it important I be there?"

"Since you're so concerned about being fair, I want to show you how fair the other side can be. In other words, I want you to get the full malpractice picture. So far you've seen only half of it: the corrupt doctor. What you haven't seen yet is the corrupt lawyer—but you will if you're in court tomorrow."

"Hammond?"

"That's his name, and he's a real sharpie. So watch

what *he*'ll do to win a case and *then* tell me if you think I ought to quit."

"I'll be there," Dan assured him. "Well, I've had enough steam for tonight. Still interested in dinner?"

"Sure." Sloan rubbed his jaw and grimaced. "A liquid one."

Dan smiled, hesitated, and said, "One last matter we ought to clear up." Angela, he thought; he supposed it would be a long time before he could think of her and what they'd briefly shared without a stab of longing. He was almost sorry she hadn't gotten pregnant. But short of that, she was too imprisoned by the past to let him into her present life.

"What?"

"Angela."

Guardedly Sloan asked, "What about her?"

"If you really are jealous, there's no reason for it. Oh, there might've been, but not now. Believe it or not, she's still stuck on you."

A wistful expression crossed Sloan's face. "I guess I knew that, really."

"Sure," Dan mocked. "But I didn't think it would hurt to remind you. After all, you're the one who told me you had a thick skull."

# 26

Dan drove directly from his home in Wayland to the Suffolk County Courthouse the next morning to keep his promise to Nick Sloan. Gordon Donnelly drove in with him and listened raptly to all Dan had to tell him about the relationship between Charles Sprague and his son, Sloan.

"What do you think of Sprague now?" Dan asked when he had finished.

"What I've always thought," Gordon replied. "That he's a hell of a lawyer. It's Nick Sloan that fascinates me. Maybe the medical profession needs more grand inquisitors like him."

"Maybe. As long as they operate in the open. Any idea what Nick meant when he said he wanted me in court today to see the other half of the malpractice picture—the bad lawyer?"

"Chances are he's talking about a bribe. But if Sloan knows about it, so does Sprague, and there'll be hell to pay."

Dan dropped Gordon off at his office, parked at the rear of the courthouse, and then walked around to the front, where he was to meet Sloan. A fair-sized crowd was gathered on the steps. From random remarks he overheard, it appeared as if half the reporters and law students in town were trying to get in.

Minutes later, to his surprise, he saw Nick Sloan and Angela arrive in the same cab. While Nick paid the driver, Angela strolled up to Dan.

"Good morning!" she said cheerily. "I hear you almost broke my ex-husband's jaw last night. Oh, don't apologize," she added as Dan looked abashed. "It seems to have started his brain working again. The job in Miami sounds exciting."

"Think he'll take it?"

Angela shrugged. "The way he was talking—or trying to talk—with his swollen jaw at breakfast this morning, he just might."

"And you? Would you go with him?"

But before Angela could answer, Nick Sloan came up to them and slapped Dan on the shoulder. "Morning! How you feeling?"

"Like I've got orchestra seats for the best theater in town."

"That's not far from the truth."

"Well," Angela said, extending her hand to Dan, "I've got to leave you two and meet Charles. I'm a working girl, you know."

"Shall we?" suggested Dan, starting to follow her up the courthouse steps.

"One second," Sloan said, gripping his arm. "I wonder if you'd do me a favor."

"Depends. I don't give B-12 shots or false testimony."

Sloan ignored the wisecrack. "My father's not been feeling well lately, and I'd like you to see him."

Dan stared. "You want *me* to take Charles Sprague on as a patient? Good God! I spend days trying to find out the name of the doctor who's been prescribing his nitroglycerin, and now you want me to do the prescribing. That's a twist!"

"He's been on roughly the same amount of nitro for

years, so I don't think his heart's the problem. But ever since he caught a bad cold a month or so ago, he's been feeling lousy, and it's beginning to worry me."

"Lousy in what way?"

"Well, a lot of headaches, mainly in the neck area, and dizzy spells, with an element of true vertigo causing a staggering gait. The spells seldom last more than a few minutes, but they're hitting him harder and more often lately. When I met him at the plane yesterday, he could hardly make it down the ramp."

"Where's he been?"

"All over the map. From Washington, D.C., to Port-au-Prince, looking for a potential witness."

"Did he find him?"

"He sure did. Brought him back in his private jet practically handcuffed to make sure he shows up in court this morning. I asked him to see an ENT man at Georgetown Hospital while he was there, but he didn't have time."

"Why an ENT man?"

"I thought he might've developed Ménière's syndrome following his upper respiratory infection. But he hasn't responded to the usual antivertigo drugs at all, and I'm afraid his symptoms might be neuro. So I'd really appreciate it if you'd take a look at him."

"Sure," Dan said. "Bring him to my office around six tonight."

As usual, Courtroom 229 was packed with spectators. Seeing Dan enter, Ned Josephson went over to him. "Dan! I didn't expect to see you here," he said.

"I hear it could be an interesting morning."

"I don't know where you heard it, but trust the source. We're putting our last, and best, defense witness on the stand: Joanne Lorris, the nurse I told you about."

"Good," said Dan. "I hope she helps."

"How about you?" Josephson asked, drawing him aside. "Learn anything useful?"

Dan hesitated. "Yes, quite a bit. But nothing of any immediate value to you—except for maybe one thing.

Ned," he said reluctantly, "you're playing all this straight, aren't you?"

"What do you mean?"

"I mean, I consider you a good lawyer, just as I consider myself a good doctor. But there are bad lawyers, too. What's your opinion of Hammond?"

Josephson looked pained. "I don't know if it's ethical for me to answer that."

"Why not? Gormann hired him; you didn't. Would you have, if it were up to you?"

"Okay, Dan," Josephson sighed, "I get your drift. He's too high-priced in my opinion—which means in the same price range as a Mel Belli or Lee Bailey, but not nearly as hardworking or as good. So he's being paid to deliver the goods, and he's got one last chance —Lorris—to deliver them. But he's calling the shots on this one."

"Well, for his sake, I hope he calls them straight."

"You know something I don't?" Josephson asked anxiously.

"I know you were right about Sprague. If Hammond's dumb enough to pull a fake rabbit out of a hat, Sprague'll top him with a live one!"

Dan took the seat next to Nick Sloan as the starting time of the trial neared.

"I spoke to my father," Sloan told him. "He'll be at your office at six tonight."

"Where's he now?"

"Resting. He got hit with another dizzy spell this morning and barely made it in. Both Angela and I tried to get him to go home, but he's stubborn as hell and won't budge."

The next instant Dan saw Charles Sprague enter the courtroom through a side entrance and sit down between Angela and the Harrison boy at the plaintiff's table. Sprague's hair and beard were neatly trimmed, and he wore the same vested suit that Dan had seen on him before. Yet, in the light of what Nick Sloan had told him about his father, Dan's discerning eye detected a few disturbing differences. Not only was Sprague's gait broad-based and unsteady, but from the way he held the sheaf of papers in his hand up and to one side, Dan suspected he was having trouble focusing his eyes.

"Tell your father I'll see him at noon," Dan whispered to Sloan. "I don't like the way he looks either."

Grimly Sloan nodded. "I'll bring him down to the first-aid room on the second floor."

At nine o'clock, Justice Jacob Richman convened the court session, thanked the members of the jury for their forbearance during the long trial proceedings, and told them he had been assured by both parties that this would be the last day of testimony. He then called on Sidney Hammond to present his final witness for the defense.

Hammond rose, brimming with confidence, and summoned Joanne Lorris, a slender woman in her early thirties, to the stand to be sworn in.

Lorris squirmed slightly as she settled into the witness chair, and her voice quavered as she replied, "I do," to the oath. But she soon shed her tenseness under Hammond's gentle questioning. He began by asking her to summarize her years of training and experience in the field of nursing, particularly her three-year stint at Bradford Medical Center. He then got her to describe the large number of Dr. Gormann's patients she had cared for during this period and to give her opinion of him as a conscientious, hardworking, unfailingly cheerful physician. Finally, after some prodding by the judge, Hammond zeroed in on the events surrounding Delia Harrison's deterioration and death.

"Did Mrs. Harrison run a low-grade fever postoperatively and develop a purulent drainage from her incision site?"

"Yes, she did."

"Was Dr. Gormann notified of this?"

"Yes!" Lorris stated emphatically; she had notified him personally.

"At what hour of the day or night?"

"After midnight," Lorris replied. "Immediately after the patient had spiked a fever of 103 degrees and suffered a shaking chill."

"And what did Dr. Gormann instruct you to do?"

"He ordered Mrs. Harrison placed on antibiotics."

"What antibiotics?"

"Tetracycline."

"By what route?"

"Intravenous."

Hammond paused for effect. "Now, Mrs. Lorris, think carefully before you answer this next question. Exactly how much intravenous tetracycline did Dr. Gormann order?"

"I . . . thought he ordered one gram QID."

"QID—meaning four times a day?"

"Yes, sir, that's right."

"And that's what you wrote down on the order sheet?"

"Yes."

"Is there any possibility—any possibility at all—that you might have misunderstood Dr. Gormann's order?"

Lorris lowered her eyes and voice. "Yes, there is."

"Please speak up," Hammond asked.

"Yes."

"In what way?"

"Well, I was working a double shift that day and was awfully tired, and I guess I might've thought Dr. Gormann said QID when what he really said was QD—once a day."

"In other words," Hammond said in a loud, firm voice, "what Dr. Gormann intended Mrs. Harrison to receive was a daily dose of *one* gram of intravenous tetracycline, not four times that amount. Is that correct?"

"Yes, I believe it is."

"A daily dose of *one gram*," Hammond emphasized, "which we have already established through expert medical testimony is a perfectly safe dosage of that drug. But because you were so fatigued from overwork, you misunderstood him and wrote down a different order—an order that resulted in Mrs. Harrison receiving four times that dose."

"Yes. May the good Lord forgive me, but I believe I did."

"Thank you, Mrs. Lorris, for your forthright testimony. No further questions, Your Honor."

"Very well," Justice Richman replied. "Mr. Sprague, have you questions for the witness?"

A hush fell over the courtroom, and every eye turned toward Sprague as he rose, slowly, stiffly, to his feet. Watching intently, Dan saw him start to fall backward before grasping the edge of the table for support. "No, Your Honor," he rasped, "I have no questions at all for Mrs. Lorris."

A murmur of surprise swept through the courtroom, followed by a buzz of excited whispers.

Dan turned to Nick Sloan. "What's going on?"

"You'll see," Sloan said expectantly.

"Why doesn't your father try to shake her testimony?"

"It's shaky enough."

"Has she been bribed?"

Sloan nodded. "Thirty thousand dollars' worth. A doctor-friend of Gormann's just bought a condominium for that amount and is going to let her live there rent-free."

"Can you prove it?" Dan asked.

"Probably—given a few extra days."

"Then why don't you?"

Sloan smiled sardonically. "And cause a mistrial? Besides, it's Gormann's money. One hundred thousand dollars more goes to Hammond, leaving the not-so-good doctor with liquid assets of around four hundred thousand dollars; which, by strange coincidence, is exactly the amount we're asking in excess of what the State Mutual Fund will pay out in damages."

"Providing you win the case," Dan reminded him.

"Which we are about to do. Watch!"

Justice Richman banged his gavel to restore order and turned to Charles Sprague. "You surprise me, counselor. Are you sure you haven't a single question for Mrs. Lorris?"

"Quite sure, Your Honor. I would, however, like to call a rebuttal witness to the stand."

"Hmm," Richman murmured appreciatively. "And the name of this witness?"

"Mr. Andrew Vivienne, registered pharmacist in the states of Massachusetts and Maryland."

"Very well," the judge said. "Will Mr. Vivienne please come forward."

A blond, bearded young man in beige slacks and sweater rose from the second row and mounted the witness stand.

Sprague quickly established his credentials and the fact that after graduating from the Massachusetts School of Pharmacy he served one year as a pharmacy intern at the Bradford Medical Center.

With his voice growing progressively weaker and raspier, Sprague then got directly to the point. On the fifth postoperative night after Delia Harrison's hysterectomy, was Mr. Vivienne on duty at the hospital pharmacy and did he receive Nurse Lorris's request for four one-gram ampules of intravenous tetracycline sent to the floor?

"I did," Vivienne answered.

"And did you fill that order without question?"

"No!" Vivienne stated emphatically. "I did not."

"Why not?" Sprague asked curiously.

"Because the dosage seemed excessive to me."

"Then what did you do?"

"I called Dr. Gormann at his home to verify it."

"I see," said Sprague, nodding approval. "Very sensible. And what was Dr. Gormann's response to your inquiry?"

"He became angry."

"Angry?" Sprague repeated. "At you?"

"Yes, sir. He said he knew exactly what he was doing and didn't want any smart-ass pharmacy intern questioning his judgment."

248

"And what was your reply?"

"I repeated that I thought four grams of IV tetracycline daily was an excessive dosage, and said that I would have to report it to the chief pharmacist in the morning."

"And what was Dr. Gormann's response to that?"

"He swore at me, but then seemed to calm down. Told me to send up the initial one gram and he'd look up the maximum permissible dosage in the morning."

"Did he?"

"Not to my knowledge."

"Did you then report the incident to your supervisor?"

"Not right away."

"Why not?"

"I took Dr. Gormann at his word."

"Meaning that he would look up the proper dose of intravenous tetracycline in the morning, as promised, and change his order accordingly?"

"Yes."

"But obviously he didn't."

"No, Mrs. Harrison received the full four grams he originally ordered."

"And did you report this fact to your supervisor?"

"Yes—too late. It happened during the week I was taking my State Board exams, so I didn't find out about it until the next time I took night call, five days later. By that time the patient had died. Of postoperative complications, I was told."

"I see. One final question, Mr. Vivienne. Where've you been the last six months?"

"In Haiti."

"Doing what?"

"Volunteer medical work for my church. I'm a Seventh-Day Adventist."

"And when did you first hear about this trial?"

"I didn't hear about it at all until the U.S. consul, at your request, told me of it and asked if I'd be willing to talk to you in person."

"Which you did. And so it is your sworn testimony that Dr. Gormann *knew* that night that the daily dosage of IV tetracycline he had ordered for Mrs. Harrison was *four* grams, not one?"

"Yes, sir!"

"Thank you, Mr. Vivienne. No further questions, Your Honor."

Justice Richman nodded. Then, glancing sternly in the direction of the defense table, he said, "Your turn to question the witness, Mr. Hammond."

Hammond hastily consulted with Josephson and then said, "In view of this surprising development, Your Honor, I'd like to request a ten-minute recess to confer with my client."

"Any objection, Mr. Sprague?" asked Richman.

Hammond and Josephson rose, anticipating none. But before Sprague could reply, Darryl Harrison, emitting an anguished cry of "Butcher!" leaped up and flung himself across the gap between the tables to grab Carl Gormann by his coat lapels. Pulling and twisting him off his chair and across the tabletop, he clamped both hands around Gormann's throat. For a long moment the spectators, including the two bailiffs, were immobilized by surprise and horror. Then several rose, cried out, and rushed forward to stop the assault.

"Jesus!" Dan and Nick Sloan gasped simultaneously from their second-row seats and bounded toward the struggling pair. From opposite sides of the courthouse, Dr. John Reaves and Dr. Gary Gogal did likewise. But it was Charles Sprague, reacting with amazing quickness and agility, who reached them first and struggled fiercely to wrench the enraged youth's hands from Gormann's throat before his thumbs crushed his windpipe. Harrison kicked and elbowed Sprague, finally sending him sprawling against the exhibit table. But before he could dig his thumbs back into Gormann's throat, a uniformed bailiff and a burly spectator seized and held him secure as he continued to scream, "Butcher! That butcher killed my mother!" Then, spotting Reaves, he stopped and stared at the psychiatrist with frightened, pleading eyes.

Breathing heavily, Charles Sprague pushed himself off the exhibit table and was starting to straighten up when he suddenly gasped, clutched his head with both hands, and collapsed on the floor.

Seeing his stricken look just before he fell, Angela shouted, "Charles! Oh, dear God! Nick—help! It's Charles!" and rushed to him.

Hearing her cry above the din, Nick and Dan pushed and shoved their way through the crowd to Sprague's side. Quickly Dan turned him over, took a pulse reading at the neck, ran a finger through his mouth, and then pried open his eyelids to check his pupils. "He's still alive and breathing," he told Sloan, "but his pupils are pinpoint. Call an ambulance, and then let's get him down to that first-aid room where we can go over him."

Straightening, Dan dug a key case out of his pocket and handed it to one of the two bailiffs Angela had summoned. "You'll find my car, a brown Datsun, 280-Z, parked in the front row of the back lot. License number's on this tag. Please bring the medical bag in the trunk to the first-aid room."

The bailiff nodded and hurried out.

"Need a stretcher, Doc?" asked the other bailiff.

"No," Dan said. "The three of us can carry him—quickly and carefully."

A path was hastily cleared through the curious but cooperative crowd, and they carried Sprague to the second-floor room. The bailiff with Dan's medical bag arrived almost on their heels, and after stripping Sprague down to his undershorts, Dan proceeded to examine him.

In addition to pinpoint, light-unresponsive pupils, the unconscious man showed a slight weakness of his right facial muscles and the peculiar, bent-elbow, outwardly twisted wrist and hand sign known as decerebrate posturing on that side. Yet what puzzled Dan was the complete absence of the other signs that usually accompany a massive cerebral hemorrhage or thrombosis: deviant eye movements, limb weakness, change in deep tendon reflexes, abnormal toe signs.

Seeing the baffled look on Dan's face, Sloan asked, "What do you think it is?"

"I don't know. It acts like a stroke in some ways, but in other ways it doesn't. Has he had any serious illnesses in the past?"

"None that I know of, except his chronic angina and a traumatic hearing loss suffered during World War Two. He seemed in pretty good health until he caught cold a month ago."

"You sure it *was* a cold, or are you merely assuming it was?"

Sloan looked uncertain. "Assuming."

"Run through the symptoms again."

"Headaches, mainly in the occipital area, occasional nausea and vomiting, severe dizzy spells. Still sounds like a postviral Ménière's to me."

"Yes, except for two things: a gait disturbance, which is rare with Ménière's, and the fact that he's now comatose."

Suddenly Sprague emitted a soft moan, prompting Dan to return to him, test his pain response to neck flexion and thumb pressure over the eyebrow, and amend his last statement. "I take it back," he told Sloan. "He's not comatose—he's merely stuporous."

"From what?"

"Not from Ménière's. But I'm beginning to get a handle on what might be going on." Dan moved to the sink and turned on the cold water full force. Then, he dug into his medical bag for a fifty-cc plastic syringe.

"What are you going to do—calorie testing?" Sloan asked as Dan filled the syringe with water.

"Yes. Here," Dan said, handing Sloan the syringe. "You inject the water into his right ear canal while I check his pupillary movements."

"Nothing!" Dan reported at the end of the procedure. "No oculovestibular response at all."

Sloan grimaced. "Meaning brain stem hemorrhage?"

"Maybe," Dan replied. "Or maybe something not so bad. With brain stem hemorrhage there ought to be conjugate eye deviation, which there isn't, and long tract signs—hemiplegia or quadriplegia—which he doesn't show either. So what does that suggest to you?"

"Oh, Christ!" Sloan groaned in self-disgust. "Thank God one of us can be objective at a time like this. It suggests cerebellar hemorrhage or infarction—which means he might just have a chance."

"He might—if we can get him to a hospital and a neurosurgeon in time. You know as well as I that if we can't get his posterior fossa decompressed soon, he'll herniate his whole brain."

"Okay. I'll tell the ambulance to take him to Palmer Memorial, which is closer, but you look after him."

"Gladly. But I'm not a neurosurgeon, remember? Got any preferences?"

"For posterior fossa lesions, I think Bill Schramm's as good as anybody."

"Schramm?" Dan gave him a look of bemused wonder. "You want Bill Schramm to operate on your father?"

"Yes," said Sloan, puzzled. "What's wrong with him?"

"Oh, nothing!" Dan hastily answered. "In fact, I'd be glad to call him myself."

"You want *what?*" growled Schramm into the telephone after Dan had reached him at his office and briefly explained the urgency of the situation. "You want *me* to operate on Charles Sprague!" He emitted a high-pitched, nervous laugh. "Well, if that doesn't take the prize for the most ironic twist of the year. Twist hell, it's a goddamn pretzel! Tell me the truth, Dan. Are you doing this to me on purpose, 'cause if you are—"

"No, no, I swear. You're Nick Sloan's choice."

"Okay. Tell Sloan I'll be right along. But I want you

to realize this makes me a leading candidate for saint-hood. If I operate successfully on Sprague and he goes back to suing doctors, I've had it in this town. And if I don't operate successfully, one of his partners will probably sue me!"

# 27

Shortly after the ambulance bringing Charles Sprague to Palmer Memorial Hospital arrived, Bill Schramm bustled through the same emergency entrance and was directed to the room where he had been taken.

"Hi, Bill," said Dan, while changing the bottle of intravenous fluid dripping into Sprague's arm vein.

Schramm nodded at him and Sloan. "How's he doing?"

"Not so good," Dan replied. "I'm running in a pint of mannitol now in hopes it might reduce his cerebral edema a bit."

"Let's take a look," said Schramm, opening his small black instrument bag. Briefly but expertly he examined Sprague. Then, without discussion, he ordered the nurse to take him directly to the operating room.

Sloan, slumping against a side wall, did not question the decision, but Dan did. "Don't you want a CAT scan first?"

Giving him a mildly scornful look, Schramm said, "Of course I want a CAT scan! I *love* CAT scans—and with the size of his lesion it would just be lovely to add

255

to my teaching file. Or protect me from a malpractice suit. But I also want a live patient to operate on. Look, Dan, I'm pretty sure of the diagnosis and what has to be done. I figure the mannitol you've given him might—just might—buy us an hour's time. And it'll take at least that long to get him ready for surgery. So it's either a pretty CAT scan or a fast decompression. Take your pick."

Dan gestured docilely. "You're the boss. Want me in the OR with you?"

"With his history of angina, you're damned right! Besides, if I pull off a miracle here, I'll need your documentation. So let's get the show on the road."

Schramm lifted Sprague's head and shoulders and Dan his legs, and they eased him off the examining table onto a wheeled stretcher. In the corridor Schramm, spurning the nurse's offer to call an orderly, sent her to notify the operating room of their imminent arrival and wheeled Sprague to the elevators himself.

"What do you think his chances are?" Sloan asked Dan.

"Not good, but not hopeless either. Schramm's a damned fine neurosurgeon—and fast. If anybody can save your dad, he can. Look," Dan said, seeing the deepening lines of despair on his face, "why don't you go find Angela and take her to the doctors' lounge off the OR? I promise I'll keep you closely informed."

Bleakly Sloan nodded and went off in the direction of the waiting area while Dan headed for the elevators.

The moment Schramm wheeled Charles Sprague through the double doors of the operating room suite, he began shouting orders to the nursing personnel for special instruments, equipment, and an anesthesiologist. The nurses, understanding the urgency of the neurosurgical procedure and tolerant of "Wild Bill's" blustery behavior, immediately scattered to accommodate him.

In the doctors' locker room Dan shed his street clothes, slipped into a starchy surgical scrub suit, and went looking for Schramm. He found him in the corridor outside the operating room that was hurriedly being prepared for him shaving the hair from Charles Sprague's head with mechanical barber's clippers.

"How come you're doing that yourself?" Dan asked curiously.

"If you want something done *right,* you do it yourself!" Schramm snapped. Then he shrugged and smiled. "Truth is, Dan, I've always done it. Maybe 'cause I'm superstitious, or maybe 'cause it helps calm the jitters I always get before operating."

"After all these years you still get jittery?"

"Damned right! The brain's a delicate organ and doesn't like being violated. I still feel the same sense of awe and inadequacy every time I look at a live one."

Dan nodded understandingly.

"Well," Schramm said, removing the last tufts of hair from the nape of Sprague's neck, "the patient has now been scalped. Funny," he said, turning to Dan with an ironic smile. "A week ago I would have gladly tarred and feathered this guy and now . . ."

Dan gazed down at the elderly lawyer and grimaced slightly at his altered appearance. Shorn of hair, his scalp was large-pored, wrinkled, and sallow, and his ears looked disproportionately large. Dan couldn't help being reminded of photographs he had seen of Nazi concentration camp victims. He was glad Nick Sloan could not see his father now.

The next instant Dr. Cal Siemens, the anesthesiologist, came out of the operating room and asked, "Okay to bring him in now, Bill?"

"Yeah," said Schramm. "But positioning him for a posterior craniotomy is going to be a bitch. I want that table raised and jackknifed until his ass is practically hitting the ceiling and his head about chest-high. Which won't leave too much room for us to work, you know."

Siemens nodded. "Well, let's move him inside so I can intubate him."

In the operating room Sprague was temporarily strapped to the operating table while Siemens attached adhesive, disklike electrocardiogram leads to his limbs and inserted intravenous catheters into both hands. He then tested Sprague's level of consciousness, found him completely unresponsive, and slipped a plastic endotracheal tube into his throat without pretreatment with the usual sleep-producing and muscle-paralyzing drugs. Once the tube was in place, he connected its outer end to a pleated hose on the gas machine to feed oxygen into Sprague's lungs.

"How's his vitals?" Schramm asked Siemens.

"So-so. BP one sixty over ninety, pulse sixty, respirations ten."

Satisfied, Schramm stepped forward, donned rubber gloves, and using a double-edged razor blade attached to a surgical clamp, and special soap, proceeded to shave Sprague's pate clean. Following that, he disinfected it by swabbing on several coats of Betadine, an iodine-containing compound that stained the scalp clay-yellow.

"All right," Schramm finally said to the others in the room, "let's all lend a hand and roll him over in the prone position."

With all the tubes and wires attached to Sprague's body, the mere act of turning him onto his stomach proved no easy matter, but under Siemens's expert direction it was eventually done.

Schramm then left the operating room to scrub at the outside sink. Working the foot pedals that released the liquid soap and water, he cleaned the dirt from under his nails with an orange stick, soaped his hands liberally, and then, picking up a small brush, began the methodical scrub at the lateral aspect of his left wrist and thumb. Presently Dan joined him to discuss Sprague's case in private.

"Okay," Schramm said, "here's the story. He's suffered a massive cerebellar lesion—either infarction or hemorrhage. If it's an infarct, he's got a seventy- to eighty-percent chance of making it; if hemorrhage, it drops to twenty percent. But even if he does make it, there's no predicting how functional he'll be. He may end up more of an idiot than most lawyers."

"I understand," Dan said.

"I know *you* understand. Just make sure Sprague's people do! By the way, what's Nick Sloan's role in this? You call him in?"

"No. He's Sprague's doctor."

"His *doctor!*" Schramm exclaimed incredulously. "Sprague's suing him, for Chrissake! How can Sloan be his doctor?"

Dan hesitated. "It's a long story, Bill. But the tag line is that Sprague's withdrawing the suit."

"Well, that's good. Listen, anybody out there to sign the operative permit?"

Dan nodded. "I'll have Nick Sloan sign it."

"What? You need a relative or guardian."

"Sloan *is* a relative. In fact, he's Sprague's son."

The small brush slipped from the neurosurgeon's fingers and clinked into the sink. With his eyes bulging and his mouth agape, Schramm momentarily resembled a man being choked. "Dan—that's crazy!" he spluttered. "What the hell's going on here!"

"It's a long, *crazy* story. You sure you want to hear it now?"

"No!" Schramm hastily decided. "Later! Jesus knows I've got enough on my mind now. Just tell me one thing. Did you know any of this the last time we talked?"

"No, Bill, I swear. I only learned about it a few days ago."

"Okay, I believe you. Otherwise I'd wash my hands of more than mere dirt. Well," he said, staring suspiciously at Dan, "any more stunning revelations to tell me? I mean, Sprague's not a Jehovah's Witness—or Jehovah himself—is he?"

"No, Bill," Dan assured him, "nor is he on Medicaid."

Leaving Schramm shaking his head in consternation, Dan went to the doctors' lounge, where he found Nick and Angela talking quietly over coffee.

"How're you holding up?" Dan asked him.

Sloan shrugged. "Being a doctor sure as hell doesn't make it any easier."

"No," Dan said softly, "I imagine not. But Schramm's about ready to start, so we'll know what's going on soon."

Dan glanced at Angela holding tightly to Sloan's hand, smiled reassuringly at her, and left.

When Dan returned to the operating room, the surgical team was in its final stages of preparation. Sprague lay prone on the jackknifed operating table, his entire body, except for a patch of yellow-tinged scalp at the back of his skull, concealed by blue cloth drapes. His face rested on an air-filled, doughnut-shaped cushion with a special groove in it to accommodate the endotracheal tube, and the corneas of his eyes were protected from damage by Vaseline pads under a tight bandage. Cal Siemens sat on a stool to the left of Sprague's head, his anesthetic machine behind him. The scrub nurse stood next to him, her instruments neatly arranged on a special tray overlapping the operating table. Across from her stood a tall, brown-skinned neurosurgical resident by the name of Sharma, who had been called to assist Schramm.

Dan was introduced to Sharma, who, unable to shake hands in his sterile garb, bowed politely. Finally Schramm entered the room, donned fresh rubber gloves and gown, and strode to the head of the table.

"Thanks for coming, Vish," he said to the neurosurgical resident. "This is going to be a tough one."

Sharma nodded.

"Did you meet Dr. Lassiter?" Schramm asked.

Again Sharma nodded.

"Not only doesn't Vish talk much, he has a great pair of hands," Schramm explained to Dan. "Which is why I always ask for him."

"It's always a privilege to work with you, Dr. Schramm," Sharma said.

"Don't bullshit me, Vish," Schramm taunted. "A year out in practice and you'll be as temperamental with your residents as I am."

Above his mask, the skin around Sharma's eyes crinkled, but he said nothing.

"All right," Schramm said abruptly, "bring up the Bovie cautery and suction."

The circulating nurse wheeled the large cautery machine closer to the table and passed the sterile segment of the suction hose to the scrub nurse, who pinned it to the drapes below the operative site.

"Set Bovie to number-three current and test suction," Schramm ordered next.

The circulating nurse turned knobs and valves, and the suction tube gurgled.

Suddenly the room grew silent, except for the *kik kik kik* of the heart monitor, as Schramm took a deep, calming breath. Finally he turned to Dan, shrugged as if to say, Here goes, and ordered, "Knife and sponge."

The instrument nurse, her eyes peering intently above her mask, passed them to him promptly.

Holding the scalpel with a light touch, Schramm barely broke the skin above Sprague's occiput with its tip as he outlined the flap of scalp and underlying bone he intended to remove. A thin red trickle of blood followed in its swath. Then, gripping the scalpel more firmly, he sliced deep into the scalp while Sharma, holding the suction tube in one hand and a gauze sponge in the other, removed the blood spurting from small arteries or seeping from capillaries almost as rapidly as it appeared. The major bleeders were then cauterized and the minor ones controlled by a series of small plastic clips attached to the wound's edges. Finally the flap was undermined and reflected back, exposing the vellumlike, periosteal membrane overlying the occipital portion of the skull.

Suddenly Siemens said, "Trouble, Bill. Blood pressure's up to one eighty over one ten, pulse fifty, and respiration's getting slower and shallower."

"Shit!" Schramm groaned. "Go ahead and bag him until I get my first burr hole in and then hyperventilate him on the respirator. Watch his EKG, huh, Dan?"

"Slow but steady so far," Dan reported.

"Craniotome with number-two drill burr," Schramm requested with surprising calm. The scrub nurse nodded and hastily attached a blunt-headed burr to a foot-long cylindrical metal drill driven by compressed air and handed it to him.

Schramm aimed it at the upper right corner of exposed bone and pressed the start button. The craniotome emitted a high-pitched whine and raised a fine spray of bone dust as it ground out a nickel-sized hole in the occiput. Holding a large syringe in his hand, Sharma directed a steady stream of cold salt solution at the site to reduce the heat and dust generated by the drilling.

The skull was thinnest in this area, and Schramm withdrew the craniotome the instant he felt the slightest easing of resistance to indicate he was through the bony table. The burr hole he had made resembled an inverted cone whose apex impinged on the dural membrane protecting the base of the brain. Schramm then took a goosenecked rongeur, a strong forceps used to gouge out bone, and enlarged the hole until he could actually see the pearly white dura bulging up from the bottom of the cone.

With Sharma's nimble hands following his own with sponge-sticks, cautery, and sucker, Schramm stuck his finger through the burr hole and used it as a guide to pry off a fist-sized plate of bone with the rongeur. Underneath it lay the taut, glistening dural membrane covered by a network of engorged purplish blue veins.

"Pulse down to forty per minute and irregular," Dan announced.

Suddenly the operating room seemed electrified with tension as Sprague seemed to hover between the living and the dead.

"Want more mannitol?" Siemens asked.

"No, prayers! I'm opening the dura now," Schramm said, and after sinking an anchoring stitch into the membrane, made a four-inch-long incision in it with a scalpel. The moment the fibrous dura was rent, the lopsided cerebellar cortex bulged through it like wet dough rising.

"Jesus!" Schramm exclaimed. "Look at that pressure!

If it were any higher, his brain would jump across the table!" Then, after carefully examining the protruding, cross-striated tissue, he muttered, "I'll be damned! He hasn't hemorrhaged after all. Just infarcted a good hunk."

Dan moved closer to the table to take a look.

"Huh!" Schramm grunted after double-checking the finding. "One thing you learn in this business is to always expect the worst, so you can sometimes be pleasantly surprised. But how do you figure, this, Dan? It certainly isn't because the guy's lived right."

"Not him," Dan corrected. "You! *Saint* Schramm," he proclaimed, rolling his eyes.

Schramm shot him a sarcastic look and returned to work.

Two hours later, Schramm had successfully resected the infarcted portion of cerebellum, placed drains in the wound, and was ready to suture the dura. With Sprague still unconscious but now breathing on his own, he felt confident enough of the outcome to allow Dan to break the news to Sloan.

Taking his lead from Schramm, Dan was cautiously optimistic in his report. "Obviously it'll be quite a while before we can determine how successful the surgery's been," he concluded, "but so far the signs are good."

"You mean there might be permanent brain damage?" asked Angela with concern.

"More apt to be some slight physical impairment," Dan replied. "But he might even get by without that."

"Then he could practice law again?"

"Do you think he'd *want* to?" Sloan said in a soft voice. He waited for Dan to pour coffee from the metal urn and then faced him with a tormented look. "I . . . I almost killed him."

"Oh?" Dan uttered. "How do you figure that?"

"The symptoms were all there. I'm qualified in neurology. Yet I kept thinking it was inner-ear disease."

Dan took a sip of coffee, put the cup down, and began massaging the small of his back. "Are you trying to tell me you made a mistake, Nick?"

Chagrined, Sloan nodded.

"Well, how about that!" Dan said, regarding him with wry forbearance. "Because *you* missed the diagnosis, your father lost half his cerebellum. Which means he'll never be able to bust broncos or play the violin or pilot a rocket ship to the moon. Grounds for a malpractice suit if ever I heard one!"

Sloan stared, uncertain of his meaning at first, and then reluctantly broke into a grin. "Is that what's called rubbing it in?"

"No, it's called *begging* you to let go, Nick."

Sloan sighed. "I think I'm ready. Angela and I've been talking . . ."

"We're going to try Miami," she said. "Providing—"

"Providing I stick to medicine and leave the courts to her," Sloan explained.

"Sounds reasonable," Dan said. "How soon you planning to leave?"

"In another month or so. If my father can travel by then."

"He has to wake up first," Dan cautioned, "but he's getting there. Well, Nick," he said, rubbing his aching back again, "I'll miss our handball games, but I'm glad things are finally working out for you."

"Thanks, Dan. But not only am I leaving the courtroom work to Angela; I'm leaving you something, too."

"What's that?"

"The problem of what to do about bad doctors."

Wincing, Dan remarked, "How generous can you be?"

Sloan shrugged. "It's just a bequest of sorts. You don't have to accept it. But since you wield a lot of clout with the medical society, maybe you can do something."

"Maybe," Dan conceded. "Only I'll have to find a different approach from yours. I'm not the medical avenger type."

"Not yet, anyway. But—" Sloan smiled sardonically, "you never know. Oh, by the way, Nate Clineman's flying into town next week to visit dad. They're old friends. He's also in the process of organizing a multicenter drug-testing program and would appreciate talking to you while he's here."

"Sure. I'd like very much to meet with Nate and find out what he's up to these days." Suddenly Dan paused, trying to frame his next words tactfully.

Anticipating him, Sloan spared him the effort. "Feel free to ask Nate whatever you wish. I'll tell him I have no secrets from you."

Sprague's cardiac rhythm disturbances, a common but worrisome complication of extensive brain surgery, kept Dan on the surgical intensive care unit for the next twelve hours. By morning, however, Sprague's heartbeat had stabilized, and he could be weaned off the respirator. That evening he began to regain consciousness, and by the following morning he was fully alert.

Five days later, when he was making steady physical improvement but beginning to show the periodic disorientation and reversal of normal sleep pattern that were typical of the "intensive care unit syndrome," they transferred him to a private room where he could rest more comfortably.

When Dan came by to examine him the next evening, he found him much more lucid. As he was about to leave, the lawyer suddenly said, "Stay awhile and talk, Doctor, if you've got the time."

Delighted, Dan said, "I've got the time," and drew a chair up to the bedside.

A faint smile flickered over the patient's worn face. "I thought you'd feel that way. Knowing as much as you already do, you must have questions. Nick told me I could speak openly, and so I shall. What can I tell you?"

"Well, first," said Dan, his brain teeming with curiosity, "how did this—this working arrangement between you and your doctor-son get started?"

"How'd it start?" said Sprague wistfully, and in a slow voice, sometimes husky with emotion, the lawyer spoke so revealingly of its beginning that Dan seemed to witness the transformation of Charles R. Sprague from enigmatic scourge of the medical profession to all too fallible human being. "With a phone call from Nate Clineman informing me that my grown son, whom I had not seen or heard of since he was a year-old baby, was flying across the country to see me; would, in fact, be arriving the next day. Well, to me, that was an appalling prospect. It's hard to justify the way I felt, but back then the last thing in the world I wanted was any contact with anyone from my marriage. You see, Nick's mother had put me through such a degrading, devastating divorce—they weren't so easy to get in those days —that in one of the most heartless acts of my life I swore I'd never see her or my son again. So when I heard Nick was coming, my initial impulse was to refuse to receive him on such short notice. But when Nate told me of the hellish tragedy that had befallen my son and grandson. and how much Nick needed my help, what could I do? I saw him. And it was like seeing a younger version of myself. The way he walked, his mannerisms, even the troubled look in his eyes—it was myself all over again."

"When was this?" Dan asked.

"End of 1962 or thereabouts. I had established a lucrative law practice in Hartford at the time, but even then was beginning to experience my usual wanderlust and getting ready to move on. So Nick and I met and, after a few strained moments, talked all night. By morning it was settled. He was to become a doctor. I would pay all expenses, including financial support for Angela and the child. Nick helped out in my law office while trying to get into medical school, and we became very close during this time. So close, in fact, that when he finally got accepted at the University of Lausanne, I decided to go to Europe with him. I had an old friend heading the international law division of the Max Planck Institute and went to work with him."

"Why didn't Nick take Angela and their son with him?"

The question produced a pained look on the lawyer's face. "We talked about it. Even though I wasn't to meet Angela until years later, I've grown very fond of her. Very fond, indeed. But Nick said he was afraid to see Billy again; afraid it would make him lose control—throw him into such a vengeful, even violent, state that he couldn't possibly cope with his medical studies. He still loved Angela; of that I'm sure. But please keep in mind that his plan to get his M.D. degree and then specialize in medicolegal work was just getting under way and was all very tentative. Nick had grave doubts that he could last through four years of medical school and beyond. He was especially afraid of hurting Angela without intending to."

"In what way?"

"His moods were very unstable in those days. Up and down like a monkey in a tree. Nate Clineman was quite correct in diagnosing him as manic-depressive. Which in a strange but very real way made me feel even guiltier . . . You see," Sprague continued in response to Dan's questioning look, "I'm one myself. Oh, not overt. I'm not afflicted by the full-blown condition, just the tendency, and never needed medication for it. Yet the pattern of my life, my career, never practicing the same type of law in the same place for more than a few years, never laying down roots, is pretty good evidence of it. So it's quite likely Nick inherited the disorder from me. Then there was one further complication about taking Angela to Europe that I hesitate to go into."

"Up to you," said Dan, watching Sprague intently.

"Yes, of course," sighed the lawyer. "But you've already proved trustworthy. There's no hard evidence of this, but I have a powerful hunch that Nick did something violent the night he found out Billy's condition was hopeless. He's always refused to discuss that night with me or, to my knowledge, anybody else—with the possible exception of Nate Clineman."

"Angela worries about that, too," Dan said. "You don't think he actually killed anyone, do you?"

"Well, not Bauman, at any rate. Whether he killed

or injured some totally innocent party—in a fight, in a car wreck—I don't know. But whatever he did do, or came close to doing, haunted him enough that he was afraid to live with Angela until he had that dark side to his nature under control."

"Was he manic-depressive in medical school?"

"Very definitely in the beginning. It almost followed a seasonal pattern—worse in the late spring and fall. He nearly dropped out of medical school twice because of it. Then two very beneficial things happened. Nate Clineman decided that the data on lithium for the treatment of manic-depression looked good enough that, despite the ban existing on its medical use in several countries, Nick ought to go on it. Nate obtained a supply of the drug from a Danish doctor at the University of Aarhus and spent a month in Lausanne personally supervising the treatment until he hit on the proper dosage. That helped stabilize Nick's mood considerably. Then, during his clinical years at the University Hospital he became intensely interested in medicine—as if it were his natural calling. He graduated with top honors in several subjects and for a time seriously considered giving up his vendetta against Bauman and incompetents like him and devoting himself full-time to internal medicine."

"Why didn't he?"

Sprague smiled wryly. "He tried. But the more medicine he learned, the more malpractice he saw being committed. And each act, particularly if it harmed an infant or child, brought back bitter memories of Billy. Then his career took another ironic twist, changing its course but not its goal. While serving his internship in Los Angeles, Nick took care of a woman made paraplegic by totally botched back surgery. Moreover, her surgeon was notorious among his colleagues for doing too many disk operations and doing them badly. But as you might guess, the hospital's surgical conduct-and-review committee did nothing to discipline or even deter him." Sprague paused to gather breath. "Nick couldn't get the poor, crippled old woman out of his mind. So he talked me into taking her case. Then another mistreated patient came under his care, and that's how it started."

"So instead of going into medicolegal work, Nick decided to take full-time hospital positions to ferret out such cases?"

"More or less—although he had something more definitive in mind. Not *all* acts of malpractice are committed by quacks and butchers, you know. Occasionally, though rarely, a good doctor commits one too. What Nick really wanted was to identify and eliminate the small number of incorrigibly bad doctors. And to do that took more than hearsay. He felt he had to have firsthand knowledge, absolute proof, of their incompetence before acting against them. And that—as you well know—could best be obtained through a hospital teaching position."

"Yes," Dan said reproachfully, "I *do* know. It's still a point of contention between us."

Sprague shrugged. "Take Carl Gormann, for instance —who incidentally just declared bankruptcy after the jury awarded Darryl Harrison the full amount we asked in damages. From what I know of him, I wouldn't consider Gormann an inherently corrupt or evil man. Yet he committed one of the most flagrant acts of malpractice I've ever seen. Any idea why?"

Dan pondered and shook his head.

"Because you—meaning the medical profession—let him. You placed no real limits on how far he could go with his patients."

"But other hospitals don't operate that way. Many— possibly most—have much more effective disciplinary committees."

"Many do," Sprague conceded. "Especially in Los Angeles, Denver, and Detroit," he added with a faint smile. "But the point is this. Nick and I concluded a long time ago that there were basically only two types of doctors: those who *know* what they don't know, and those who *don't know* what they don't know." With his voice hoarsening to a whisper, Sprague paused to sip water.

"Maybe that's a bit too simplistic for you, Doctor," he went on, "but hear me out. The first type, mediocre as many might be, are reasonably safe. They only handle the simple cases and refer the difficult ones to more competent colleagues. I wouldn't want one of them treating me for some life-threatening disease but I wouldn't mind seeing him for a cold. The second type, though—of which Gormann is a prime example—represents an out-and-out hazard. If ever the charge can be fairly leveled that some doctors like to play God, then it applies almost exclusively to this type. Their incredible arrogance makes them believe that if they can't cure a particular patient, nobody can!"

Dan sighed and nodded. "I know a doctor like that. Several, actually, but one who's a particular thorn in my side."

"We have them in the legal profession too." Sprague paused a long time before he spoke again. "You know, Dr. Lassiter, even though I've been rendered hairless and partially brainless, I'm glad it's finally brought Nick to his senses. He and Angela deserve another chance at a normal life. And frankly, so do I. You see, even before I was felled by my stroke, I was already a very tired, old man."

"Yet you kept going—and performed brilliantly!"

"Yes," sighed Sprague, "I kept going, for Nick's sake and, in a curious sort of way, for the medical profession's sake as well."

"I could argue about that," Dan declared.

Sprague smiled tolerantly. "I'm certain you could. And I'd be well versed in most of the arguments you'd use. But except for the threat of a malpractice suit, what else protects the public from bad doctors? What other deterrent would be nearly as effective?"

"I can think of one. In fact, it's an idea I've wanted to discuss with you for some time. I was even on the verge of making an appointment for that very purpose before things got out of hand. Simply stated, my proposal is this: Why doesn't the medical profession convert to the military system of justice; make the punishment of bad doctors commensurate with their misdeeds?"

"Interesting concept," Sprague murmured, "provided you realize that the military code of justice is far from perfect."

"So I found out," Dan said. "I was an officer in Korea."

"And I was with the Judge Advocate General's Corps for four years." Sprague chuckled. "Might've stayed longer if I hadn't tried to improve on the way they did things. Spent six months on a long, scholarly recommendation for modernizing the court-martial system so that its primary purpose would be to provide justice for the accused, rather than 'good military order and discipline,' as they put it. Caused quite a stir at the time."

"In what way?" asked Dan.

"Well, you know how military justice used to work. A soldier wasn't court-martialed unless his base commander recommended it. The same CO then chooses a panel of judges from among his subordinates—which is like having a civilian jury composed entirely of prosecuting attorneys. So I proposed mobile courts-martial, bringing in panels of officers from bases not under the jurisdiction of the local commander. But most of the commanders were MacArthur-type war heroes who didn't like having their authority diminished. So the upshot was that my report was shelved and so was I. I got out and went back to civilian practice."

"But do you think something similar to the court-martial system could work for doctors? I mean, if punishment for poor medical practice were meted out by a panel of physicians, picked for their outstanding credentials, leaving awards for damages to arbitration or the courts?"

"If the members of such a panel were from another community than the doctor under review, I think it could. Hell, one study I know of indicated that as many as two million medically induced injuries—'potentially

271

compensable events' we call them—occur in this country annually. And thirty-five percent of those are due to negligence on the part of doctors or hospital personnel. So the deterrent effect of a malpractice suit is obviously minimal when you're dealing with those kinds of figures."

"So what's the solution?"

Sprague shrugged. "Well, your idea of impartial medical tribunals is one—in fact, the only one that'll give the doctors any say in the matter. Otherwise your colleagues will simply have to abide by the golden rule: Those with the gold make the rules!"

"Meaning government control?"

"Exactly. Something similar is already happening with the closed-panel-versus-open-panel debate over union-sponsored prepaid legal-aid plans. Just as the union bosses want some say in deciding what lawyers their members consult, to make sure they're sympathetic and don't cost them a bundle, the HEW bureaucrats want the same thing. Once national health insurance is enacted, they'll get it, too. If a given physician fails to pass their audit because he's practicing poor medicine or overbilling for his services, they'll simply suspend payment to him until he straightens out."

"But all that'll do is lower the cost of health care, not improve its quality," Dan protested.

"Probably, which is why your idea is better. But will doctors listen while there's still time?"

"They might—if they heard it from you."

"Me?" Sprague exclaimed. "Why in the world would I want to solve their problems after all the abuse they've heaped on me?"

"Because you owe them—at least a few of them—your life."

Sprague stared hard at him. "Dr. Lassiter, possibly because I'm missing part of my brain, I find that a difficult argument to refute. All right," he sighed, "put some of your ideas down on paper and we'll go over them tomorrow."

"One last question," Dan added. "How did you get your air force 201 file lifted?"

Sprague grinned. "That was a cinch. I had a friend of mine in air force intelligence investigate me for alleged subversive activities. The file was sent to him in Heidelberg for review, and being a careless sort, he somehow misplaced it."

Dan shook his head in wonder. "I thought destroying official government documents was illegal?"

"I thought so, too, before Ford pardoned Nixon."

Toward the end of the week Dan had dinner with Nate Clineman, hoping Nate might fill in the few remaining gaps in his knowledge of Nick Sloan's strange metamorphosis from lawyer to doctor.

Clineman was a dapper man in his late fifties with flowing white hair, a trim beard, and piercing blue eyes that seemed to snap with intelligence whenever his brain was unusually active.

"You know, Dan," he began, "it's a secret I've kept locked inside me for so long that even now, after all that's happened, I find it hard to talk about. Anyway, the evening Nick learned the truth about Billy's condition, he broke into Bauman's canyonside house to kill him. But Bauman never came home that night. So the next afternoon Nick trailed him as he left his office, intending to run him off the road on his way home. But Bauman surprised him again by driving to keep an appointment with me, since I was treating him for depression. Then the damnedest thing happened. Instead of following Bauman as he left my office, Nick walked in and asked to see me. Told me the whole tragic story. So I took him on as a patient. But despite my best efforts I couldn't get him to file a malpractice suit against Bauman or relent in his determination to destroy the man. Nor could I warn Bauman without violating patient confidentiality—which put me in a hell of a bind. Moreover, it became increasingly apparent that Nick had manic-depressive tendencies and was becoming more manic—and murderous—with each passing day. So in desperation I tried another approach—one carefully constructed to incorporate Nick's respect for the law with his compelling need for revenge. I suggested he go to medical school and then specialize in medicolegal cases, thereby protecting the public from not merely one bad doctor but many. This intrigued him—enough so that he became less obsessed with Bauman. But he lacked the money to finance it until I put him in contact with his father, whom I happened to have known at Yale. So in 1964 Nick applied to and was accepted at the University of Lausanne, and his father took a post at the Max Planck Institute to be near him. The rest of the story you know."

"Yes," Dan said. "And I think it was a brilliant stroke on your part to get him to go to medical school. But once he got started on his medical vendetta in earnest, couldn't you do anything to stop him?"

"I tried. Believe me, I tried innumerable times, but I simply couldn't dissuade him. Maybe the reason I couldn't was because I was never sure in my own mind that he was wrong."

"But he *was* wrong!"

Clineman gestured futilely. "You might well be right, Dan. But the truth is, I'm still unsure. There are a lot of bad psychiatrists, you know. Many more than bad internists. And I know very few of my colleagues who are doing much to stop them. What Nick Sloan did was certainly unorthodox, and I'm glad he's given it up, but to this day I don't honestly know if it was wrong."

# 28

When Dan got to his office early the next morning to tackle a week's backlog of paperwork, he felt more relaxed and rested than he had in months—a mood that lasted all of one hour. At eight A.M. Jim Hermanson phoned and insisted on seeing him as soon as possible.

Almost pleadingly Dan asked, "Can't Spencer Walt handle it?"

"Afraid not, Dr. Lassiter," Hermanson stated. "This one requires your personal touch."

"All right, Jim," Dan said reluctantly. "But I can only spare you a few minutes. How fast can you get up here?"

"About as fast as it takes you to hang up the phone."

Dan steeled himself to hear all about the house staff's latest hassle with Dr. Peter Trombley. But what Hermanson ended up telling him far exceeded anything Dan had expected or could tolerate.

"Remember that patient of Trombley's, Harry Jukes, I asked you to see a month or so ago?" Hermanson began. "The one with severe heart failure and high enzyme levels that Trombley thought had hepatitis and we thought different?"

Dan nodded. "I remember him very well."

"Then you'll remember how Trombley refused to consider our diagnosis of acute pulmonary embolism until you stepped in and let us give the guy a trial on heparin."

"Yeah. How's he doing?"

"He did great in the hospital. His breathing improved dramatically, his heart failure cleared, and his enzyme levels returned to normal. Even his lung scan was highly suggestive of pulmonary emboli, though not conclusive, as they seldom are. So the house staff taking care of him felt pretty good about it. That is, until he was re-admitted two nights ago worse than before."

"How come? Did he quit taking his oral anticoagulants?"

"No, he didn't quit. Trombley never prescribed any for him when he left the hospital. Says he wasn't convinced of our diagnosis, so why run the risk of bleeding."

"I see," Dan said, scowling. "Well, he's back on heparin now, isn't he?"

"No, he isn't."

"Why not?"

"Because you don't anticoagulate a corpse! He died twelve hours after admission. Trombley never would let us restart heparin."

Dan paled with anger. "Did you get an autopsy?"

"Yeah, we did—despite Trombley's interference. Fortunately, the guy's daughter is a nurse and wanted to know."

"And what'd it show?"

"Multiple pulmonary emboli. That was the main and *only* cause of death."

"Huh!" Dan grunted disgustedly. "That's really a damned disgrace! Make sure to send his chart to the medical conduct-and-review committee."

"Don't worry, I will."

"And thanks for telling me," said Dan, rising from his chair and hoping Hermanson would follow.

"There's more," Hermanson said grimly.

"On Trombley?"

The chief resident nodded.

"Go on," Dan sighed, sitting back down.

"The other patient of Trombley's I asked you to see—the guy who developed respiratory arrest after a shot of morphine and didn't get straightened out until we treated him for myxedema. Well, he's not doing so hot either."

"Oh, Jesus!" Dan groaned. "Don't tell me Trombley stopped the thyroid on him?"

"Not exactly. But since the guy improved so much on the IV thyroxine we gave him, Trombley decided to taper the dose to see if he really needed it. He's now on one-quarter grain."

"Good Christ! Is he into faith healing or something? Doesn't he know a destroyed thyroid gland never regenerates?"

Hermanson shrugged. "Anyway, the guy's no dummy. He wants you to see him again—only Trombley hasn't written the consult yet."

"Does the patient know that?"

"Nope. Trombley's been telling him you're too busy. Want me to turn that case over to the medical conduct-and-review committee too—before the autopsy?"

"No, I'll take care of it right away. What room's he in?"

"1202. And Dr. Trombley? Do you intend to take care of him, too?"

Dan slumped, head down, seething in silence for a long moment. Then he looked up at Hermanson and said, "Are you trying to tell me Trombley doesn't belong in the medical profession?"

"Dr. Lassiter, you're amazing. You just read my mind."

"Yeah? Well, to show you it's no fluke, let me read your next thought, too: When the hell am I going to use my position around here to do something about him?"

"Like I said, you're amazing!"

"Well, show's over for today. I'll let you know what I decide."

"In other words, don't call you, you'll call me?"

"Not quite. I've somebody else in mind to call. You know, Jim, in some states a doctor is liable, himself, if he sees malpractice and doesn't report it."

"Makes sense."

"Sure. It also makes every doctor the judge of every other doctor. You residents think you have it tough—having to take care of patients with an attending man always looking over your shoulder. Well, maybe that's the way it's going to be for all of us from now on."

Hermanson's eyebrows lifted. "Yeah, I see what you mean. But getting back to Trombley—"

"No." Dan cut him off. "I've got some hard thinking to do about him—alone. So, if you'll excuse me . . ."

"Sure, Dr. Lassiter," said Hermanson, rising abruptly and striding out of the office.

Sighing deeply, Dan moved to the windows, trying to decide between two opposing courses of action: the first, to let the medical conduct-and-review committee deal with Peter Trombley, despite the fact that its chairman, Will Renton, was a close friend of his and might mute the charges against him; the second, much more drastic and definitive. He remembered his statement to Nick Sloan that he wasn't the medical avenger type and Sloan's prophetic reply: "Not yet, anyway."

Well, if Sloan's such a good prophet, he ought to be honored while he's still around, Dan thought wryly. Briefly he reconsidered, trying to recall and heed his own arguments against such a precipitous step, but a vivid image of Harry Jukes expressing his gratitude to him for a second chance at life kept intruding on his thoughts.

Finally deciding further procrastination was futile, Dan returned to his desk, buzzed his secretary, and told her to get Dr. Nicholas Sloan on the phone.

"Hello, Nick," he said a moment later. "Look, I wonder if I could ask you a favor—a couple of favors really. The first is for you and Angela to have dinner with me tonight."

"Sure," Sloan said. "We've been meaning to do that anyway. What's the second?"

"You might not like this, but the second is for Angela to delay her departure for Miami a few months."

"What for?"

"Because there's one more malpractice case I'd like her to take on. Involves a doctor on my staff named Trombley. Angela already knows something about him, and I'll make sure she gets the referral."

There was a long pause on the other end of the line. Finally, Sloan said, "Dan, are you sure you've thought this through carefully?"

"You're not going to try and talk me out of it, are you?"

"No," Sloan said softly. "But I hope you realize that's how I—"

"Don't say it," Dan cut him off. "I know, I know . . ."

## ABOUT THE AUTHOR

Physician, writer, teacher—MARSHALL GOLDBERG is professor of medicine at Michigan State University College of Human Medicine and chief of endocrinology at Hurley Medical Center in Flint, Michigan. He was recipient of the Outstanding Teacher Award at Michigan State College of Human Medicine in 1972, and a past president of the Michigan Association for Medical Education. A close personal friend of Mayor Charles Evers of Fayette, Mississippi, Dr. Goldberg won the NAACP Humanitarian Award in 1974 for instituting a project which helped provide medical care for Fayette, and he serves on the board of directors of the Medgar Evers Foundation. His previous novels are *The Karamanov Equations, The Anatomy Lesson*—the first in the Dr. Daniel Lassiter series and a "cult" book among medical students—and *Critical List. Critical List,* incorporating portions of *Skeletons,* was produced as a television mini-series by Mary Tyler Moore Enterprises and aired by NBC in the fall of 1978. *The Anatomy Lesson* is currently in production as MTM's first feature-length motion picture. In addition to publishing numerous articles in medical journals and popular magazines, Dr. Goldberg appears weekly on CTV's *Canada A.M.* as its resident health expert. He is currently working on the fourth novel in the Lassiter series, tentatively entitled *Sensorium.*

A Special Preview of
the entertaining opening pages of
the provocative new novel by
the author of ASPEN

# WHY NOT EVERYTHING
## by
## Burt Hirschfeld

"Hirschfeld's romp of a book is funny, sad, pointed,
crazy in the happiest sense."

*Publishers Weekly*

Happy endings are out of style.

So says Walter and Walter knows about such meaningful matters. Walter, my husband, is a man of sober single-mindedness, a trait I greatly admired when first we met.

Walter is a committed literary person. That is to say, he reads a great deal, informing his brain with large chunks of knowledge, common and extraordinary. Walter reads history, biography, novels, whodunits, Screw magazine, memoirs, Commentary; whatever comes his way. Walter belongs to seven book clubs, subscribes to twenty-seven periodicals, including the Times Literary Supplement, The New York Review of Books, even Rolling Stone; and Walter loathes rock music. If those big-money quiz shows were still on TV, Walter could win a fortune. And, boy oh boy, could we use the cash.

Personally I prefer movies. Especially the kind they don't make anymore. Old-fashioned pictures with fadeouts, dissolves, halos of light around the faces of the leading women. I like my movie stars to look like movie stars, special, that is. Larger than life, an aristocracy of beauty and talent. What I enjoy most in movies is plenty of kissing, poetic declarations of love and eternal fealty. Also fireworks going off instead of naked men and women fooling around with each other.

Blue movies put lots of strange and unsettling ideas into my head. That makes me nervous. It becomes hard for me to concentrate, harder still to get to sleep at night. Besides, those old pictures always had happy endings, and that's what the world needs more of these days.

Which brings us back to Walter. Walter is a

practical man. He insists sad endings are inevitable and realistic, even if painful. True to life is the way Walter likes his movies, plays and books. "Most people never get what they want," he is fond of saying. I say, "Why shouldn't people get what they want?" Why shouldn't I? Living happily ever after strikes me as a pretty good idea.

Here I am, reasonably pretty. Attractive, at least. Well, I used to be. What I've got is an okay face. My eyes are exotic, sort of. Not exactly Chinese, but heading in that direction. My skin is on the pale side and I have to be careful in the sun and about the kind of makeup I wear. Not that I've been using it often lately. As for my mouth, it doesn't amount to much. Too wide, too much lip. I've always admired girls with thin lips, cool and neat. The kind of mouth Cici Willigan has, a perfect mouth. And then there's my hair, kind of wiry and rebellious. There are times when I let my hair go its own way much of the time. As for my figure, it's good enough. Not what you'd call petite, except in the chest area, but slender, and with a shape. Men used to look at me a lot. Not as much as they looked at Cici, of course, but they looked. Some of them. Some of the time.

I perceived myself as an incomplete puzzle, parts scattered all around. Put them all together and—voilà! key elements still were missing

*Give me back my parts! . . .*

For too many years I had labored in an arid garden of self-pity that gave up weeds of discouragement in return. A West Side zombie was what I'd become, jailed by bars of my own making. A rising tide of unfocused anger left me flushed, trembling, more and more out of touch with myself and the real world. I wanted desperately to take charge of my life. Change it at least. To get a firm hold on one small segment that would belong only to me. Was that so unreasonable? Was it wrong to do what I wanted to do?

I gave it a great deal of thought and came up with a solution, which I presented to Walter. "I think we should leave the city," I told him one evening.

"Leave the city." Walter had a tendency to repeat what I said.

"Yes. It's awful, living here."

"Where would you like to live?"

"In the suburbs. Long Island, maybe. Or Connecticut. We could buy a house," I ended with an anxious rush.

"Have you forgotten," Walter replied slowly, "I'm out of work?"

I gave that one up and thought about the problem some more. And discovered another answer to my unsettled state and presented it to Walter the following week.

"What would you say if I told you I want to have another baby?" I didn't really mean it. I was all for zero population growth, at least in my own case.

He put aside the book he was reading, assessed me gravely. He frowned. In horror, I assumed. I noticed Walter was showing more gray at the temples. If anything, he had become better looking as he grew older. Not that Walter was old, far from it. Just sliding without protest into middle age.

"Another baby?" he said. "You don't mean it."

"Stevie is almost five years old. Wouldn't it be nice ... ?"

He shook his head regretfully. "I'm out of work, remember."

Walter's logic was sturdy and unshakable. I needed another, a much sounder plan. It took nearly three weeks of hard thinking before I came up with one.

It was a marvelous idea. Exciting, stimulating, and scared me half to death. I began to quiver and was unable to get warm.

I would get a job. Go to work. Make a career. What an awful idea. I was jumpy, suspicious, exceedingly afraid of the Demanding Demons that I was about to unleash. It was a personalized fear, like the fear of being punished, a night fear trodding heavily into my consciousness. This beast could destroy me.

I found Walter behind the *Collected Poems* of James Wright. I stood erect and cleared my throat, waited for him to pay attention.

"Yes?" he said eventually.

"Suppose I told you I wanted to go back to work?"

"Go back to work."

"Get a job."

"Get a job—you?"

A convulsive shock broke over me. I really meant it. Really wanted to find a job, purposeful and productive work, create a special place for myself in this world. I braced myself for Walter's response, afraid he might mock me, even laugh out loud. Not Walter, that wasn't his way. His eyes glinted and his jaw seemed to square itself, like some terrific TV hero.

"Soon," he said evenly, "I'll be back at work."

No matter what I suggested, it seemed to turn Walter's thoughts back to his own employment situation. Obviously, in his mind, we were inexorably linked up so that any movement at one end of the chain gave off a sour clunking at the other.

Walter had been out of work for nearly a year. We lived off unemployment insurance, food stamps, and had used up almost all of our savings. Not to mention my meager emotional reserves.

"One day runs into another," I said. "It's as if I exist in a fog. What happened to the Libby I once was? I want to do something with my life."

"After six years of marriage, of not working, one does not simply go into the marketplace and announce one's availability. Times change. Skills once in demand no longer are. A new generation of workers is on the scene."

"It can't hurt if I try."

"Who will take care of our son?"

"A housekeeper."

"A good housekeeper will cost more than you're likely to earn."

That sent a chill through me. "There's always day care."

"Not for my son."

"Lots of working mothers . . ."

"I don't think so."

"We could put Steven back in nursery school. Next fall he'll enter kindergarten and—"

"The afternoons. That leaves the afternoons."

"I'll arrange it, Walter."

"I must be frank, I believe you'd be wasting your time."

Had he given his assent? My hopes rose. "Oh, I really need to go to work, to accomplish something, something that's mine alone." I began to weep.

Walter changed his position. Any overt display of emotion made him uneasy. He assumed a wise expression and delivered his all-purpose explanation for my loss of control. "You must be premenstrual."

I gagged on my resentment. "That's not it."

"Check your calendar."

"I already did."

"Then you must be coming down with something."

You bet. A bad case of depression and defeat. "I'm fine," I lied.

"Take two aspirin."

"I'll be all right."

"People don't cry when they're all right."

He brought me two aspirin, one Valium, and a glass of water. The water had a sickly gray cast to it.

"Would you like me to take your temperature?"

"No, thank you."

He kept insisting until I agreed to a trade-off:

I'd get into bed and he'd bring me a cup of hot tea. He sat on the foot of the bed, not wanting to contract my disease, and read to me out of James Wright. Poetry couldn't fix what ailed me. I was tripping along a narrow line searching for dignity, self-respect, tilting crazily toward disaster, at the same time picking at the bare bones of my thoughts. What would it be like to have a job again? To do good work again? To know that somebody depended on me and was willing to pay for what I did, believing that what I contributed was mine alone and special. That made me feel good. Although I knew damn well nobody in his right mind was going to hire me. That's when the shivering started all over again.

The next morning Stevie woke me, yelling that his bed was wet. Stevie, beautiful fruit of my womb, my hope for the future, a four-year-old nag. A raucous reminder of my maternal shortcomings. Okay, kid, you peed in your bed, you can lie in it and suck your thumb. Oh, the guilt ...

Stevie's relationship with his thumb played havoc with Walter's emotional stability. Walter gave no credence to the sucking instinct or other forms of oral gratification.

"You know what it means?" Walter couldn't bear to give the sucking a name.

"What?" I replied with assumed innocence. There was in me, you see, a niggling quality of character which I detested. Oh, I understood Walter's attitude very well. He perceived the pernicious traces of faggotry in every suck in the same way Tailgunner Joe McCarthy used to see Bolsheviks in every federal closet.

"What's wrong with you?" Walter said it mildly, in complete control of his emotions.

Only two things, I almost answered. My fears and my anxieties. Otherwise mark me down as being in tip-top condition. That comes from the eminent Dr. Xavier D. C. Kiernan, M.D., Ph.D. Former seminarian, former authority on urban affairs, former instructor in Latin at Fordham University. Kiernan, one of the world's foremost dispensers of advice, fancies himself as a laureate among shrinks when what he really is is greatly full of shit. It took many, many painful and expensive sessions for me to discover that Xavier D. C. Kiernan knows very little about human people.

Question: If I'm so smart, why do I feel so bad?

Next to me, Walter stirred grumpily. Why grumpily, you wonder. When it comes to body language, Walter is a linguist. When it comes to verbal communication, however, Walter suffers from emotional lockjaw. All Walter's feelings have been deposited in a well-guarded cerebral vault. Safety first, and very little interest paid.

"Steven is crying."

"I know."

"You should do something about it."

You do something about it, I wanted to say. Just one morning, you get up first. You make the coffee. You squeeze those damned oranges. You go to Stevie, peel off those clammy, smelly pajamas. Instead I said, "I'll take care of it." Which was kind of funny since I didn't feel capable of taking care of anything. But why let on?

I opened the drapes and sneaked a look outside. The bright sunlight made all the pollutants in the air dance and sparkle, and in the distance the skyline seemed to shimmer. On such a fine morning, a right-minded wife and mother should wake up feeling good. Full of the old get-up-and-go. Instead I felt like a lost and lonely little girl. I doubted I could make it all the way through my life and was terrified by the awful possibility that I might.

"Ah." Walter had the covers up to his chin and his eyes were closed. "What a nice day."

I put on an old flannel robe but it didn't help at all. I was still cold.

"A good day to take Steven to the playground."

Playgrounds and playpens. I'm troubled by anything with bars. "I'll see." I went into the bathroom.

Walter opened his eyes when I came back into the bedroom. "You're old enough to shut the door," he said, right on schedule. Walter believes in lofty principles by which to live, beauty in all things, and privacy in the john. The splash of my pee sets Walter on edge, relatively speaking, that is.

"Next time." I gave him my most conciliatory smile and pulled on my old lavender sweater with the big C.C.N.Y. on it. There were holes in the elbows and the cuffs were frayed, but it was strung with good memories and kept me warm. A really nice sweater.

"You didn't flush."

If it weren't for Walter, how could I get along? I went back into the john and flushed. When I reappeared, Walter nodded his approval.

"You really should take Steven to the park."

"I have a very low opinion of Central Park."

"It's becoming a phobia."

"You may be right."

"Of course, I'm right. You're afraid."

"Afraid, yes. I admit it."

"There's nothing to be afraid of."

"Just muggers, purse-snatchers, rapists . . ."

"Don't exaggerate. It's safe enough during the day."

"That's how much you know."

Walter sat up and tugged at his T-shirt, which had gathered under his armpits. "What are you trying to say?"

"Last time out some weirdo flashed his pride-and-joy at me."

"His *what?*"

"His ding-dong."

"His penis?"

"That's the word, Walter."

"Is that your idea of a joke?"

"Aired it out and played rub-a-dub-dub . . ."

"In Central Park?"

"In broad daylight so nobody could miss anything."

"In the playground?"

"That was his game."

"What did you do?"

"Do! I didn't do anything. Did you expect me to lend a hand?"

"You could have left."

"I couldn't move. I was paralyzed with fright. The sonofabitch watched me every minute."

"Watched you?"

"Watched me watching him."

"You watched him do it?"

"There was a certain fascination."

"I don't understand you."

"A thing like that can ruin all your fantasies."

"Fantasies. Are you saying you fantasize about things like that?"

"Well, not exactly like that."

"I don't understand you."

"That's what Dr. Kiernan says."

End of discussion. Walter, the great reader, didn't read Freud. He didn't believe in psychiatry. I wasn't sure I did, either. But what else was there?

It required a massive effort on my part not to respond to Stevie's continuing howls, but I managed it. In the kitchen, I made coffee. It was flavored with mother's guilt. Or was it that I simply made lousy coffee?

I was halfway through that first cup when Walter appeared in the doorway. He wore only his underwear and a look of disapproval.

Walter walked into the kitchen, his Fruit of the Loom ass clenched and hardly moving. There was a time when I believed Walter had the most beautiful ass in the world. Either his ass had changed a lot or I had. . . .

Picture me. Huddled up in the lower playground envying Stevie the sand, and shivering. Asking the same old question—What Is Going to Become of Me?

Take a peek at my past glories. Most Likely to Succeed in my class at the Bronx High School of Science; you have to be pretty bright just to get into that place. Magna Cum Laude at City College; a major in math, a minor in psych. Plus courses here and courses there, taken out of sincere intellectual interest or to fill in empty spots in my social life, which were many.

Beginning in my second year in high school, I held a variety of jobs. At night, on weekends, on holidays, summers, piling up a wide and somewhat disconnected experience. There must have been a hundred jobs. Some paid well and seemed to promise an unlimited future. Others were ordinary and offered nothing beyond a small paycheck.

Taken in total, it all looked good. Even now it looks good. A background that must inevitably lead to Success. Status. Riches, even. Except it didn't work that way. From High Potential, I had slipped steeply down to Emotional Loser, your everyday West Side schlepp. What happened? Who did it to me? Where did I go wrong?

Why?

Please, God, show me the road back.

A job was the answer. Plunge into some rewarding work. At least a job that paid well. After all, Walter was still without gainful employment and showed no signs of altering the situation. Walter, who had the hots for the printed word like nobody I'd ever known. Not to mention an M.A. from Columbia and a Ph.D. from the University of Chicago, no less. Walter, who had been without a job for the full gestation period, was overdue.

All that was getting born was my disgust and dismay. Walter was getting on my nerves. Do you think I should have left him? Just split with Stevie?

If I really had the nerve, I'd've left them both. Together. That would certainly have made a serious dent in Walter's reading time. Instead, I hung around and took it.

Unemployment insurance, our savings, food stamps; that's what we lived on. Also an occasional loan from Walter's brother, Roger, a completely and utterly despicable, but rich, human being. We also borrowed on Walter's life insurance. Not much; Walter owned only enough insurance to get him a decent burial. Then there were Sybil's CARE packages, which helped in an odd way. Sybil Markson was my mother, but more of Sybil later.

"Libby Pepper!"

I jumped up. Like a sybaritic schoolgirl caught in the midst of some shameful act. Afraid I'd come under attack, I took up a vaguely defensive stance, ready to fight or run. Preferably run.

"Libby, it's been so long!"

Accusation; I was ashamed, anxious to make amends, wishing I had acted in a more considerate fashion. I squinted through the polluted air at the woman who confronted me. The Manhattan vapors cleared long enough for me to make out her features. That *face*. That glorious, unforgettable, perfect face. Carole Cynthia Willigan.

"Cici!" I took an uncertain step in her direction.

She smiled indulgently. "Dear Libby."

Through grade school, high school, even unto that Gothic enclave on Convent Avenue, Cici Willigan had been my dearest, closest, most intimate friend. My only friend, come to think of it. In concert, we had plotted grand strategies meant to carry us to victory over our enemies, as well as other dramatic and rare accomplishments. We had reveled in anticipatory joy over the superb love affairs that would come our way with handsome and tireless sexual adventurers. Not to mention marriages to shamefully rich merchant princes.

"Cici!" I flung myself at her.

"Libby!" She clasped me to her bosom.

She felt great. She smelled great. She let go of me before I was ready to let go of her.

"Four years, Libby. For shame."

"You're right." Boy, did she look terrific.

"You could have phoned, Libby. . . ."

"You're right." A telephone works both ways. Why hadn't she called me? I didn't dare ask.

"I thought about you often, Libby. Wondered what happened to you."

"The usual stuff."

"There was nothing *usual* about the Libby I knew. I'll bet you have your own business by now, rich and incredibly successful. I've been published, you know."

I knew, I knew. All those articles in *Cosmo* and *New York* magazine. "You are a beautiful writer, Cici."

"What kind of work are you doing, Libby? I've got a piece coming up in the Sunday *Times* magazine next week."

"That's fantastic. I—"

"All this time, and you never called even once."

I apologized.

"I understand," she said. "Life fills up. It can become overwhelming. There are just so many hours in a day, days in a week. . . . Good friends should not be apart so much. It isn't right."

"Not right at all."

She sure looked good. She'd always looked good, of course. But not this good. By some magic trick she'd acquired the face of a *Vogue* model and the body of a Hollywood sex kitten. She looked good enough to eat. At once I felt perverted, grotesque, depressed by the dirtiness of my mind. It occurred to me that I had forgotten to comb my hair.

"Still not wearing makeup," Cici said.

"You're not wearing a bra." I blushed and

took in those tight pink hot pants, thigh-high French leather boots, and a lot of flashy rings on her lovely, tapered fingers. Oh, how I envied her those fingers.

"The natural look," she said. "That was always Libby's way."

I felt frumpier than usual.

"The twins," Cici said, with a gesture.

I peered around her. There stood a pair of neat and beautiful miniatures of Cici, watchful, silent, polite. The twins.

"Scottie and Brucie."

One after the other, they offered clean hands in a manly handshake. How Nice to Meet You, each of them said. Mother's Told Us All about You, they said. Compared to the twins, Stevie looked like a savage. "Nice boys," I said, and maneuvered to screen off Stevie from view.

"I," Cici was saying, "am ticketed for lunch with Bella. Do you know Bella? Of course you do. At Tavern on the Green. A series of interviews is what I'm up to. With women who count. The out-front women, breaking new ground for us all, if you know what I mean."

I didn't know what she was talking about, but I wasn't going to say so.

"*Good Housekeeping* is interested," Cici said. "None of your common women's crap shit, these are to be straight-from-the-shoulder pieces. Tell it like it is. Hit 'em where they live. Next week it's Betty, the week after, Gloria. Maybe I can do a story about your career, Libby. From Grand Concourse to Grande Dame. That has a certain ring, don't you think? We must talk about it. The Movement, the Movement, my true passion. What are we if not sisters in blood, tears and oppression?"

I felt as if I were a couple of paragraphs behind, on a cerebral treadmill with no chance to catch up. I didn't have a career. . . .

"Cici . . ."

"Poor Hedda," Cici said.

"Hedda?"

"Hedda is my housekeeper, Hedda Svenson. Beautiful woman but not reliable. Without a sense of time. Do keep an eye on the twins for me, Libby, until Hedda shows. Won't be more than a few minutes. Is that your son over there? Looks a great deal like you, Libby. Darling, you and—what's his name?—your husband, must come to dinner. One night next week, I insist. Let's say seven-thirty on Wednesday. No, that will never do. Next week is a bitch of a week. The week after. Tuesdays are out, all those gallery openings. You must make the rounds with me sometime, all those painters . . . Oh, damn, damn, the week after is a drag, all filled up. Anytime after will do. Tell you what, you call me, sweet? We'll arrange it. You will call? Bye-bye, now . . ."

She swept out of the lower playground and it was as if the sun had suddenly gone out leaving me in a world bare, gray and lifeless. I began to shiver again.

Seeing Cici again brought back all the old hungers, all the thwarted fantasies. The worlds left for others to conquer, the peaks I never attempted to scale. Not trying, that's the Original Sin. Anger and cowardice existed side by side in me, and weirdnesses and shortcomings; giving birth to passivity and inaction. Libby Pepper, a half-person, crippled and incomplete, dealing out duplicity with every breath. . . .

All the old lines of thought, past dreams of glory and achievement came rushing at me. All the victories that were supposed to come my way. None of it had happened.

I had surrendered all my dreams when Walter, the man in my head, became the man in my bed. He had given me what I wanted—a husband, a home of my own, a son. Conflicting inner forces rose up, gave me trouble. Part of me wanted to blame Walter for what had happened to me—or didn't happen. For allowing me to let go of what once I had been, slipping into the soft coma of indecision and inaction. If only Walter were to blame, I could hate him and that might make it easier.

Or was it my mother? Did she encourage me too much to became a wife and a mother, to steer me away from any other kind of life?

Or was it the dream itself that was at fault? Should I have recognized it as empty and false from the start?

Cici had stirred everything up. One look at her said it all loud and clear for me. Cici had all the parts of her life in perfect working order. Husband, children, home, job. She was beautiful. Smart. She had figured life out. She must have all the answers. I would ask for her assistance, sit at her knee and absorb her wisdom. There was only one thing wrong; I didn't even know the questions.

As for me, just a sweet little job would satisfy me. Paying a modest little salary. Nothing pretentious, nothing grand. Some remote corner of the universe where I could lie low and function without much pressure in mild and quiet competence. Something that belonged exclusively to me.

Was that too much to ask for?

I made up my mind to give it a try. When I grow up, I said to myself, I want to be exactly like Cici Willigan.

Fat chance.

Libby decides to go for the brass ring . . . a job, a lover, success and her erotic fantasies fulfilled. She unexpectedly discovers that getting the prize may be less important than winning the battle.

(Read the complete Bantam Book, available July 1st, wherever paperbacks are sold.)

# THE LATEST BOOKS
# IN THE BANTAM
# BESTSELLING TRADITION

# Bantam Book Catalog

Here's your up-to-the-minute listing of over 1,400 titles by your favorite authors.

This illustrated, large format catalog gives a description of each title. For your convenience, it is divided into categories in fiction and non-fiction—gothics, science fiction, westerns, mysteries, cookbooks, mysticism and occult, biographies, history, family living, health, psychology, art.

So don't delay—take advantage of this special opportunity to increase your reading pleasure.

Just send us your name and address and 50¢ (to help defray postage and handling costs).